CW01497540

# SAVAGE GAME

## A KYLE PAYNE THRILLER

## JT SAWYER

INKUBATOR
BOOKS

Published by Inkubator Books
www.inkubatorbooks.com

Copyright © 2025 by JT Sawyer

JT Sawyer has asserted his right to be identified as the author of this work.

ISBN (eBook): 978-1-83756-652-5
ISBN (Paperback): 978-1-83756-653-2
ISBN (Hardback): 978-1-83756-654-9

SAVAGE GAME is a work of fiction. People, places, events, and situations are the product of the author's imagination. Any resemblance to actual persons, living or dead is entirely coincidental.

No part of this book may be reproduced, stored in any retrieval system, or transmitted by any means without the prior written permission of the publisher.

*I would like to thank my amazing editor Lorie Jones for bringing me into the Inkubator fold. Many thanks to my publishers Brian Lynch and Garret Ryan and all of their talented staff at Inkubator Books. I am eternally grateful.*

# PROLOGUE

If Micah Brezny had seen the killer's eyes watching them from the tree line, she would have grabbed her friends and paddled back across the lake before the sun dipped below the horizon.

Before then, the canoe trip had been glorious and carefree. After a week of recreational paddling along nine of the forty-three lakes in the Birch Lake Wilderness Region, the two young women, along with April's boyfriend, Ryan, had felt like they owned the world. All three of them had grown up in the outdoors, being raised around logging towns dotting Alaska and working on trail crews during their summers since their mid-teens.

And Micah lived for the summers, when she could escape from her lecherous foster father and the hovel he claimed was home.

Now, duty called, and Ryan was headed to Army boot camp in two weeks, while April had a forestry scholarship at the University of Oregon in Portland. And Micah—she was on a fast track to nowhere in particular, as long as it was as far from Anchorage as possible. She'd saved enough money working on the trail crew these past few months to camp out in the woods outside of Homer, or some other tourist town, where she hoped to get a job as a server in one of the many diners dotting the peninsula.

Micah heard the crackling of the campfire near their tents as she squatted behind a large spruce to relieve herself. A pine cone struck her in the head, and she turned to see April laughing from the next tree over.

Micah picked up a small ball of tree sap. "You want this in your hair, you gutter rat?" She flung it, the crystalline projectile barely missing April's head.

"Good shot, dumbass. You always did suck at baseball."

Micah flicked her head toward the tents. "And the rumor is you were always good at sucking. Is that why Ryan hung out with you all summer?"

"Ha-ha. I told you he hit on me, not the other way around."

Micah stood, pulling up her shorts. "Did he take you to the clinic first and have you tested?"

"You won't be mocking me when I drag your sleeping bag into the lake tonight." April slid up her sweatpants and then smashed a mosquito on her neck.

They turned, watching Ryan a hundred feet away. The orange sun hung low over the lake's glassy surface, casting long shadows that stretched like grasping fingers across their small campsite and onto the young man's muscular frame. A second later, he got up and walked to the tent on the right, rummaging through his backpack by the entrance.

Micah took a step forward, then froze as she saw a blur of movement shoot from the shadows behind the tent.

She was about to call out to Ryan when a figure emerged from the dense woods on the opposite side of their camp. Tall and dressed in dark clothing that seemed to absorb the dying light, the man moved with predatory silence across the twenty feet of open ground.

The stranger was almost upon Ryan now, and the glint of metal in his hand made Micah's blood freeze.

Ryan looked up from the tent just as the killer struck, burying the curved gutting blade into the young man's abdomen, then slicing upward. The knife flashed in the fire-light, and Ryan's startled cry echoed across the water before dying into a terrible, gurgling silence. His body crumpled beside the firepit.

Micah muffled the scream balling up in her throat. She grabbed April's wrist, pulling her deeper into the forest.

But the killer's head snapped up at the sound of a breaking twig beneath Micah's foot. His eyes swept the tree line until he locked onto the girls' position. Dark blood stained the front of his plaid shirt, and a slow smile spread across his bearded face.

"Run," Micah whispered.

They burst from the trees and crashed through the under-growth, abandoning any hope of getting to their canoe. Behind them, they could hear him coming.

The forest grew thicker as they fled from the lake, the canopy above blocking out more and more of the fading daylight. Micah's lungs burned, but she pushed forward with April's hand still clutched in hers.

"Let's go this way, instead," April said, pulling her toward what looked like a game trail winding between two boulders.

But in her panic, April missed the exposed root that snaked across the path. Her ankle caught, twisting viciously, and she went down hard with a cry of pain.

"April!" Micah dropped to her knees beside her friend, trying to help her up. "Come on, we have to—"

"I can't feel my toes." April's face was white with agony.

The sound of footsteps crushing through dead leaves grew closer, like an unstoppable force flooding over the earth.

"Go," April whispered, pushing Micah away. "Please, just go."

"I'm not leaving you—"

The killer emerged from the shadows between the trees like something conjured from a horror film. Micah couldn't understand how he had closed the distance so fast. In the dying light, his white teeth were accentuated against his dark beard. He raised the knife, Ryan's blood still dark on the steel.

"No!" Micah lunged forward, but her own boot got hung up on the tangle of roots, and she fell back.

The blade descended along April's abdomen with surgical precision, and the teenager's scream cut through the evening air before fading into a terrible silence.

Micah stumbled to her side, her vision blurring with tears and abject terror.

The killer straightened slowly, his attention now fixed entirely on her. More blood darkened the front of his shirt, and his shaggy hair and maniacal eyes made him seem wolflike.

Somehow, she sprang up and found herself in an all-out sprint, crashing through the brush and ferns until her legs began to give out. Her breath came in ragged sobs, and she fought back the urge to vomit as the reptile part of her brain pushed her to keep running. She could hear him coming, never seeming to hurry, his steady pace increasing but never rushing.

*God, why is this happening? Who is this psycho?*

The ground began to grow soft and spongy beneath her feet. The air became thick with the smell of stagnant water and decay. She was approaching the marshlands that bordered the eastern edge of the forest that they'd seen on their afternoon approach. If she could reach the swamp, maybe she could lose him in the maze of thick vegetation.

She heard the sickening sound of branches snapping to her right, wondering how he could have gained so much ground in that direction. Reflexively, Micah picked up a rock and hurled it towards the noise, hearing a dull thud, followed by a groan. The armed man staggered from the shadows, pressing one hand to his jaw while fixing his gaze on Micah.

She grabbed two more rocks and threw them with all her strength, not waiting to see if they connected.

She turned and plunged into the deepening shadows of the swamp, praying the darkness would hide her long enough to find a way out of this nightmare.

# CHAPTER 1

## WOLF LAKE LODGE - THIRTEEN MILES SOUTHEAST OF BIRCH LAKE

Kyle Payne let the ax sail through the seasoned spruce, splitting it neatly in half. He tossed the severed pieces onto the growing pile beside him and took a moment to stare at the vista of Wolf Lake in the distance.

If the topography of a land matches a man's soul, then Payne was exactly where he needed to be right now.

Five weeks earlier in Seattle, Payne and Carrie Walker had admitted what they'd both been avoiding—that a few months of dating couldn't bridge the gap between her need for purpose within the system and his need to escape it entirely. They had said their goodbyes before she left for a new assignment with the FBI, and he took his Indian motorcycle on the ferry bound for Alaska.

Walker was probably finishing her first field assignment by now, and he wondered if she was staring out at the Atlantic Coast. He had briefly entertained the idea of going with her, but he'd had his fill of the congested East Coast, and especially Virginia, which was one step too close to his old employer at Langley. And he still had places to see, wild shores to fish, and miles of open road in the US that he craved to explore.

After briefly visiting Juneau, he continued north on the ferry to Seward and spent two weeks touring the Kenai Peninsula on his motorcycle until arriving at Wolf Lake Lodge, nearly a forty-minute drive west of the small town of Saxon.

He'd first seen the ad for a temporary caretaker at Wolf Lake Lodge during a pit stop in Skagway. The Xeroxed flyer on the general-store bulletin board in the lobby was probably aimed at locals, but it sounded too appealing to pass up: a free cabin at a remote property owned by a former wildlife biologist who catered to nature photographers and outdoor enthusiasts. Six days a week of property maintenance, woodcutting, and supply runs to town—and all the king salmon a person could eat. That latter part was one of the real draws.

As much as he enjoyed seeing Alaska from his motorcycle, he could go without the constant airborne assaults by the vampire legion of mosquitoes, black flies, and no-see-ums, which always found ways inside his helmet during every drive. During the last half-hour stop along the highway near Soldotna, where a sow grizzly bear and her cubs had halted traffic while foraging on berries beside the road, Payne figured he donated a quart of blood to the local insect population.

A cabin instead of a tent and a world-class view on a wilderness lake near Denali National Park in exchange for some honest manual labor sounded idyllic. The lodge was situated on a half mile of rugged shoreline and consisted of a main dining hall, staff quarters, and admin office at the north end, while eight timber-framed cabins and a shower house were on the edge of the forest beside a grassy meadow overlooking Wolf Lake. At the south end was the tool and woodshed and a lone trail that wound through a tree-draped pathway to the caretaker's cabin.

When Payne first saw his new abode, he wondered if he should cancel his ferry ticket back to Washington at summer's end and stay on over the winter.

Now, with only six days left on his contract, the open road was calling him again, and he wanted to spend his last weekend halibut fishing down in Homer before heading east towards Wyoming and the Dakotas.

As he split the last round of dried spruce, his boss, Gus Freed, ambled up from the beach, where he'd been checking the engine on his float plane. While visitors arrived on the plane, there was a twenty-six-mile-long dirt road that accessed the region, allowing for the company truck to haul in bulky food orders that arrived weekly in Saxon.

Since Payne had begun his work-trade arrangement, the lodge had seen a flurry of visitors, mostly couples and families from the lower forty-eight, but Gus indicated that this last week of August was intentionally devoid of clients because of the start of the school year and the need to prepare for the fall onslaught of visitors that began with Labor Day.

"Just saw a bull moose swimming across the northern cove; probably going after those new pond lilies that emerged a few days ago," Gus said, sitting on a stump under the open-faced woodshed while resting his Ruger .375 rifle across his lap.

"Everything's gotta work for a living," said Payne, burying the Swedish ax in the chopping block and sitting down across from his employer.

"Speaking of that—when you gonna get started? I coulda had this all split up hours ago."

Nearly every morning was like this, with Gus making his rounds on the property, then stopping by to rib Payne before returning to his indoor duties in the main lodge.

"Pff—I was out here at dawn while you were still waiting for the ibuprofen to kick in so your joints don't creak like a rusty gate."

Gus chuckled, pointing at Payne's face. "You got something glistening on your forehead that I ain't seen since you got here. And maybe you've never seen at all."

He dragged a shirtsleeve across his sweaty brow. "Yeah, my boss is a real hard case, driving me like a pack mule."

"Just doing my part to shape tomorrow's generation, though you may be beyond redemption."

"And you say you never wanted kids of your own—can't imagine why with your overdeveloped optimism in others."

"Not sure why your dad didn't leave you in the woods when you were a kid."

"He did, plenty of times, mainly 'cause I begged him to."

"Well, those Ohio cornfields must have been brutal for ya."

Payne grinned, not responding, knowing Gus was aware of his upbringing in Michigan's rugged Upper Peninsula since the two men were always trying to outdo one another on fishing, tracking and hunting exploits, mostly because Gus constantly poured fuel on that fire.

"They teach you where Ohio was at in that one-room schoolhouse you attended back in the eighteenth century?" said Payne.

"Son, I'm just old and wise, not ancient. And just remember, I was radio-collaring wolves when you were still figuring out which end of a crayon to use."

"I'd never call you ancient. Antique or maybe prehistoric, but never ancient."

Gus grinned. "I could still out-paddle you on the lake any day."

While Gus had served in the Marine Corps after high school, it was his decades in the bush that had given him a hard exterior, but beneath all the joking, there was a patriarchal figure who cared more about the people and wildlife around him than turning a huge profit at this out-of-the-way slice of paradise.

At sixty-three, the older man moved with the deliberate pace of someone whose body protested every morning, but his mind was still sharp as a scalpel. He'd spent half of his life with the Alaska State Troopers as a conservation officer and had retired seven years earlier after his patience for bureaucratic nonsense had grown thin. His beard was more salt than pepper now, and his eyes had the permanent squint of someone who'd spent decades peering through binoculars at distant wildlife, back when researchers lived for extended periods amongst their subjects in the field rather than spending all season crunching statistics behind their desk.

He had used his savings to purchase the rustic property and partially renovate the dilapidated structures. After several prominent photographers boasted of his place online, his reputation had grown, drawing in small groups seeking a pristine backcountry experience where bears, moose and eagles were never more than a few hundred yards away on any given day. Payne had never been in a place that was so imbued with the spirit of its owner.

Gus stood. "Well, Jasmine's got a pot of coffee on, like always, and there's still plenty of hash browns and eggs, so come on up, if you want—unless you were gonna take a nap."

"I prefer the term 'siesta,' and I'm not due for it until at least 1 p.m."

"Figured you for a slacker. Sure you weren't in the Army or Air Force?"

Both men laughed.

Payne yanked the ax from the stump and walked it over

to the toolshed. A second later, he heard footfalls approaching.

Jasmine, the brunette administrative assistant who handled the reservations, marketing, and website, was moving briskly past the bathhouse towards the two men. While Gus was the resident expert on all things Alaska, Jasmine handled the day-to-day reality of keeping the business afloat. The woman was clad in jean bibs and a red flannel shirt with her long curly hair bouncing along her shoulders with each step. At forty-eight, Jasmine could have easily passed for someone in her late thirties, her bright eyes and athletic figure giving her an almost timeless appearance that had originally caught Payne off guard.

The woman picked up her pace, moving with a quick step across the grassy meadow towards them.

"She's upset about something," whispered Gus. "Never a good sign to see that particular look on her face."

Jasmine's walk increased to a trot for the last thirty feet. "Wish you'd carry your damn phone. It's that new state trooper, Lieutenant Nolte. Says it's extremely urgent." She handed him the device and leaned a hand on an upright beam, catching her breath. "Something about a bear attack at Birch Lake."

Payne and Gus gave each other concerned looks, and Gus pressed the phone to his ear. State Trooper Lieutenant Robert Nolte was talking loudly enough that Payne could make out most of the conversation. Four people brutally mauled at three primitive campgrounds spread around the lakeshore northwest of Saxon. A seasonal ranger in his boat had discovered them this morning while doing routine permit checks. Nolte needed Gus to confirm it was a bear attack since the ranger was a newbie from the lower forty-eight. He asked Gus to meet him at the Saxon airfield in sixty minutes so they could fly out together on a helicopter.

Payne had met Nolte once during a supply run to town and briefly spoken with him after the man learned that Payne was the new caretaker at Wolf Lake Lodge. Payne recalled the trooper had moved down here from a post on the outskirts of Anchorage three months ago after spending nearly two decades working in a liaison role between the Alaska State Troopers and Anchorage PD. He seemed like a fish out of water in Saxon, but hinted that the laid-back lifestyle out here was better for his blood pressure and his marriage, in that order.

Gus agreed to help with the investigation and handed the phone back to Jasmine, giving her a concerned look. "Better remove the canoe itinerary for Birch Lakes and the surrounding waterways from our website. That area's probably gonna be shut down for quite a while."

"And if people ask why?" she inquired.

"Tell 'em the state temporarily closed the region and that's all you know for now." He glanced at Payne. "Gimme a ride to the airfield, will ya."

Payne nodded, removing his leather gloves and stuffing them in his back pocket. "Let me get my stuff first."

He bounded down the trail to his twenty-by-thirty cabin, grabbing his daypack, snacks, and jacket.

Afterwards, all three of them walked along the meadow towards the lodge.

Payne had experienced numerous bear encounters during his youth, but those were black bears and not the grizzlies that roamed in these parts and could remove a person's head with one swipe of their shovel-like paws. He vaguely knew the Birch Lake area and recalled it was part of a cluster of nearly forty other interconnected lakes that were only accessible by canoe or air taxi. It made him wonder if one of the campers had broken the rule of not cooking where you sleep, or had forgotten to properly stow their grub in one of the steel bear boxes found at every campsite in the state.

*Still, how would that account for four people being mauled to death? Maybe this bear was rabid.* He sighed. *Helluva way for those campers to meet their ends.*

As they walked the last few feet towards the front porch of the main lodge, he glanced at the still woods to the left with a sense of both humility and dread that he'd had since first arriving in Alaska—humans were no longer at the top of the food chain, and nature could remind you of that in a heartbeat in this rugged land.

———

A FEW MINUTES LATER, when Payne climbed into the weathered Chevy Silverado belonging to the lodge, Gus was already sitting inside. The old man was rubbing his right leg, and Payne wondered if it was from an approaching low-pressure system.

"You alright?" asked Payne, starting the engine and pulling out from behind the lodge, heading along the narrow dirt road that led to town.

"Yeah, nothin' a few painkillers won't help with. Damn knees are just worn out from too many years of hiking. The buggers ache like hell when the weather's about to change."

"Maybe you can get Nolte to carry your pack for you," he said with a chuckle as he drove down the dirt road.

"You got a good sense of humor, Kyle. You oughta use it sometime." He thrust his thumb towards the back seat. "Besides, I brought an extra rifle for you. I could use another set of eyes on the ground, and with your wildlife experience, you'll be a good fit."

"I appreciate your confidence in me, but I thought the

Alaska State Troopers had their own wildlife officers in the county who handled this sort of thing."

"They do, but our resident expert is out on sick leave from back surgery, and the rest of the guys are spread thin down by Homer and other popular fishing spots because of peak season. Nolte seems like a competent fellow, but he's a recent transplant to these parts, and I'd be surprised if he can tell the difference between a chipmunk and a squirrel. By the way, we don't have counties out here. We have boroughs, and they're all handled by guys like Nolte—troopers in charge of their designated posts, or what you'd call precincts or departments down in the lower forty-eight."

Payne gave Gus a surprised look. "Thanks for the lesson in bureaucracy, but you sure he's gonna be alright with someone he barely knows mucking around his investigation?"

"He's not going to object, especially if he wants a thorough examination of the area, and my goddamned joints might prevent that."

"Like I said before, I'm just your pack mule. I see how it is."

"You're a lot smarter than you look, Kyle."

"It's not because of the company I keep."

"My hat size is a bit bigger than yours, lad."

Payne laughed. "It certainly matches your ego."

———

THE SAXON AIRFIELD stretched across a narrow clearing carved from the dense spruce forest; its single asphalt runway was flanked by weathered windsocks that danced in the mountain breeze. At the eastern end, a cluster of utilitarian buildings huddled together like survivors against the wilderness—a corrugated metal hangar large enough to shelter the lone Alaska State Trooper helicopter and maybe two small aircraft in the wintertime, alongside a cramped administrative building that doubled as flight operations and the local coffee stop for pilots.

Three float planes bobbed gently at the wooden dock extending into the adjacent lake, while a pair of bush planes with oversized tires sat parked in the corner of the tarmac like mechanical grasshoppers. The gravel parking lot, barely large enough for a dozen vehicles, was hemmed in by evergreens that seemed to press inward, as if the forest were constantly plotting to reclaim this small scar of civilization.

Payne parked near Nolte's cruiser, all the men exiting their vehicles. Payne heard the roar of a Cessna's engine and watched a small passenger plane take off, bound for a sight-seeing tour around Denali.

Forty-two-year-old Lieutenant Robert Nolte had an unblemished tan backpack on his right shoulder, and his open black blazer was flapping in the wind. From his polished boots to his crisp brimmed hat, the trooper looked like he had stepped from the pages of a law-enforcement catalog. The man was clean-shaven and kept his blond hair high and tight, like he was fresh out of boot camp.

The men exchanged handshakes, and Nolte emitted an irritated glance when Gus mentioned having Payne along for his tracking and wildlife experience. "Hope you don't mind the sight of blood. This sounds like a fucking nightmare," said the lieutenant.

"Most bear attacks are, unfortunately," Payne replied. He gestured at the forest in the direction they would be heading. "Just curious…are the National Park Service or Forest Service guys involved?"

Both Nolte and Gus shook their heads. "The area we're going to is one of those weird checkerboard regions made up of a mix of federal, state, and borough lands," said Gus. "The shoreline campsites along Birch Lake are on state land, while the area a quarter mile beyond that is owned by the borough, and the lake itself is federal, if you can believe that."

"Lucky me," quipped Nolte. The lieutenant glanced at the pilot in the Bell 260 helicopter, who gave a thumbs-up. "Alright, let's get this over with."

Payne noticed the reluctant tone, wondering if the trooper was just eager to get back to his climate-controlled office, or if he was dreading the responsibility for shouldering the forth-coming investigation that he probably had never planned on encountering when contemplating the job of a small town lawman.

# CHAPTER 2

The pilot set the bird down on a flat grassy area a quarter mile northwest of Birch Lake where the seasonal ranger met them, clutching his Remington 870 shotgun. Derrick Landry was around twenty-three, but his ashen face made him look frail and much younger. There was a faint stain of vomit on his jacket, and his eyes were bloodshot. The bronze name badge on his issued jacket indicated he was with the National Forest Service.

From what Nolte revealed on the flight out, Landry had graduated with a degree in adventure education, whatever that was, and had previously spent three summers as a rafting guide in North Carolina, so he had been a shoo-in for the solitary federal position that was usually hard to fill. From the petrified expression on the young man's face, he was probably wishing he'd taken a job at the visitor center in Denali.

After Nolte, Payne, and Gus did a weapons check on their rifles and gathered their packs, they followed Landry through the forest. Other than the scolding sound of a red squirrel in the treetops, the lakefront was silent.

During the past three weeks, Payne hadn't ventured this far out. It would take a day of hard paddling under windless conditions, along with numerous portages, to make it past the four other lakes between Birch Lake and Gus' place. But he could understand the appeal. At least, before today.

Following five minutes of walking along a game trail, Landry stopped. He glanced at the tranquil waters to the right, then back towards the other men before lowering his eyes. "I had just helmed my canoe through the narrow passage connecting Birch to Swanson Lake when I came across the first camp. There was still smoke coming off the campfire, but the, um, the tent, it was shredded." He lightly raked his fingers along his abdomen. "And the guy was...he was just..." Landry pursed his lips.

Gus rested a hand on the ranger's shoulder. "Why don't you just take us to the first site, son. We'll piece things together from there, and then you can fill us in as we go."

Landry nodded and turned, continuing along the trail.

While they were walking, Payne kept his Ruger Hawkeye Alaska .375 rifle at low ready. Unlike Gus' other hunting rifles, this one wasn't equipped with a scope. Iron sights and a point-and-shoot approach were what would be needed for an approaching leviathan like a grizzly. Payne had hunted black bears before in Michigan, but a grizzly was built like a tank and had a more aggressive nature by comparison. Early on, Gus had hammered home the difference between the two creatures by explaining that, during flyovers of the tundra, black bears ran away from the approaching plane while grizzlies stood up and pawed at them.

The trail rose for twenty feet, then dipped to the lakeshore. An unkindness of ravens suddenly erupted as Landry and the others approached the grisly scene. A yellow tent was flattened and had long parallel shred marks on the right side. Beyond that was a splayed body thick with congealed blood around the torso. The forty-something man's eyes were wide, and his mouth hung open. Beneath it, the torso was riddled with deep incisions, which had caused the intestines to spill out. The man's sleeping bag must have been cut in the struggle, and hundreds of flecks of goose-down insulation made it look like it had snowed. If snow were crimson.

"Jesus," said Nolte, leaning over and studying the man's filleted abdomen. "This guy never had a chance, but why didn't the bear drag him off and eat him?"

Payne pointed to the dead man's ribs. "Those cut marks are too narrow for bear, plus there'd be five parallel marks since bears have five claws."

"I agree," said Gus. "And I'm not seeing any bear tracks."

"Could it be cougar?" asked Nolte, who'd backed up and was photographing the entire campsite with his iPhone.

"Not many cougar in Alaska in general, and certainly not this far up," said Gus. "Plus, cougar tend to lick off a lot of the facial tissue on their victims, and I'm not seeing any evidence of that."

Nolte gave the old man a concerned look. "And I thought things couldn't get any more disturbing."

Payne glanced around the shredded tent, using a stick to lift up a section of nylon fabric. He examined the backpack, then gazed down at the green Old Towne canoe tethered to a stump by the shore ten feet away. He glanced at the dead man's boots, which had a waffle-pattern tread, then followed a set of tracks down to the canoe.

Payne scanned the forest, then returned to scrutinizing the gear strewn about the tent, some of which consisted of photography lenses along with some sealed Ziploc bags of trail mix and dried fruit. "Guy has some pricey camera stuff here, and his backpack and food are untouched."

"I noticed that, too," said Landry. "Campers are required

to stow their food in bear boxes of their own or in the ones we provide at each lake, but this guy's chow was by his stove." He gestured towards a dark brown metal container shaped like a trash barrel but with a twist-off lid that was bolted onto a cement pad thirty yards away.

Payne moved up beside Nolte. He studied the wounds again but this time from an attacker's perspective. *This dude was caught off guard and gutted by his fellow kind. Helluvan agonizing way to die. But there are other ways to quickly and quietly kill someone with a blade—why gut him like this?*

Landry retreated slightly to the trees, leaning against a trunk and taking in several deep breaths. "I already checked the permits on the canoes. This fella here was out of Indiana. The next guy was from Anchorage, and the couple around the bend were from Homer. At least, the permit indicated a couple, but I only saw…saw one body."

"Are the other victims like this?" asked Payne as he glanced over at the young ranger.

"Pretty much." Landry led the way again, keeping his shotgun leveled at the trail ahead.

After the second time Landry made a wild swing to the right at a chattering bird, Payne had to speak up. "Would you mind putting the safety back on and keeping that pointed a little lower?"

The kid gave a nervous nod and complied, his lower lip trembling. "The victim ahead is the worst."

This time, Landry remained a little farther out, letting the other three men walk past him.

Payne approached the camouflage tent and felt his gut constrict as he stared at the carnage. Another butchered figure, but this person was seated by a stump, his tent still intact. The man had a salt-and-pepper beard and looked to be in his fifties.

"Looks like he was eviscerated," said Gus.

"This is ten times worse than the other guy. Were the ravens all over this body when you arrived?" Payne asked the ranger.

"A few, but he looked like that when I paddled up," said Landry.

The men stood in a circle, staring at the unraveled pile of innards beside the victim's disemboweled abdominal cavity.

Gus removed his hat and placed it against his chest. "My God, in all my years, I've never seen anything like this. This sure as hell ain't no bear. We've got a psycho on the loose out here."

"Compared to the first victim, this wasn't just a simple stabbing. The killer took pleasure in it," said Nolte. He waved his hand at the upright orange backpack against a tree and the personal items strewn on the ground. "And whoever did this wasn't here to rob these people."

After Nolte finished his initial photography work, he motioned for Landry to lead them to the final site. This campground was a hundred yards farther down the beach and tucked away in a small cove.

The next victim was a young male who appeared to be in his early twenties. His sandy blond hair was about the only part of him that wasn't splattered with blood. His torso looked like it had been slashed over twenty times with a few of the marks extending from the hips to the shoulders. It reminded Payne of revenge slayings he'd seen in an African village, where the rebels had so badly hacked up their victims that it was hard to tell the individual bodies apart. "Whoever did this was either amped up on drugs or just filled with rage to go this ballistic on someone."

"Or both," said Nolte. He pointed to the two tents and shot a glance back at Landry. "But where's the other person who was camped here with him?"

The younger man shrugged, his face turning green just before he leaned over and began vomiting into the bushes.

Payne stepped back and studied the ground, then gestured towards the forest. "Bunch of tracks heading off this way." He walked alongside the plethora of boot prints, stepping over a log and continuing for fifty feet before stopping at a large spruce tree.

"Soil's dug up here, and there's some remnants of toilet paper sticking up," he said as Gus and Nolte followed behind. "And two different sets of boot-tread marks. These are much smaller than the guy at the campsite, quite possibly women."

A few feet farther, Payne kneeled. "Looks like they were squatting here, but not using the bathroom."

"How the hell can you tell that?" asked Nolte.

Payne pointed to the tracks with a stick. "No disturbed soil and the imprints are deeper and more defined on the front toe regions—happens when a person remains in one spot for a while, compared to the more shallow prints left when you're just walking through a place."

Nolte shouted towards the beach, "Landry, who was registered at this site?"

"Couple out of Homer. It was listed under a Ryan Kemp."

"Just the two of 'em?"

"Yes, sir. The other name was listed as April Mason."

"Not unusual to get tag-alongs who sneak in," said Gus. "Coulda been a friend who joined at the last minute."

"Still, they're supposed to list everyone on the permit," said Nolte.

"And people are not supposed to drink and drive," replied Gus.

"The women must have witnessed their friend getting killed and hightailed it out of here," said Nolte, who was searching the forest.

Payne stood, sweeping his hand towards the woods as he discussed avenues of escape, while examining the topography. "The trees on my left are so thick that it would have been impossible to run through that, and those are all blackberry briars to the right near the shoreline, so we should continue straight. Hopefully, we can pick up some tracks by the edge of the swamp ahead once we get past all these pine needles."

Forty feet ahead, Payne saw a flurry of disturbed soil and clumps of crushed vegetation, which resembled the pattern someone made when they were sprinting. He surmised the two women had crept into the bush, then carefully made their way to the swamp.

*Hoping to hide, or were they going to skirt around it and keep going?*

To the right, he caught sight of another trail intersecting that corresponded with the appearance of the disturbed soil. He thrust a finger at the larger boot marks in the soil. "The killer was after them now, so they musta run like hell."

A few feet beyond, his pulse quickened. Just beyond a fallen log was another bloody corpse. The woman was lying flat on her back, her dark hair spread around her head. The sight of the blade wounds in her abdomen made his stomach churn. *Who could've done this?*

Payne high-stepped over the log and stood beside the path while Nolte and Gus just stared, both of them remaining on the other side as if crossing over was too much. Several frogs hopped around the bloody entrails, flicking insects off the spilled remains. With the lack of wind this far in, the smell was nauseating, and Payne stepped back, pulling his shirt collar over his nose.

Eventually, Nolte and Gus moved closer and examined the victim while Payne continued his tracking efforts. "Got some good signs up here," he said.

The two men joined Payne near the far end of the two-acre

marsh. Here, the trees gave way to a mucky area filled with cattails but devoid of any surface water. Somewhere a red-winged blackbird's scolding sound emerged from the vegetation.

"Looks like the other woman got this far, then stepped on a bunch of rocks to cover her prints before taking off again in the woods." Payne pointed to the faint clump of mud on some flat stones near the edge of the cattails. "Smart lady."

"Doesn't mean she got away," said Nolte.

Payne nodded at the patch of torn-up dirt on the right and kneeled down. He bent forward until his nose was only inches from the soil. A minute later, he sat up, grabbing a dead twig and using it to outline his new find. "That trail with the big boot prints...I was mistaken about it being just one person—pretty sure there were two big guys chasing the women."

# CHAPTER 3

"How's that?" said Nolte, leaning over Payne's shoulder and squinting at the ground.

"Two identical sets of tracks. Same star-shaped pattern like you see in a lot of hiking boots but"—he waved the twig over the center mark in one of the prints—"see how the *b* in the Vibram logo on the right boot is chipped and worn down while the others are crisp and newer."

Nolte turned on his iPhone's light and shone it over the tracks. "I see it but just not sure I make of it what you do. All these boot prints look identical and appear to be the same size."

Payne canted his head up at the lieutenant. "This isn't a subjective thing I just invented. Tracking is about science—presenting data and then supporting it, and the ground clearly shows a distinct difference in one set of prints compared to the other. There were two killers out here."

Nolte glanced around the marsh, then focused his gaze on Gus. "What do you say? You agree with Payne?"

"Sounds plausible, and he seems a lot more experienced

in man tracking than me. My thing was mainly large fauna like moose, bears, and wolves."

Payne stood, facing Nolte. "Make of it what you will. I'm just along to help out, but we should push on and find the other woman. She's probably still hiding out somewhere."

"What makes you think she's still alive?" asked Nolte.

He pointed to the trail that led back to the lake. "Because it looks like this was as far as these two meatheads went, and by how wide the trail is, they were crashing through the brush, trying to get out of here, when they turned around."

Nolte glanced at both of his companions. "The way these folks were killed has a lot of similarities to a murder that happened north of Saxon about five years ago. Does the name Jimmy Dean ring a bell for you, Gus?"

"Of course. I knew Jimmy and his parents, but this wasn't his doing. No way."

"How can you be so sure?" asked Nolte. "He hacked up his old man in the exact same fashion. I know because I was called in as an expert witness on that case."

Payne chimed in, "Besides being the brand name of America's greasiest breakfast sausage, who's Jimmy Dean?"

"He was an abused thirteen-year-old who couldn't take watching his old man beat his mom any longer," said Gus. "A short time after she died from smoke inhalation in a house fire, Jimmy lost it one night after getting slapped around by his dad."

Nolte narrowed his eyes at Gus. "Your memory is too kind. Jimmy went ape-shit. He didn't just cut his dad one time to defend himself, he gutted him like it was salmon season."

———

THE ATTEMPT TO locate the remaining woman had come to a halt a half mile from the tracks at the swamp, and Nolte indicated he would get a search-and-rescue helicopter in the air to patrol the region. After he took additional photos and gathered up the victims' IDs from their packs, they returned to the helicopter for the flight back to Saxon.

Landry remained at Birch Lake to provide assistance to the incoming troopers and forensics team that Nolte was sending.

Once back at the airfield in Saxon, Payne and Gus drove behind Nolte's police cruiser, a 2007 tan and white GMC Yukon. Given that the population of Saxon was only three thousand people, it took five minutes and one stop light to arrive at the troopers' post.

The modest one-story brick building was situated at the north end across from a hardware store. For Payne, Saxon reminded him of nearly every other small town he'd been in along the West Coast during the past year. The exception being that this one often had moose or a wandering black bear bringing traffic to a halt.

They pulled their vehicles in at the rear, alongside several mud-crusted trucks whose drivers were hanging around the tailgate. Nolte's troopers—all four of them, though he indicated more would be en route from the outlying posts.

After handshakes and hasty introductions, Nolte relayed the findings from the campsite while Gus occasionally interjected comments ruling out a grizzly-bear attack. Payne watched the troopers' faces alternate between shock and horror as the gruesome descriptions percolated through their psyches.

Nolte gave two men assignments to set up a roadblock to prevent access to the Birch Lake canoe put-in point, while the other two would be flown out with the county coroner to the campsite to join Landry and begin the tedious process of cataloging the crime scene before the coming storm later tonight. Generators for the lighting and a full-blown incident command post with more staff inbound from the nearby Seward State Trooper post would follow in the coming hours.

The focus now was on preserving evidence and finding the sole survivor. Bears, ravens, and coyotes were going to be encircling the campsites, and manpower was necessary to protect the crime scene. Canopies and tarps would need to be strung over the three campsites to prevent the rain from washing away tracks, blood, and DNA.

From experience, Nolte mentioned how the location would eventually leak out to the public, which would cause a deluge of curiosity seekers and self-anointed podcasters who'd be doing flyovers in their private planes and drones. Containment was the crucial first step in the investigation.

When Nolte finished his briefing, the troopers gathered their packs and rifles and piled into one vehicle for the drive to the airfield.

Gus and Payne followed the lieutenant inside, needing to relay their observations to Nolte's secretary, Carlie, while the details were still fresh. Payne didn't envy the woman. Her world view was about to drastically change and so was the serene atmosphere of Saxon.

Payne kept running through the bizarre string of tracks on the ground at the last campsite. Clearly someone had gotten away. There were really only two possible outcomes: the woman had succumbed to injuries, or she was on the run, trying to make it to town. If the latter was the case, she would be in for quite a trek since it was nearly twenty-three miles as the crow flies from Birch Lake to the nearest off-grid home, according to Gus.

*Or she's lost and heading deeper into the wilderness and facing an even more grueling ordeal.*

He thought about the personal items around the last

campsite. All the backpacks were faded and well-worn; the cooking pots had the unmistakable layer of soot from months of campfires; their canoe paddles were heavily nicked and abraded; and there were hand-carved cedar spoons in their coffee cups.

*Those three were experienced in the outdoors, compared to the other two campers with their off-the-shelf gear and shiny canoes.*

He glanced up at the clouds one last time before heading inside, hoping the survivor was as resourceful as the tracks indicated.

———

WHILE HE WAITED for Gus to finish giving his statement to Carlie, Payne sat in the cramped staff lounge, which consisted of three folding chairs and a musty couch that looked like it was a prototype from when furniture was first invented.

Nolte's tense voice was evident in his office in the next room as the man called in requests with other law enforcement posts up and down the region. The last call was the most interesting, both in Nolte's tone and his demands, as he barked at someone in Anchorage about unsealing Jimmy Dean's juvenile records. The conversation ended with the lieutenant slamming the landline phone down on the receiver, followed by pacing around his office. A second later, his door opened, and the man strode down the hallway with an empty coffee mug in his hand.

Nolte stopped abruptly in the doorway of the lounge upon seeing Payne, before continuing his march to the coffee maker in the corner. "You heard all that, I'm guessing?"

"Heard what?"

"Good man. I'd appreciate it if everything you saw and heard today stayed out of public consumption."

Payne gave him a two-fingered salute.

The trooper walked to the counter and poured himself a fresh cup of coffee, then added in four teaspoons of sugar. Nolte turned around and sipped his drink while eyeballing Payne. "You provided considerable help and input at the lake. Where'd you learn how to do all that man-tracking stuff, anyway?"

"Grew up with a dad who's a game warden in Michigan. He spent a lot of time tracking down poachers over the years, and it rubbed off on me as I got older." Payne left out the part about hunting down insurgents and enemy combatants in Africa and the Middle East. Those manhunts ended with a very different outcome than anything poachers faced in this country.

"Well, you sure made my job easier. Now, if I can just locate that missing girl, I'll sleep a little better."

"Not sure if any of us are going to sleep for a long time after what we saw at those campsites."

Nolte sighed. "Certainly not after I call all the families of the victims. Those poor souls. Who woulda thought that a laid-back canoe trip would end like that?"

Payne studied the stress lines on the sheriff's face, which seemed to have multiplied since the flight out to Birch Lake. "Probably not what you expected moving to a small place like Saxon."

He shook his head. "I've seen a lot of disturbing shit in my time working near Anchorage: turf wars between drug dealers, murdered prostitutes dumped in the boonies, domestic violence, and holdups gone wrong, but nothing as savage as today. It takes a special kind of sick mind to do something like that."

"And with a knife...that's someone who wanted to see his victim's eyes before they died, up close and personal."

Nolte paused in mid-sip. "You know, I looked into you, Payne. Had to, since I needed to know who I'm vouching for in my reports with the crime scene interpretation. You worked in risk management overseas, eh, handling safety for big companies and all that?"

Payne nodded. "Had my fill of ugliness in third world countries where kidnapping and ransom are a part of daily life. The outcomes on a lot of those cases didn't always end up like Hollywood films, with smiling families being reunited. More like a machete-riddled corpse or burnt remains being sent home."

"That why you're up here working for Gus? Needed to get away for a while?"

"For good, actually. I had my fill of that line of work. Just taking some time to figure out what to do next."

An odd frown crept out. "Well, a few days ago, I would have told you to put down some roots in a small town, but it sure doesn't seem like evil abides by location."

Payne stood after seeing Gus heading down the hall. "Well, Lieutenant, I wish you the best. You know where to reach me if I can provide further assistance with the tracking end of things."

The man extended his hand, and both of them shook. "Much appreciated. Unless you know how to storm a house and take down a murderous criminal, I probably won't be calling you anytime soon to be deputized."

"Sounds terrifying. Sure glad you and your crew have nerves of steel."

———

PAYNE EXITED the staff lounge and headed to the front door. He paused to step aside in the hallway as a young woman and her little boy walked past. The mother looked distraught and barely glanced at Payne.

He stopped by the desk in the lobby and leaned on the

counter to talk with Carlie. "Was that someone connected with one of the victims from the lake?"

She shook her head, staring down the passage as the woman and child entered Nolte's office. "Suzy Reynolds. Her husband, TJ, went missing a few weeks ago. She visits the lieutenant periodically to check on updates. She probably figured something was up after all the activity here and at the airfield."

Payne recalled the numerous flyers of the missing man plastered all over town. "He the geologist who disappeared in the backcountry?"

"Yep, though you could say that about a half-dozen people in these parts each year."

"They get lost or injured?"

"Or gulped down by a griz, or fall through the ice, or get drunk and tumble off a ridge, or any number of things."

"Or murdered during a canoe trip."

Her lips grew flat. "Yeah, that too."

# CHAPTER 4

Three hours after Payne and the others returned to Saxon, two figures emerged from the woods six miles east of Birch Lake. They stayed on the leaf-littered shoulder of the narrow jeep trail to avoid leaving obvious tracks. A mile later, they veered down a recently created pathway for sixty yards and stopped at a faded brown pickup truck that blended into the dense forest.

Thirty-two-year-old Andre Groh removed the suppressed Weatherby rifle from his shoulder and set it on the hood. His partner, Karl Hatch, who was a decade younger, dropped his camo daypack and stretched his arms up to the sky while yawning. It had been sixteen hours since the lakeside massacre.

It was supposed to be a short assignment: murder the four occupants spread out along three campsites, then return to their vehicle and head north. Except there had been a fifth person—a teenage girl who had proven to be very resourceful. *And fierce*, thought Hatch as he rubbed his swollen cheek caused by a rock the girl had thrown just before disappearing into a marsh.

Now, they had a major loose end and one that could inter-fere with their plans. So they'd spent the night and early morning hours scanning the forests and nearby lakes with night-vision scopes from the stolen boat and trekking on foot. But the girl was gone.

*Hopefully in some grizzly's stomach by now.*

Hatch opened the rear door of the Ford F-250 and retrieved their duffel bags with spare clothes, tossing Groh's across the vehicle to him. Hatch pulled off his blood-dappled plaid shirt, then kicked off his boots and slid down his jeans which were more crimson than their original blue. He placed all of his accouterments into a large trash bag and sealed it up before placing it in the back seat. These items would be burned later.

Hatch glanced up at the low string of cumulus clouds drifting to the north. "You think she made it?"

Groh removed the portable police scanner from his belt, turning up the volume. "We'll know soon enough, but we can't risk sticking around the area any longer with search-and-rescue combing the woods soon, as well as more troopers trickling into Saxon. I'll put the word out with some of my contacts in the area to be on the lookout. In the meantime, we have two more people on our list who need to be handled."

"Where?"

"First is in Anchorage. The second one is near Homer."

"Damn, why'd they have to be spread out north to south like that? That'll eat up a lot of time with driving."

Groh removed his plaid shirt, which matched the pattern and color of Hatch's.

The younger poacher caught himself staring at the scars peppering Groh's pale torso. Like other poachers around Alaska, he had heard the rumors about Groh's legendary hunting exploits at home and abroad. "Get those four marks on your ribs from a cat or something else?"

"Leopard. Northern India. I should have known better to approach a mostly dead predator."

Hatch didn't ask about the other scars, some long, others deep, while a few were divots from major puncture wounds. Instead, he ran a finger along a six-inch scar below his beard. "Older brother tried to strangle me with barbed wire when we was kids. Just missed my carotid. Kicked in his front teeth. Never did bother me again after that."

Groh kept on his leather gloves as he removed his muddy boots, which were identical to Hatch's. When he was done, he placed the footwear into a separate trash bag. These would not be burned.

———

HATCH HAD BEEN both shocked and aroused by his knife work on the victims. So much blood. And muffled shrieks. He was surprised by their chortled, bronchial sounds bleating out from their trembling lips before their life force drained away.

He'd shot, trapped, speared, and gutted a lot of wild animals before, but the eerie sound that emanated from his victims' nostrils as their innards were shredded was something he'd never forget.

Of course, the cocaine flowing through his system amplified everything, making it seem surreal. But the dried blood in his beard reminded him he was now a mass murderer. He had looked up the definition before they ventured out on their killing spree. The FBI defined an event where four or more people are killed in a single incident to be a mass murder. Hatch felt a tinge of notoriety laced with his fleeting pride at the thought, but it was undercut by the bile in his gut, which had been threatening to erupt as the cocaine wore off.

He recalled the look on Groh's face just after knifing the

old man at the middle campsite. Groh was like a maestro, perfectly composed as he artfully wielded the blade that neatly sliced through the navel, then arced down to the hip bone before continuing back up in a comma shape, which ended at the sternum. Hatch had been skinning foxes, bobcats, and beaver for his father's fur-harvesting business since he was eight, but this was bladework on another level, and he wondered how many times Groh had executed the moves.

They had arrived at the southwest end of the mile-long Birch Lake in the stolen motorboat earlier that day, before the campers arrived. After going ashore a few hundred yards from the campsites, they waited and watched as each canoe pulled up to their designated site and set up their tents.

Groh decided dusk would be the best time to attack, given the way the fading light plays on the forest, creating helpful shadows but not fully obscuring the available light. Again, Groh would know. He had hunted on five continents and himself had been raised by a renowned poacher who had taken nearly every creature that flew, swam, crawled, or ran back in the day before Alaskan conservation laws and officers made it impossible to live in the bush like a free man.

They had watched with interest as the occupants at the last campsite to the east set up two tents for a third person who wasn't listed on the official permit required by the authorities. She was a lanky but athletic girl who looked to be no more than seventeen. Hatch had stared at her tan legs through his binoculars until Groh had forcefully nudged him, reminding him to stay focused on the coming objective: use their designated blades on the abdominal region and, most importantly, leave no one alive.

———

WHEN THEY'D FINISHED CHANGING and scrubbing their hands with sanitizer, they stowed the rest of their gear and hopped into the truck. Groh started the engine and slowly moved along the pathway back toward the seasonal jeep trail. The coming rains would soon obscure the trampled vegetation and reduce any signs that someone had been there. Groh wasn't too worried. There were hundreds of dirt roads and pullouts crisscrossing the surrounding forest west of Saxon, and at this time of year, those saw a lot of use by loggers, fishermen, and woodcutters. Though, that was about to change once news of the slayings went public and the stolen boat was discovered adrift near the west end of Birch Lake.

The midday sun punching through the thickening cloud cover cast a gray tint on their furrowed faces, making them seem more weathered than they should be for their ages.

Hatch glanced over at Groh, a smile emerging. "Not a bad paycheck for only a few days' work. I could get used to this."

"Yep, and more of that in the near future if you play your cards right."

Nine miles later, they hit the blacktop road. Groh turned left. They had one crucial stop to plant some false evidence before heading to Anchorage. He turned up the volume on the police scanner, making sure the route to the next location was clear.

# CHAPTER 5

Micah Brezny crawled through the knee-high bracken ferns and came to a stop before a moss-covered fallen log. Her eyes and ears strained for the presence of the two killers, but all she heard was the wind in the pines and the incessant hammering of a downy woodpecker in the distance.

She lay on her side, examining her arms, which were covered in lacerations and scrapes, but found nothing life-threatening. Micah felt the sting of what she surmised were small cuts on her face and neck where mosquitoes were busy taking advantage of tiny wounds.

Her green shorts were tattered around the edges, and she noticed something black on the side of her right shin, hastily plucking off a bloated leech and smashing it against the log.

It seemed like everything in these woods was out for her blood.

From her wilderness first-responder class last summer, she recalled the importance of doing a pat-down on her extremities and torso to make sure there were no grievous wounds. She went through the motions and patted her face and scalp again. *Nothing that'll do me in.*

Micah couldn't say the same for her two friends, April and Ryan. *God, what happened back there? How can they be gone?*

Tears streamed down her cheeks, and she pulled her legs up to her chest as she fought to muffle her sobs. Despite physically being in one piece, she felt like the gnawing pit in her stomach was going to implode. With the latest adrenaline rush fading, the feeling of terror and soul-shredding loss was conspiring to swallow her up.

Her only friends in life were dead, hacked up by some deranged lunatics who were still out there. She had come on this trip to get away from her despicable foster parents, biding her time until she turned eighteen and could escape the hellish home she was trapped in. Now, she was the target of more predators. She would much rather face down a grizzly bear than her own kind.

*You don't see the animals out here fucking each other over like people do.*

She turned on her back, staring at the cottony clouds, and whispered April's name. Micah bit on her lip, hoping to wake herself up from a nightmare, but it seemed like this was her reality, being life's punching bag again. It was like she was ten all over again and learning of her parents' deaths on the highway.

Her senses shot back to the present when a branch snapped to her right. She grabbed a rock and angled towards the noise, seeing a Sitka deer browsing on some grass. Micah shuddered out an exhale and lay back down. Sheer exhaustion drifted over her, and she felt like her limbs were encased in concrete. She glanced over at the faint yellow orb beyond the clouds in the south and figured she had been moving due east the entire morning.

She vaguely recalled the access point on the first lake a week ago. *Or was it a month ago?* That spot was in the very southeastern corner of the wilderness region. The two-lane highway they'd taken from Saxon to the put-in point should be another five to ten miles past that.

In between, she'd seen a handful of cabins tucked away in the woods off the dirt road that led to the access point. If she continued east, she would eventually hit the highway or get to one of the private homes, and someone could call for help, or she could steal a vehicle.

Then she could tell the troopers what had happened, and they could hunt down the psychos before they killed more people.

And she had evidence showing who the butchers were. Shortly after April was murdered, Micah had seen the two men scouring the forest. She managed to video them on her iPhone from her concealed position in the cattails. Eventually, the men retreated and were heard later in their boat, searching the shoreline with their flashlights.

Micah felt a bolt of hope rush through her veins. She rolled onto her left side, grabbing the phone in her back pocket, but only felt fabric. She gasped and shot up, glancing around the ground, then back along the path she'd crawled.

The deer froze, staring at her, then bounded off.

She swiveled around and retraced her movements, crabbing forward on her elbows and knees as she frantically searched the forest litter. Nearing the creek she'd crossed earlier, she stopped, her eyes scrutinizing the muddy embankment on the other side. She slumped down and began cursing, slamming the rock onto the earth, imagining the faces of the two men as rage filled her trembling body.

———

THE NEXT TWO hours of hiking were easier than what she'd previously endured. The forest was interspersed with large grassy meadows. She skirted along the edge rather than walking in the open, to avoid standing out. For a second, she thought she'd heard a helicopter in the distance but wondered if her weary brain was playing tricks on her.

The whole time, she kept replaying last night's horrific events, trying to grasp why it happened. And what was being done now since other canoers or the park rangers must have come across the gruesome sights.

*Someone has to know by now. They have to.*

The only problem was there would be no listing for Micah Brezny on the backcountry permits, as April had left off her name so Micah's foster father couldn't locate her.

As her mind raced over the dizzying outcomes, she heard a faint rumble ahead. It sounded like a diesel truck chugging along a bumpy road.

Micah felt her heart punch through her chest. She broke into a trot, jumping over logs as she raced along the meadow's edge until she saw movement ahead. A dirty green pickup was descending a slope.

Micah stopped near the road, squatting beside a large pine stump and examining the driver. From this distance, the details of his face weren't very clear, but he looked older and didn't resemble the two bearded psychos from last night. And his dog was sticking its head out the passenger's window, the basset hound's floppy ears flung back by the wind.

*Do psychos have dogs—probably not happy ones like that?*

She felt her shoulders ease slightly and stepped out onto the road, waving down the driver. Her luck had finally turned.

The man abruptly stopped the vehicle and exited, coming around the front bumper and staring at Micah. He kept one hand on a weathered revolver on his right hip. He looked like a lot of other Alaskans who lived in the bush full time, with a furrowed face resembling driftwood, except this one was offset by a particularly long chin beard that looked like strands of floss glued to his lower jaw.

"My God, you alright?" he said. "You get lost?"

"They're all dead. Murdered." Micah felt like the words were lodged in her throat. Her head was spinning from the adrenaline, the exhaustion, and the sheer terror. "Two guys killed my friends at Birch Lake and some other folks, too."

She leaned her hands on the side of the vehicle, sucking in the pine-laced air. She saw her reflection in the windshield and realized her face was riddled with blood droplets, mud, and lacerations.

The man kept his distance for a moment, then stepped back to his open door and retrieved a tattered canteen, sliding it across the hood. "Take a drink. You look mighty dehydrated. Then you can fill me in on what you're talking about."

She drank like she'd run a marathon. Which she had, but the only trophy was survival. After several gulps, she forced herself to slow down. She didn't need to vomit and get further dehydrated.

The guy moved around the front bumper and examined her again. "Don't see any major wounds or injuries, so that's good." By the way his eyes lingered on her body, Micah was sure the fifty-something man was doing more than just a first-aid check.

She handed the empty canteen back, taking a few steps to the rear. The hound's face jutted out, and she reached out towards the friendly dog, stroking its neck.

"So what happened, exactly?" His wispy chin beard moved with each twist of his head, which served as a distraction from his yellow teeth whenever he opened his mouth to speak.

"Can you please take me to a troopers' post?"

"That's fourteen miles in the opposite direction from where I live. My house is just a few miles away. You can call from there. But first, I'd sure like to know what the hell you're talking about a bunch of killings."

She pressed her back into the truck and rested her hands on her knees. "Two guys with knives hacked up my friends and at least two other people, maybe more, at Birch Lake last night."

"What? Dear Lord." He canted his head. "How'd you get away?"

"What does that matter? I ran. Like all hell, and made it around the other side of the lake, and then ran some more." She waved a hand at the forest. "Look, I'd rather not stick around here in case those guys are in the area. Can you just drive me to town?"

The man again rested his hands on his pistol. "I been out here most of my life. Last time a little kid went missing, they had helicopters and search crews all over the place. I ain't seen nobody in these parts or heard anything on the radio. And Birch Lake is a helluva long way to run on foot." He glanced at the woods beyond his truck. "For all I know, you're giving me a story while your friends ransack my place."

*Jesus, this guy's paranoid.*

Suddenly, she felt her heart sink, wondering if this was one of the attackers. She glanced over his weather-beaten face and his spindly figure and eliminated the thought. The two guys from last night were big and moved with predatory aggression. This old-timer looked like a scarecrow that could fall over from the slightest wind.

"Do you have a cellphone?" she asked. "You can call the troopers from here."

He shook his head. "Flip-phone and it only gets reception in a few places. My home phone is the best bet." He gestured to the open bed of the truck. "You hop in back and stay where I can see you in my mirror. I'll drive you to my place, and you can call from there. If, at any time, I think you're bullshittin' me, or I see anyone sneaking around my property, I'll let out Brutus, my Rottweiler. He's a mean sum-bitch and would take you down in three bites."

Micah gazed down the road in either direction. It was going to be a long walk to the blacktop highway, and she could still run into the two maniacs. She would have to rely on the stranger for now, so she decided to at least ease his worries by sharing something more personal.

"My name is Micah, and what I told you is true. I was canoe-camping with my friends April and Ryan. And I...I just want to get out of these woods." She dragged a sleeve across her moist cheeks, stifling a cry.

"Name's Ernie, by the way. And we'll get this sorted out." He walked around to the driver's side and told her to get in the truck bed. "Ten minutes. Hang on to the sides, as it's bumpy as hell the last mile."

# CHAPTER 6

Micah was sure she lost a filling on the gnarly road leading up to the old man's house. He either didn't have the money to maintain it, or he kept it that way intentionally to keep people out.

And home was an understatement. The L-shaped dwelling looked like places Micah had seen in history books about Alaska's earliest settlers. The siding had mostly disappeared and was covered with tar paper in various stages of decay. The windows had a beige sheen with tattered white curtains hanging at odd angles. And the warped porch looked like it required two hands to navigate.

On the right side of the abode was a car port with a faded green tractor and an ATV inside, amidst workbenches filled with junk. A mechanical splitting maul and piles of firewood were on the left side. A moose hide was strung up on a drying rack leaning against a tree, not an unusual sight in the Alaskan backcountry.

Strangely, there was a well-maintained garden in elevated cedar boxes in front of the house with a wood-chipped pathway between them. Micah wondered if there was a Mrs. Paranoid who lived here as well.

The man parked the truck near the woodpile and stepped out, followed by his hound. His eyes swept around the woods in all four directions of his property; then he headed to the side door. "Just stay put. I'll be right back with my cordless phone."

Micah pulled her knees to her chest, keeping her attention on the house entrances, then the outbuildings, then the road. The only comfort was the eager dog prancing around the rear bumper, who was clearly happy to have a visitor.

She felt like she was either going to die here and be tossed in a swamp, or that she'd be in the presence of the troopers within the hour.

A minute later, the lanky figure emerged with the phone in one hand, quickly closing the side door to keep the frantic Rottweiler inside. The dog's head looked to be twice the size of Micah's, and she was sure the old man wasn't joking about it swallowing her up.

"I already told the captain the basics of what you told me, but he wants to talk with ya." He stood near the steps, waving her over. "You'll have to stand here. This phone don't have great reception beyond this point."

She climbed down, the hound dancing around her and licking the dried blood on her legs. Again, she caught the man glancing over her figure, but this time he was slow to avert his eyes.

She took the phone and stood to the side, facing the owner. "Hello, this is Micah Brezny. I was camped at Birch Lake last night, and a bunch of people were murdered there. You have to send someone out there."

"Whoa, slow down," said the man. "Ernie told me the same thing, but why don't you start from the beginning."

She found it odd that the man didn't introduce himself. She tried to remain detached, but nausea conspired against her as she rattled off the details: that it was two knife-wielding maniacs in a motorboat. They came out of nowhere, at dusk. And how she and April were taking a bathroom break when Ryan was killed. The terrible fight with the large man in a plaid shirt who rushed at them and how she had hit the man in the face with a rock.

The anguish-laced story flooded out of her until she finished with the part about meeting Ernie on the road. When Micah was done, she felt a vein throbbing in her neck and gulped down a breath.

The old man sat on the steps, stroking his hound's side while scanning the woods.

"So, you said the two men were dressed in plaid shirts and had beards. Any other details?" asked the voice on the phone. "What did their knives look like?"

"They were hook knives, like the kind hardware stores sell for carpet cutting." She was surprised at how robotic the man's voice was. There was no compassion or concern for her safety, or recognition of her overcoming horrendous odds to make it this far, or any inquiry about her background. She'd had plenty of encounters with cops in Anchorage and wondered if Alaska State Troopers were really that different.

"Alright, Micah, I think I have—"

She interrupted him. "What's your name? I never got that."

"Officer Tomlinson. Denali borough. Now, can you hand the phone back to Ernie so I can coordinate picking you up."

Again, rote voice. No emotion. Not even mildly irritated for being called out on his poor manners. *And state troopers don't usually call themselves officers. That's a term used by cops in Anchorage and Fairbanks. And Denali's a national park, not a fucking borough.*

Micah thrust the phone back to the old man, who stood

up and walked towards the woodpile despite just saying the device didn't have great reception.

Ernie paced around the chopping block, stopping occasionally to punt a black beetle. Behind her, Micah could hear the heavy breathing of Brutus on the other side of the wooden door.

"Hey, is there a bathroom or outhouse I can use?"

Ernie pulled the phone away, gesturing towards the rear of his home. "On the other side of the back porch, there's some fuel barrels you can go behind."

She hopped up and moved to the other side of the structure, skirting along the screened-in back patio. Micah paused, seeing a phone set on a table. She glanced back, not seeing the old man. She walked up the steps and slowly opened the door and removed the phone from its charging cradle, keeping her other hand pressed against the speaker.

The lawman's voice was no longer monotone. He was barking orders at Ernie. "You did a good job selling your story about being suspicious of her. Now, find a way to entertain her. Make her lunch and offer her a shower...whatever it takes to keep her there until I arrive this evening. She's the bitch who got away from us."

Micah felt like the porch was constricting. She fought to breathe, pressing a hand against her side. *No. No. This can't be happening. Not again.*

Ernie's gruff voice flooded into her ears. "She's not gonna buy that the authorities can't get here for eight hours."

"Tell her the troopers are all out at Birch Lake, handling the crime scene. Slip some drugs into her food—just do whatever it takes to keep her there."

Micah returned the phone to the cradle, trying to steady her shaking hand. She felt her stomach churning again. She stepped back, bumping into a table. Turning, she saw it was covered with wood handles, brass pins and half-moon-shaped blades—the exact weapon used by the killers.

Her eyes widened, staring at the components, then at the metalsmithing tools alongside dozens of knives of different designs. She felt like her feet were glued to the floorboards, having just wandered into a spider's lair.

*He not only knows the killers, he's in deep with them.*

She opened the door and backed down the steps right into the guy.

"Guess the cat's out of the bag. Now, you're coming with—"

Micah didn't wait for him to finish. She sent a vicious shin kick into his groin and then punched him in the lip. The man groaned and fell back, the phone dropping from his hand as he hit the ground. She rushed up and grabbed the keyring off his belt and his folding knife, then sent a kick into his ribs.

The basset hound was barking at her now but ran onto the porch as she trotted by.

Micah bolted past the truck and into the carport, hopping on the ATV. She fumbled with the keys, finding the smallest one, then started the vehicle.

She throttled the engine and sped out of the carport, pausing by the truck. She flicked open the folding knife and stabbed the air valve on the rear tire. A second later, she fled down the road as the old man limped towards the front of his cabin. She heard the crack of pistol shots and saw splinters of wood on the trees around her as she fled.

The ATV fishtailed on the muddy road as she fought to keep it upright. Behind her, she heard Ernie shouting curses, followed by the thunderous barking of Brutus—one hundred fifty pounds of pure muscle and fury crashing through the underbrush with the single-minded determination of a freight train.

*Holy shit on a cracker!*

Another gunshot rang out, closer this time, and tree bark exploded inches from her head as she leaned low over the handlebars, weaving desperately between the towering spruces while the Rottweiler's massive paws pounded the earth behind her, gaining ground with each stride.

The path curved sharply ahead, and Micah took the turn at full throttle, rear wheels sliding sideways on the slick soil as Brutus lunged for her back tire, his massive jaws snapping shut on empty air. The beast's hot breath had been so close she could smell his rank saliva as his teeth scraped against the plastic fender, missing her leg by mere inches.

She swerved left as Brutus made another desperate lunge, his claws raking against the metal frame while she fought to keep the ATV from rolling, then jerked right as he came at her again, foam flying from his muzzle as he snapped at her boots.

Only when she hit a straight stretch and opened the throttle completely did she finally leave the creature skidding in the mud. Ernie's curses echoed through the woods for a few seconds until she sped up the hill and disappeared over the side, escaping another brush with death.

She prayed it would be her last.

# CHAPTER 7

After they finished at the troopers' post in Saxon, Payne and Gus drove back to Wolf Lake Lodge. The tone in the truck was somber, and Payne could see the tension on the older man's face. While the grisly scenes at Birch Lake would be enough to turn anyone's mood dark, it seemed like his attitude had further soured after discussing the Dean kid's case.

Once they arrived at the lodge, the two men gathered their packs and rifles and stood under the eaves of the back porch.

Gus shot a glance at the glassy lake as if he were searching for something below the inky waters. "Just don't see how it coulda been the Dean boy. He didn't strike me as being wired to be a mass murderer."

"Knew him well?"

A faint scowl formed on Gus' face. "Knew his piece-of-shit father. And I use that paternal term lightly. He treated that kid like an animal. I'm not the only one who was grateful to hear that the old bastard had been put down. Just wish it hadn't been by his own son."

Gus kicked a pebble down the slope. "Jimmy's mom used

to run a small bakery in town when he was little. I'd go in there most mornings on my way to work and grab a coffee and pastries. Jimmy was always there, since he was home-schooled. He was a good kid. When his mother died in a house fire after her drunken son-of-a-bitch husband passed out with a cigar on the couch, life went from tolerable to brutal for Jimmy. Didn't see him for a long time, and whenever I did, he looked like a beaten dog."

He shook his head and waved a meaty hand at the lake. "You don't see other species torturing their own kind and kicking 'em around. And man thinks he is somehow above all the other creatures and has dominion over the Earth."

"I hate to say it, but spending his teenage years in juvie lockup would have changed Jimmy. He survived by adapting and becoming something else."

"You're right to a degree, but it just doesn't turn a boy like that into a psycho." Gus pursed his lips. "I visited him once when I was in Anchorage for a conference. He'd been in lockup for maybe two years at that point. He was no longer a scrawny kid and held himself like I did after coming out of boot camp. He had a strength in him, but behind it all, I could still see a hint of that sweet little kid. It hadn't all been driven out."

"I don't think Nolte is going to share your sentiments, but he's an experienced trooper and will hopefully put his time in the trenches to good use getting to the bottom of what happened at that campground."

Gus nodded and turned towards the main lodge. "I'd better check on next week's client list. If you wouldn't mind replenishing the firewood in the cabins before it rains tonight, I'd be grateful. Then come up for some supper, if you'd like."

"Will do."

The older man walked off.

Payne wondered if Gus' challenge in keeping staff was

because he never talked like the boss, and instead asked his employees to help as if they were doing him a favor. Payne had no problem complying and was looking forward to swinging an ax in the remaining hours before sunset, and finally going halibut fishing down in Homer for the weekend. He just hoped the change of scenery would be enough to wash away the images from Birch Lake.

Payne headed in the opposite direction, walking across the meadow, then down the long wood-chipped trail that led to his isolated cabin. He grabbed a banana and a Clif bar, stuffing them in his pocket, then took a swig of the tepid coffee left in his cup on the counter. After grabbing his leather gloves and a water flask, he retraced his steps down the trail, veering off toward the woodshed.

The twenty-foot-long building had two open-faced bays containing a ride-on grass cutter, tractor, and wheelbarrow, along with an ATV with a snowplow on the front.

In the right corner was Payne's Indian motorcycle, sitting dormant for the past three weeks. On the far left was the tool room. Though it had a rusty padlock on the door, it was never used, and Gus always joked that if someone drove out here on the rutted dirt road and stole some items, then they needed them more than he did.

Payne walked to the tool room, grabbing the handle and pulling the door open. It was then that he noticed the faint speckle of blood in the dirt.

The rush of movement in the dim light caught him by surprise, and he jumped back as something blurred towards his head. The sound of wood cracking against wood shattered the stillness as a hickory ax handle slammed into the door frame, narrowly missing his nose.

He shuffled back, grabbing the ax resting on a stump to his left. The faint outline of a woman was silhouetted by slivers of sun slipping through cracks in the wall. Her long hair was disheveled and peppered with twigs and leaves.

"Stay the fuck away from me," she yelled as she thrust the hickory handle like she was a fencer.

"Easy. I work for the lodge. I was just coming to split some firewood." Payne lowered his ax by his side. Now that she had stepped into the light, he could see the look of abject terror in her eyes. She resembled a caged animal ready to bite off an approaching hand.

Payne glanced at the lacerations on her bare legs, then down at her muddy hiking boots. "You've covered some ground getting here. This place is a long way from nowhere."

Her stare alternated between Payne's hands and the open meadow that led to the main buildings in the distance. "Where am I?"

"Wolf Lake Lodge, about twenty-five miles west of Saxon."

She stepped out, holding the hickory handle like a baseball player as she glanced at the property, then back at Payne.

He gazed down at the dirt, seeing the same tread pattern from the last campsite at Birch Lake, confirming his suspicions. He stepped back a few feet, keeping the ax handy. "Thirteen miles is a long way to trek, especially after what you've been through."

Her gaze slowly shifted to his. "I don't know what you're talking about. I just got lost after my ATV ran out of gas a few miles back."

He removed the Clif bar and banana from his jacket and set them down on the stump. "I was at Birch Lake with the local trooper most of the day, going over the crime scene and interpreting the tracks. I can't imagine the hell you witnessed last night. But I know you must be tough as hell to escape that kind of ordeal."

She scurried forward, grabbing the Clif bar and tearing off

the wrapper with her teeth while keeping the stick weapon raised. The snack was quickly devoured. The girl wiped a tear from her cheek and slinked back against the door frame of the tool room, her confident façade suddenly deflated.

He knew she was in shock on many levels, and her exhaustion was only kept at bay by sheer will and adrenaline, both of which had to be nearing depletion. He tossed his water flask at her feet.

She kicked it away. "How do I know it's not drugged?"

"You really think I figured a stranger was hiding in the woodshed, so I went back to my cabin to prepare a concoction to drug you?"

She raised an eyebrow. "This inbred motherfucker who tried to trap me at his house earlier today looked like you, and he came off like he was going to help me, too."

Payne chuckled. "I've been called a lot of things over the years, but never 'inbred.'" He leaned the ax against the stump. "I'm Kyle Payne. I'm the groundskeeper here, at least for a few more days."

She glanced up at his face while grabbing the water bottle and taking a swig. "You look like a biker."

"An inbred biker or just a regular one?"

"Not sure yet."

He canted his head towards his Indian. "Funny you mention that, because I'm traveling the US on my motorcycle. Just took this gig to have a home base and see the wilderness out here. The owner of this lodge needed some temporary help, so here I am."

He stepped closer, grabbing the banana and tossing it to her. "What about you? You from the Saxon area?"

She greedily peeled the covering off and began eating as the first raindrops began pattering the tin roof. "Nice try. You share a tidbit of your personal life and then try to pluck out my background. You a therapist or social worker in your previous life, Kyle?"

It wasn't the response he was expecting. Why hadn't she spilled what happened at Birch Lake? And why hadn't she asked for him to call the troopers or get a ride into town?

An icy chill ran down his back. Unless she was somehow involved in the killings. He quickly dismissed the idea. The tracks said otherwise. Two larger men chasing down a smaller figure who had escaped along the far end of the lake.

"You wanna tell me what happened at that campground? I'm here to help."

She tossed down the empty peel and stared out at the gray sun. Again, she wiped a tear off her quivering cheeks. "Will there be troopers on their way here soon? Because, honestly, the last thing I want right now is to be interrogated about the worst night of my life."

"The road is about to turn to mush with this coming storm, and Gus, my boss, won't risk flying out in this weather, so tomorrow I can get you to Saxon."

She glanced around the shed, rubbing her shivering arms. "Any tarps around here that aren't covered in mouse shit?"

"It's going to be in the forties tonight. With this rain and in your condition, you'll be hypothermic by midnight. There's a bathhouse halfway down the meadow on the left. Go get cleaned up, and I'll scrounge up some clothes and get you dinner from the lodge."

He walked to the front of the woodshed. "I told the lieutenant in charge of the investigation that there were two attackers, but he isn't entirely convinced, so anything you can share would sure help. You have every reason to not trust me, or anyone at this point, but the other victims who died at that lake aren't going to get the justice they need without your help."

He was about to walk off when she spoke. "You're right—there were two of them, and they were fucking barbarians."

# CHAPTER 8

## ANCHORAGE

*The view from the upstairs porch of the two-bedroom home must be incredible*, thought Groh as he scanned the groomed property with his binoculars from his truck on the cusp of the city limits.

Hatch was sitting in the passenger seat, doing a weapons check on his suppressed Glock 19 pistol while chomping on the last chunk of a KitKat bar.

"Remember, don't be too precise with that thing. I want this to look like a burglary gone badly, not a staged assassination," said Groh.

Groh watched the black Land Rover meander up the long driveway across the street, then wait in front of the middle garage door while it opened.

"Five minutes, then we head inside the house," said Groh after watching the vehicle enter and the door close.

The rain pattered the truck's windshield, and Groh was going to be grateful for tomorrow, when this storm system had pushed through. Though it did have the added value of washing away tracks and blood, which was a blessing in his line of work.

And his line of work entailed acquiring priceless objects for discretionary buyers while eliminating any obstacles along the way. Most of Groh's clientele paid premium rates for access to the world's most endangered creatures, and he'd acquired a reputation for always delivering regardless of who had to be eliminated. Most of the time that meant guiding wealthy clients to a shooting perch to take down a prized big-game animal in Africa or Southeast Asia.

But this week's paycheck was for a friend and benefactor who had provided him with the means and resources to become one of the most feared poachers in the world. After this assignment, he would ensure he didn't have to work again for a few years or more, and no expense had been spared for the weapons, comms, and men to complete his objective.

And William Evans, the man entering his posh home, was about to be checked off Groh's list.

He and Hatch had been sitting here for half an hour, parked in the truck with tinted windows along the neighborhood trailhead whose pathway snaked through the trees on the state land abutting Evans' place. The nearest homes were a hundred yards in either direction, and given the weather, the woods weren't likely to see any day hikers.

"Ever wonder if a place like this would suit you?" asked Hatch as they stared at the front of the house.

"Modern-day slave bracelet," said Groh as he rested his leathery hands on the binoculars in his lap. "The guy inside will be grateful to get a round in his chest so he isn't shackled to his ridiculous mortgage. The upkeep on the grounds alone must eat into half his paycheck."

"Never figured a surveyor to make enough cash to afford a nice joint like this."

"His old lady's the breadwinner. She's a physician's assistant."

Groh didn't know much more about his target other than that he ran his own land surveying company and had a degree in geography and natural resources. The man specialized in remote land survey, mapping out properties for landowners so far off the grid that their holdings could only be accessed by float plane or boat.

Usually, such parcels were snatched up by hotel companies wanting to build resorts in far-flung places where visitors could feel like they were staying at the edge of the world. But sometimes, guys like Evans also did work for individuals wanting to have their property boundaries staked out if it was located in contested regions near logging or mining operations.

For Groh's employer, the latter was a concern. And now the two killers were here to eliminate Evans and erase evidence of a particular remote survey from three months ago.

Groh examined yesterday's text message from one of his local contacts who had surveilled Evans' daily routine during the past two weeks. "He does Zoom meetings and calls with his clients at home on days like today, so he should be in his home office on the west side of the house for the afternoon, and the wife works until midnight."

Hatch pointed to the thick coppice of oak trees along the public trail. "Should be easy to access the side door from there."

"Use your lockpicks. I want it to seem like we were already in the house when he came home."

"Got it."

———

GROH STOOD IN THE TREES, watching Evans through the thin white curtains on his office window. The man had his back to the forest while he worked on his computer on the spacious desk, oblivious to the predators outside.

Hatch got busy with the deadbolt on the side door, unlocking it with his picking tools after a few minutes of quiet effort. Years of perfecting his skills breaking into isolated cabins where he would live for a few weeks had gotten his lock bypasses down to sixty seconds. He gave Groh a thumbs-up, and both men removed their suppressed pistols before stepping inside.

They stood on the small entry carpet, listening to Evans finish a phone call. Groh glanced down the long hallway, seeing two more doors on the right, one on the left, and a living room ahead beside a staircase to the second floor.

He'd already made sure that the Evans' family didn't have dogs, which would have been a hurdle he'd have to use poison for. Groh hated dogs more than he hated people; their only use in his world was for treeing bears and mountain lions so they could be easily shot.

Evans signed off from his call, and the office was silent. The two men waited until the surveyor began typing on his keyboard before they proceeded.

Groh took the lead, pressing against the wall and moving slowly so his boots didn't scrape the wood flooring. Reaching the entrance, he swept inside and waited for Evans to swivel around in his chair before firing off two rounds into the man's chest, followed by two in the wall, making sure not to damage the laptop.

"Easy-peasy," said Hatch, who shoved Evans' limp body from the chair and dragged him to the back of the room.

Groh sat down and began pulling up the files from this spring's surveying contracts. He settled on May, then went to the last week and examined the headings. "While I'm doing this, go grab a pillowcase full of jewelry and shit from the house and break a few things along the way."

Hatch grinned. "Most fun I've ever had on a job." He walked to the door and froze, stepping back. "Um, Andre, we gotta problem."

Groh spun in his chair, staring at Evans' eight-year-old son. "Shit. You were supposed to be in daycare after school." He noticed the boy's red cheeks and puffy face. "Did your dad bring you home early 'cause you ain't feeling good?"

The boy nodded, clutching his Captain America figure and glancing at the desk. "Who are you? And where's my daddy?"

"We're, um, friends of your dad's from work," said Hatch as he blocked the door so the boy couldn't see the rest of the room. "I think he said he was going to the garage to get something from his vehicle, so let's find him."

The boy moved back a few feet.

Hatch glanced over his shoulder at Groh. "Take care of it. And I don't mean with duct tape."

"What? You serious?" said Hatch as his mouth hung open.

"We don't have time for this shit, and maybe you forgot the part about using my name."

"He's just a kid."

Groh's eyes narrowed. He pushed past Hatch, the gunshots echoing off the walls suddenly making the house seem more cavernous than when they first entered.

———

AFTER THE SECOND round of vomiting in the downstairs toilet, Hatch returned to the hallway, averting his eyes from the bloody tiles as he walked towards the living room and headed upstairs. He shut the door on the first bedroom upstairs, where the floor was covered with superheroes. He trudged to the master bedroom at the end of the hall and yanked the case off a pillow on the king size bed. He robotically began shoving items inside from the dressers on either side of the room. Watches, earrings, necklaces, keepsakes, anything that looked shiny. He slammed a lamp on the floor and kicked over a nightstand with a vase full of fresh roses.

Another round of bile in his stomach conspired to rush up. He dropped the pillowcase and ran to the bathroom, splashing cold water on his face. When he glanced up, he saw someone who resembled his ailing grandparents.

He splashed again, then rubbed his cheeks so hard he thought the skin would slough away. The murders at Birch Lake had been so fueled by cocaine that he barely remembered who was killed first. It had almost seemed like a video game. Even the screams of the young girl seemed melodic now in retrospect, but he knew that was his brain compartmentalizing the horrific shrieks to cope with what he had done.

Now, he was sure there was no amount of drugs that would erase the image of the young boy's face. He glanced through the doorway for a moment to make sure Groh wasn't present; then he removed a small vial of white powder from his jacket.

He poured a dab on his palm and snorted the nose candy. He'd sworn off cocaine after Birch Lake, but now he knew it was a crutch he'd never live without.

He looked in the mirror and wiped away the remnants from his nostrils. Hatch glanced at the crucifix on the wall in the bedroom. *God, forgive me.*

# CHAPTER 9

Payne waited in the rain on the covered porch outside the bathhouse, mulling over the girl's appearance and the Herculean effort it must have taken to endure what she'd been through to make it this far.

While she was clearly in shock over what had happened, he was surprised at both her composure and her defensiveness to his questioning. She didn't fold or break down, which would have been an understandable response. Instead, she remained steadfast, which told him she was someone who had experienced violence in her life before, though hopefully not on the scale of what had happened at Birch Lake.

Her jaded demeanor reminded him of kids he'd seen in refugee camps in war-torn regions in Africa, where life had been driven into a corner and the only concerns were the daily quest for food, water and a safe place to sleep. Children who had seen too much horror and were reduced to either being predator or prey.

The lights went off in the bathhouse, and the girl stepped out onto the screened porch, moving to the opposite side from Payne. She was wearing a donated pair of baggy jeans, a green T-shirt and black hoodie, along with her muddy boots. Her right hand still clutched the hickory handle, though it hung loosely by her side this time.

"You can thank Jasmine, the admin assistant, for the loaner clothes in the morning, along with my boss, for not locking you up in the basement of the lodge."

"Good luck trying to do that."

He gestured towards the Tupperware container on a small table under the porch light. "Moose steak, potatoes, and green beans—and I told the chef to leave out the drugs."

She frowned before popping off the lid and plucking out the steak, then tearing into it. With her hands and face clean of dirt and blood, he could see her tan skin. So she was clearly someone used to spending a considerable amount of time under open skies. She looked sixteen, but the fearful gaze in her eyes made her seem much younger.

A long silence followed, and the raindrops on the roof muffled out the usual sound of insects and crickets.

Finally, Payne removed a folding chair from the corner and sat. "You out on that canoe trip with your friends for a long time?"

"How'd you know who I was with?"

"Because tracking isn't something new. I examined all the boot prints around the three campsites. Plus there were two tents and three sleeping bags at the last site where you were."

She froze mid-bite, staring into the pitch-black night as the rain came down heavier. For a moment her face looked pale, and Payne wondered if her stomach was about to hit the eject button on her meal.

"We were out for almost a week and got to our last campsite yesterday afternoon. April and I went into the woods to use the bathroom, when…" She set down the container and leaned against the wall. "The attacker came out of nowhere. Ryan didn't have a chance. He…he was…"

She shook her head. "April and me ran. We ran so fast. But they just moved like cats. I grew up in the woods and had never seen anyone move like that. They almost caught us. We were so close to the marsh where we were gonna hide, but April tripped."

Her lips were trembling now as she paced back and forth. "I tried to help her, but they were already on her." The girl pressed her back into the wall and slid to the ground, pressing her hands to her face.

Her story confirmed his findings from the manuscript on the ground. Two efficient but ruthless predators had emerged at the shoreline and quickly dispatched four defenseless individuals in a matter of minutes, then disappeared.

*But why? And was one of them Jimmy Dean as Nolte suspects? And why venture out into a remote wilderness region to slaughter a bunch of seemingly unconnected people?*

Payne couldn't fathom the answers. That would be Nolte's job, and he was sure the lawman was hunched over his desk, mulling over the crime scene photos. Right now, Payne's only concern was making sure the girl was safe and got some rest. Tomorrow, Nolte indicated to Gus that he would fly out to pick up the girl. After that, Payne would be on his way south to Homer on his coveted fishing trip.

"I'm sorry for your loss and for what you suffered through. It's not how it should've gone. For anyone out there. The term 'psychos' doesn't begin to describe those two guys."

She waved a hand towards the darkness. "They have friends out here."

"How's that?"

"That inbred dude I mentioned earlier. I ran into him on a road this morning, probably six or seven miles from here. He was talking to someone on the phone at his house about me— said it was a trooper, but it was all bullshit. He was coming to finish me off tonight."

"Who'd the guy on the other end of the line say he was?"

"Officer Tomlinson out of Denali, but Denali doesn't have a police force or troopers, only park rangers. Plus, I overheard him say 'she's the bitch who got away from us,' so what does that tell you?"

The whole time she was explaining things, she was intently studying Payne's face, gauging his reaction, while keeping one hand tightly clutched around the hickory handle.

"You're wise not to trust anyone, given what you've been through, but there's something about you that tells me you're probably pretty good at relying on your gut instincts, so what are they telling you right now about being here? About me? Because that will determine what happens next."

"Next?"

He gestured towards the screen door. "I don't plan to hang out on this cold porch all night. My cabin is a couple of minutes' walk from here, and you're welcome to sack out on the couch by the fireplace. In the morning you can tell a real lawman, Robert Nolte, what happened."

She dragged a sleeve across her moist cheeks and stood. "Your place have a porch like this?"

He nodded.

"If you've got a sleeping bag and pad, I'll stay there instead. I'm used to living outdoors. Worked on a trail crew for the past three summers, so the cold don't bother me."

"Suit yourself, but I like to know the name of my guests."

She seemed to weigh the simple question as if inquiries into her life always passed through a screening process. It made him think it was reflexive and not something born from the past twenty-four hours of terror.

"I'm Micah. Micah Brezny."

———

ONE MILE AWAY, four ATVs slowed along the muddy road. The drivers veered left into the woods and killed their lights before dismounting.

The camouflaged figures methodically removed the suppressed rifles from the hard-shelled cases mounted on their rear cargo racks. Each of the poachers donned their night-vision goggles, then slid the hoods of their waterproof jackets back over their heads.

Ernie Packard glanced at the GPS unit he removed from his pocket, then pointed across the road. "One mile cross-country to the southwest side of Wolf Lake Lodge. We'll do a sweep of the structures and locate the girl. According to Groh's contact, she's staying at the groundskeeper's place, which is most likely detached from the main lodge. Remember, this needs to be a quiet snatch. No shooting unless fired upon. Ideally, I'd like to wait until the lights are out and everyone's asleep, but if the opportunity to grab the girl presents itself, then do it."

He held up a photo of the blonde-haired girl on his phone that he had downloaded from the security camera on his home's back porch. He wouldn't mind slitting her throat for the beating she'd dished out, but that would have to be done off-site to avoid creating another blood-soaked crime scene.

"What happens after we get her? We gonna haul her scrawny ass back through the woods with us?" asked the goateed man to his right.

"That's the plan. Then we'll drop her body in that swamp near the Kenai Peninsula."

"After we have some fun with her first, right?" the guy asked.

Packard frowned. "It's not one of those trips this time."

"What if she talked to others at the lodge about what she saw at Birch Lake?" said a tall man who slung his AR-10.

"Won't matter. When Groh was pretending to be a cop on

the phone with her at my place, the dumb bitch gave out her name. His employer did some digging and found out she's a runaway from Anchorage. Been in and out of the court system for years, so she won't be believed or even missed." Packard looked at his watch. "Given the terrain and weather, I figure sixty minutes to get to the property, so let's get a move on it. I want Goldilocks boots up in the cattails by sunrise."

# CHAPTER 10

The front entrance of the cabin was shattered in one blow, the frame splintering apart, the wooden door breaking free from its hinges. The team of assaulters rushed inside, their rifle-mounted flashlights sweeping around the small structure.

The place smelled like beer and sweat. Lieutenant Nolte's rifle fixed on the slumped figure lying flat on the couch. Nolte moved forward as the rest of his hastily assembled five-man team searched the remaining rooms.

Once the small cabin was cleared, most of the team reassembled in the main cabin while two troopers headed out the back door.

Nolte's volunteer lawman, Miles Kitchner, kneeled beside the gaunt figure on the couch, feeling for a pulse. As a paramedic, Kitchner quickly assessed his patient, then examined the prescription bottle on the coffee table and the half-empty bottle of tequila. "He's barely alive. Pulse is thready. Must have OD'd on his Vicodin. We need to get him to an intensive care unit, fast."

"We'll have to drive him ourselves since the helos are gonna be grounded in this weather," said Nolte, who glanced at the bearded man on the left scrutinizing the kitchen counter. "Gomez, you drive my cruiser while Miles takes care of this guy. Call for an ambulance and have them meet you en route to Anchorage."

"Roger that, boss, but you're gonna wanna see this." He flicked on the overhead lights.

Nolte moved closer, examining a bloody knife that matched the description of the curved gutting tool previously used in the murder of Dean's father.

He walked cautiously around the kitchen, stopping near the bathroom door and gazing at the pair of muddy boots near the shower. He stepped inside, picking up the leather boots with a gloved hand and examining the diamond-shaped tread pattern, which was identical to the style seen at Birch Lake. He noticed the chipped *b* in the Vibram logo on the right boot, like Payne had indicated. Nolte studied the left boot, whose logo was completely intact.

*Payne may have been right.*

He retraced his steps to the main room just as another trooper entered the back door. Corporal Hicks' face was dappled with rain, but Nolte was sure that wasn't the cause of the guy's ashen expression.

"Sir, there's a boat trailer out back with blood all over the side rails and hitch. I never seen…never seen anything like it before."

"Find a tarp and cover it. I need that evidence preserved," barked Nolte.

Hicks nodded reluctantly, then disappeared into the night.

The medic had trotted out to the vehicle and returned with his trauma kit, beginning a saline IV in Dean's right arm while the two other lawmen assembled a makeshift stretcher from a blanket. When they had finished, the two troopers transferred Dean to the blanket on the ground and hoisted him up, carrying him to the vehicle, while Kitchner accompanied them.

Nolte completed his initial exam of the modest dwelling. The place reminded him of his son's college fraternity in Fairbanks. A heap of empty cereal boxes near the overflowing trash bin, a pile of dirty clothes by the bathtub, crumpled beer cans on the floor by the couch, and a bedroom that smelled like a gym.

*Except this is the home of a mass murderer.*

He scrutinized the bloody knife on the counter again, knowing he was going to need more help with this investigation. A full-blown forensics team and extra troopers to secure the area, for starters.

And one other critical element: a PR crisis management team because Saxon was about to become ground zero for a legion of gawkers and journalists intent on promoting their version of the Birch Lake Butcher.

# CHAPTER 11

Payne was sitting on the rocking chair near the stone fireplace, enjoying the warmth of the flames while reading *Don Quixote*. It was his third time perusing the classic in ten years, and each visit with the old master caused some new revelation to rise through the pages.

He was only halfway through the second chapter when the back door of the porch opened and in walked Micah. The bags under her eyes seemed more pronounced, but her expression softened when she glanced at the fireplace.

"Suffering in silence can be rough, especially when the cold is gnawing away at you," said Payne. He set his book down on a round table and gestured towards the stove. "I just shut off the pot of water, and there's hot chocolate and mugs in the cabinet beside the fridge. Help yourself."

"'Mugs'…nobody up here says that. You must be a cheechako."

"Not sure how to take that since Gus said a cheechako means 'bush idiot.'"

Micah chuckled. "That too, but it also means outsider, as in someone from the lower forty-eight."

"Fair enough. What else gave away that I'm not from here?"

She went about making herself a cup of hot cocoa. "Not your clothes...you actually look like someone used to spending time outdoors, which isn't usually the case with tourists here, who seem like they just maxed out their card at REI."

She finished stirring the drink and then hopped up on the edge of the counter like she owned the cabin. "Your accent... can't place it but certainly not from here either. This is as far as I've ever traveled outside of Anchorage, so not sure, but I've seen plenty of crime flicks, and you ain't from Chicago or New York."

"Michigan. Grew up in a small town in the Upper Peninsula that was half Swedish, part native, and a mix of ex-Canadians, so it's not the usual Midwest accent like my downstate counterparts, which, by the way, we call 'trolls,' meaning people who were raised below the Mackinac Bridge. So even we have our own elitist version of cheechako."

"I'm not elitist. I just get tired of dumb tourists coming up here and trashing our fishing areas and trails, thinking the wilderness is so vast, it doesn't matter. Then they get into trouble in the woods because they're unprepared or just plain stupid and suddenly need help."

"Sounds like you've been on the receiving end of that call. Did that happen when you were on the trail crew you mentioned?"

She sipped her drink, staring into the cup. "Sometimes. But April and I always joked that the bears..."

Micah set the beverage down, gripping the edge of the counter so hard that her knuckles turned white. She gazed up at the ceiling, shaking her head. "God, what am I doing here? We were supposed to be coming off the water today. Loading our canoes onto Ryan's truck and heading to Homer for pizza."

She slid off the counter, folding her arms as she leaned back. "What did that guy Nolte say when you told him about me being here?"

"I didn't actually talk to him. My boss, Gus, did. It sounded like Nolte understood the logistics of getting out here in this weather and that he also had his own operation underway to apprehend the guy behind the killings. Someone by the name of Jimmy Dean."

Micah's eyes widened. "The kid who killed his old man when he was thirteen?"

"Yeah, you know him?"

She shrugged. "Everybody out here knows about him. April used to say that Dean was possessed by a demon that came out of the swamp. Kids made up all kinds of bullshit stories about what happened. But it wasn't him at the lake last night."

"I know you said there were two guys, but one of them could have been Dean."

She shook her head, walking to the couch and sitting down. "Jimmy has a limp, supposedly from falling off his bunk in juvie and fracturing his pelvis when he was fifteen. No way he was at the lake. Plus, those two guys were big, and Jimmy was a stick."

*She sure knows a helluva lot about Dean. And she called him by his first name. This all sounds like firsthand knowledge.*

He glanced at her hands, noticing the faint trace of scars on her knuckles. Old scars that probably didn't come from being on a trail crew. From the way she quickly assessed her surroundings and had scrutinized Payne earlier, along with her rough edges, he wondered if she had also been in juvie.

*Is that why she seemed reluctant to talk with the troopers tonight? Is she on the run from more than just the Birch Lake killers?*

"Whoever's behind the murder of my friends and the others is trying to use Jimmy as their fall guy."

"Why? And why would they..." Payne arched up, his head canting towards the ceiling. Then he heard it again. At first, he thought it was another burst of thunder. Until he detected the sound of something on the roof. By its weight and cadence, he dismissed it as a raccoon or skunk.

A second later, the flames in the fireplace dropped to half their height, and wisps of smoke began floating into the room.

"What's going on?" Micah asked, holding her sleeve up to her nose as the smoke intensified, setting off the overhead alarm in the hallway.

Payne heard the sounds on the roof again. He bolted for the bedroom, grabbing the Mossberg 500 shotgun from the corner along with his .38 Smith & Wesson revolver hidden behind the books on the closet shelf.

*This can't be a coincidence: having the girl here and my cabin being flooded with smoke. Someone's trying to draw us out.*

He returned to the living room, motioning to Micah to be quiet and follow him, then turned off the main light switch. Payne returned to the bedroom, yanking down the blaring smoke alarm; then he removed his backpack and gear from the closet and pried open a small hatch in the floorboards for the crawlspace under the cabin.

"What are you doing?"

"Someone's trying to smoke us into the open. I'm guessing they're here for you."

"What? There's no way they would know I'm here. You probably didn't open the flue on the fireplace enough, cheechako."

"The flue isn't the problem. The hit team outside that's about to storm us is."

"You watch too many movies."

"Get below, and we can compare notes later, kid."

She glanced into the hole. "This is insane. Are you some paranoid survival nut?"

"Some people would think so, but this is no drill." He grabbed her sleeve and pulled her towards the hatch.

"Leave me the fuck alone. I'm going back to the porch while you…"

They paused, both of their heads turning towards the bedroom window, where a silhouette of someone passed beyond the curtains, followed by the raspy voice of a man. "I just heard a girl inside. It's gotta be Micah."

She turned towards Payne, her face frozen. "Oh, God, they know my name? How does anyone know I'm here?"

"Go," Payne said, nodding at the crawlspace entrance. "And don't come out, no matter what you hear."

This time, she moved as if there were an invisible line yanking her into the opening.

Payne's eyes were watering, and he fought back a cough, staying low. A few more minutes and the air would become deadly.

The fact that they hadn't burst through the doors and shot up the place meant they wanted Micah alive. *Or maybe they just don't want to turn the cabin into another massacre site.*

He slid the safety off on the shotgun, knowing the first three rounds were triple-aught buckshot while the remaining four were lead slugs. After that, it would be down to six hollow-point rounds from the .38 snubbie.

He hoped it would be enough firepower.

# CHAPTER 12

The rain had intensified, and Payne was sure there would be a breaching party entering both doors soon. They would be expecting two smoke-choked victims gagging on the floor. Right now, he needed to control the variables while he could.

Payne quickly trotted to the rear entrance, sliding the curtain aside slightly and peering through the window. There were two guys, but one man with a chin beard peeled off and ran around towards the front while the other remained. The latter goon was only a foot from the door, with a suppressed AR-10 levelled at the entrance.

Payne stepped to the side of the unlocked door, coughing and raking his fingernails along the surface. "Help. I can't reach the handle."

The door slowly opened, and Payne caught the glint of the metal barrel in the hazy firelight as the man stepped inside. Payne swung his shotgun barrel down on the rifle, then quickly pivoted his body and scythed the Mossberg's stock into the man's face. The guy's jaw crashed into the glass, shattering it as he tried to remain upright.

Payne drove the stock into the man's groin and then swung it in an uppercut that smacked the thug's chin, sending him back onto the porch. He crushed a wicker chair on the way to the floor and slammed his head against the corner studs. From the contorted position, it looked like the guy had broken his neck upon impact.

Payne removed the assaulter's 1911 pistol from his vest and tossed it aside, then grabbed the man's suppressed AR-10, leaning his Mossberg against the wall. He did a partial chamber check, seeing the faint hint of .223 brass, then made sure the safety was off.

He stepped off the back porch, making his way along the edge of the forest on the opposite side of the cabin. The mountain air hung thick with the scent of smoke and damp earth as Payne crept through the underbrush, each footstep calculated to avoid the twigs that littered the forest floor.

The rain had intensified, muffling sounds and turning the world into a hazy gray tableau that he hoped would work in his favor.

Pausing behind the large propane tank, he could make out two figures positioned ten feet away from the porch—one crouched behind a stack of firewood, the other leaning against an angled tree. Both were armed with what looked like military-grade semi-auto rifles.

The heavy patter of raindrops provided perfect acoustic cover as Payne veered into the woods and took up a position behind a massive spruce. The rough bark pressed against his cheek as he raised his rifle. His breath came out in controlled puffs of vapor.

Payne's crosshairs found the first target's temple through the night-vision scope, the man's profile sharp and clear despite the misty conditions. He controlled his breathing, feeling his heartbeat slow to that familiar combat rhythm, and gently squeezed the trigger. The suppressed rifle barely barked out, and the henchman behind the firewood crumpled silently to the wet ground.

His accomplice had less than a second to register something was wrong before Payne's next shot punched through his skull just above the ear, dropping him in a lifeless heap near his partner.

The bark splintered beside Payne's head, and he dropped to one knee, hunkering down around the far side of the tree. From the brief glint of muzzle flash, the shot had come from the woodshed.

Payne moved through the wet undergrowth, using the steady rhythm of rainfall to mask his approach again. As he passed the two dead guys, he paused to examine their facial features, not seeing the shooter with the chin beard, whom he figured was the same guy who had nearly taken his head off with that last shot.

He pushed on, circling wide to approach the shed from the blind side, where stacked cordwood created natural shooting lanes between the gaps. Through his scope, he could see the shooter's silhouette pressed into the shed's corner—a wiry man wearing a camo ball cap. Unfortunately for Payne, the guy was standing in front of the Indian motorcycle, so any shot was going to do considerable damage to his bike.

Instead of going for the kill shot, Payne shifted his aim slightly and squeezed the trigger, sending a round that struck the bearded man's right shoulder in an explosion of blood and muscle.

The shooter screamed and dropped his weapon, clutching his mangled arm as he stumbled away from the shed and crashed through the forest like a wounded animal.

Payne remained motionless for another full minute, scanning for additional threats, before finally rising from his concealed position and trotting down the trail to his cabin.

He stepped inside, closing the door. Payne made his way to the bedroom and called into the hatch for Micah.

The girl crawled back to the opening.

"Let's go. We need to get the hell out of Dodge, and right now," he said.

Micah shimmied up through the opening and followed Payne to the front door, then ran down the steps and along the trail, pausing by the dead men, whose lifeless shapes were illuminated by the porch light. "Jesus, did you do that?"

"Possibly." Payne removed the night-vision goggles off the nearest dead guy and grabbed the remaining weapons off the ground. He slid the safeties on the two AR-10s and handed them to Micah. "Sling those on your shoulder and follow me to the main lodge. It'll be safer there."

"You think they'll come back with more guys?"

"Probably not. I think they were just planning to grab you and take you off into the woods; otherwise they would have stormed the place and not bothered with smoking us out."

He could see the rollercoaster-wild look in her eyes. She was sinking into extreme flight mode, and panic was about to make her next move for her. Payne clutched her forearm. "Stick with me, and I'll get you through this. Alright?"

She stared down at the dead men and the blood streaming into the mud puddles, then up at Payne.

"Hey, you hear me?" he asked. "You're a helluva tough girl to make it this far. It's not going to end for you in the hands of people like this. You'll see the sunrise tomorrow. You got it?"

Micah bit her lower lip, nodding.

Payne pointed at the forest to the left. "We're going to skirt along those trees, following the meadow past the bath-house until we get to the side door of the main lodge. These night-vision goggles are going to give me a skewed view of things and slow me down a little, so just keep pace with me and don't run ahead."

"Okay. Can we just get out of here already?"

Hours ago, there was no place he'd rather be than in his cabin. Now, he couldn't agree more with her.

# CHAPTER 13

Groh had just reclined his truck seat to catch a few hours of rest when his cellphone buzzed.

Ernie Packard's number showed, bringing Groh a sense of relief. Until he heard the man's frantic voice and the constant wincing from being shot in the arm after the botched kidnapping at Wolf Lake Lodge.

Groh balled his fist so tight the nails began cutting into his calloused palm.

"Whoever that groundskeeper was, he knew his shit. He took out everyone but me, and I barely made it out in one piece. My right arm is fucked."

"Relax, Ernie," said Groh, trying to calm himself as much as his old friend on the other end. "You did what you could. Who could've known that there was someone inside that place with tactical know-how? But right now, I need you to take some painkillers and man up again."

"You want me to go back with more guys and assault the lodge since that's probably where the girl's at?"

"No. Freed and the newcomer will have established a defensive position and be expecting that, and I don't want to lose you or any more men. But I do need you to handle one more thing for me. And this time there can't be any mistakes."

———

AFTER HE HAD RELAYED his instructions, the phone went silent, and Groh tucked it away in his jacket.

"What now?" asked Hatch, who had just wedged a new wad of Copenhagen in his mouth.

"That girl, that's what. She keeps slipping through my fucking grasp. She got help from some local who sounded like he was ex-military. Dropped three of Packard's guys."

"If the girl talks to the troopers, it's going to be a problem. They'll know there were two of us at Birch Lake and start to wonder if Dean was really the one behind the killings."

"In Africa, when I needed to get someone out of the way without killing them, the quickest route was to publicly discredit their reputation over time. Worked well on a prominent conservation officer who was responsible for protecting the last white rhino in Namibia. Once support for him was shaken after his second arrest for drug possession, it gave me a narrow window to drop the fucking beast. That rhino's horn went on to fetch over $50K on the black market in Asia."

"But this is a teenage girl, with little to no reputation, from what you've said. She's a runaway from her foster parents."

"Exactly. And according to the inquiries my employer did, she's already known to the authorities in Anchorage and has a history of getting suspended at a half-dozen schools. The police scanner indicated Dean was already rolled up by Lieutenant Nolte, and with all the bloody evidence we planted at Dean's place, Nolte's going to see his apprehension as a slam-dunk. Once he talks to Micah Brezny, he's going to start to see holes in her story, especially once he learns about her background."

"Still, it sounds like a gamble. From what I've heard about Nolte, he's no small town cop. Worked homicide and narcotics outside Anchorage for nearly twenty years before moving to Saxon."

"He's a burnout. Came to the boonies to escape the pressure and will want to wrap up this murder investigation with a bow tie, especially once the media starts climbing all over Saxon and tourism in the region takes a major hit."

Groh removed his burner phone, finding the number for Alaska Department of Social Services on Google. He dialed the twenty-four-hour hotline, then tapped the third option for missing persons.

When the operator came on, he spoke in a pensive voice. "Yes, hello. My wife and I were just in a diner near Saxon and overheard a young woman arguing on her phone with what sounded like her mother. The girl said she was running away for good this time and would do whatever it took to fund her lifestyle, whatever that meant. She was pretty jittery like she was on something and seemed so scared. She took off into the woods before my wife could see if she needed help. Is there anything you can do? It's so cold out here tonight."

"First, thank you for your compassion. You did the right thing, sir. Most people just look the other way. Can you provide a description of the girl so we can notify the authorities in Saxon and hopefully locate her family?"

"Of course." Groh smiled as he recounted the details of the terror-stricken face from Birch Lake.

# CHAPTER 14

Payne hadn't slept at all, standing vigil on the second-floor balcony of the lodge, while Gus kept watch on the rear of the building. Micah slept in a spare bedroom, nestled between the cook's and Jasmine's bedrooms.

With the approach of dawn, Payne removed the night-vision goggles and welcomed a return to a world that wasn't cloaked in green hues.

Gus stepped onto the large porch and moved towards Payne, struggling to lower down on one knee behind the thick timber railing.

"Bring back memories from your Army days?"

"It was Marines, smart-ass, but you already knew that."

"What did I say? I thought I said Marines." Payne grinned as he nudged the older man in the arm.

"From the way you described handling the attackers at your cabin and your man-tracking skills at Birch Lake, I'd say you were former military, but you already told me you never served. And don't tell me you picked up being able to track people like that from occasional jaunts in the woods with your dad or your previous job working as a risk-management consultant overseas. I've known a few man trackers with the troopers over the years, and that's a pretty specialized skill."

Payne ran through his mental list of cover stories, but he didn't want to deceive a man he'd come to trust and respect, and who had put a roof over his head for the past three weeks. "What I told you about growing up in northern Michigan with a dad who was a game warden was true, but, later, I worked for the CIA for nearly fifteen years until resigning last summer."

Gus stared at him for a long moment. "So you did serve our country. Figured as much by some of the expressions you use and the way you carry yourself. You kinda struck me as an Army guy, except you don't walk like you got a roll of nickels up your ass or have a forty-six-inch waistline."

The older man returned to scanning the forest. "Were you a spy or an assassin?"

Payne fought back a laugh. "That sounds like Hollywood talking. At first, I was part of a unit that handled counter-insurgency issues overseas following the war on terror. Later, I worked with a smaller team that rescued case officers of ours who were in danger or on the run."

Gus nodded in the direction of Payne's cabin. "Well, it looks like you're still rescuing people on the run."

"Just until Nolte gets here; then I'm off to go fishing down in Homer, although the lieutenant might require me to stick around for another debrief, which, hopefully, won't last too long."

Gus glanced back at the door. "Look, I feel bad for what that kid's gone through, but I'll be glad when she leaves."

"Hey, man, I'm sorry about what went down at my cabin. I had no idea someone was going to come knocking on my door at midnight, especially not a team of hitters like that."

"It's not you I'm upset with. I woulda done the same thing."

"She'll be on her way to Saxon shortly, and then I'll have to see how Nolte wants to handle things at my cabin. I imagine he'll have his forensics guys head over here."

Gus frowned. "You think?" he said it with irritation in his voice.

Payne pointed to the extra AR-10 rifles on the floor. "There's some spare firepower. I'm going downstairs to check with Jasmine on Nolte's ETA."

"Roger that."

"And I'd appreciate it if you kept my past to yourself."

"You got it, kid."

Payne headed inside and paused beside the door to Micah's bedroom, listening for any movement. He figured with the past couple of days of adrenaline and running, she'd be in a deep sleep, but he heard her bare feet pacing along the floorboards, and wondered if she had been up all night.

He walked downstairs, passing through the main dining area. During busy weeks, the place would have been bustling with clients enjoying the complimentary breakfast, but the only person on the lower level was Jasmine.

The woman motioned him over, pointing to a cup of steaming coffee on the round table near the front door. "Thought you could use some liquid energy."

While Gus was reserved, Jasmine always loved to socialize and had a quick wit about her. Her graying brown hair was up in a tight bun, and her red reading glasses hung around her neck. She had been working part time at the lodge since Gus' wife died six years ago, and seemed more like Gus' personal assistant, doting on the man like he was far more than her employer.

"Two teaspoons of sugar, just like you take it," she said, sliding the cup towards him. She glanced at the AR rifle, then turned and gazed out the bay windows towards the lake.

"Usually when Gus is armed, it's for bears. Just can't believe someone would come after that young lady."

"Lady," it was the first time Payne saw Micah as such. She struck him more as a teenage tomboy who was part outdoor enthusiast and part street urchin, though which side dominated was uncertain at this point.

"Well, she'll be in Nolte's hands soon and out of harm's way." He sipped his coffee, keeping his eyes on the forest to the right and the distant trail that led to his cabin.

Payne stepped closer to Jasmine and lowered his voice. "Gus was sure intent on getting the girl out of here, and not just because he was worried about a repeat performance of last night's attack."

Jasmine nodded. "No outfitter or tourist company can afford bad publicity, but especially not this place." She moved in closer, whispering, "I know Gus makes it sound like he's always booked up, but our enrollment numbers have been way down this season. Case in point, this week is normally a full house out here, but with the economy and the cost of travel for the down-staters, and because a lot of kids are returning to school, we slotted the one couple we had signed up into next week's group. The following months are critical for income. If our numbers take a hit and people start cancelling because of what happened at Birch Lake or the attack here, we might be done for."

Payne knew the tourist trade was a boom-or-bust industry, especially at a remote site like this. But the place was paradise, and the thought of Gus' business going under was something he would never want to see happen, as long as he could help.

"You wanna know the real reason your position opened up…it was because Gus had to let his paid caretaker go. When you agreed to do a work-trade, we were sure grateful to have you, for even a coupla weeks."

"I had no idea. Gus said this week was about getting prepped for the coming rush on Labor Day, so I figured that's why there's only the staff on-site."

She tapped her finger on the edge of the table. "He's a stoic old coot and doesn't let on much about what he's feelin', but he's worried as hell. So am I."

During the three weeks since his arrival, Payne had always enjoyed his conversations with the woman, which were interspersed with colorful anecdotes about past clients, wildlife, or gossip out of Saxon that she'd heard during her other part-time job in town. Now, there was a look in her eyes similar to what Micah showed after being discovered in the woodshed.

Payne gestured towards the silver object flying over the far side of the lake as the float plane with Nolte came into view. "Well, I'll talk to the lieutenant about keeping things low profile, but I'm not sure how much sway I'll have, being a newcomer."

"That'd be a big help, newbie or not."

They both turned at the creaking of steps and saw Micah descending.

"Poor thing, she must be starving. I'll go get her something to eat," said Jasmine, who scurried towards the kitchen.

Micah moved up near Payne, giving a weary nod. Her hair was tangled, and she clutched a fleece blanket around her shoulders like it was a suit of armor. Her striking blue eyes glanced at Payne, then at the trees, searching the shadows.

"So this is it, eh?" she asked, watching the plane coasting along the lake and coming to a halt at the beach.

"I'd like you to stay here while the lieutenant and I go inspect my cabin, and I walk him through what happened. After that, he'll probably want to talk with you before you all fly back to Saxon. I imagine your foster parents will be there, and you'll be going home with them once Nolte has what he needs."

A faint grin crept out, turning into a full-blown smile. "Fuck my leering loser of a foster dad and his head-in-the-sand spouse. They have no say over my life anymore. I'm not going anywhere with them. Ever. Again."

"The lieutenant and the courts may say otherwise."

"Yesterday, yeah. Not now. It's my eighteenth birthday today, so the courts can also kiss my ass."

Payne smirked. "So that's why you were so interested in whether Nolte could get out here last night, weather aside."

She held her chin up and pulled the blanket-shawl tighter, like someone newly coronated, then suddenly her shoulders rolled forward, and a deflated look came over her face. "April and I were supposed to be celebrating in Homer. We were going to greet the sunset at the end of the pier. She joked that she was going to call in a pod of dolphins for me."

Payne went to rest a hand on her shoulder, but she slid away. "Thanks, but I'm good."

"I've lost friends before, and it can take a long time to get your compass bearings again. You got anyone else back in Anchorage you can rely on or call for help once you're done at the state troopers' post?"

"I'll be fine. You don't have to play social worker with me. I'll sort everything out. I always do."

Jasmine returned with a plate of toasted bagels, crème cheese, and sliced oranges. While Micah dove into the food, Payne exited the lodge and walked down to the docks to greet Nolte and the other trooper, Corporal Hicks, both of whom were armed with AR-15 rifles.

After Payne provided a hasty overview of last night's tumultuous events, the three men proceeded up the trail to Payne's cabin.

And what they saw caused Payne to freeze in his tracks.

# CHAPTER 15

Nolte scratched his scruffy chin, examining the bare ground where Payne swore there had been two dead bodies. "And you said you shot them with the rifle you handed me at the dock?"

Payne saw both men glancing at each other before slinging their own rifles and scrutinizing the wet ground again. The same spot where two men with gaping head wounds had been situated.

"Maybe a bear dragged 'em off," said Hicks in a sarcastic tone as he headed to the rear of the cabin.

Payne thrust both hands at the ground. "They were right here." Where there had been a plethora of muddy tracks hours before was now covered with leaves and debris that had been sprinkled over the area, and the blood splotches were gone, though he could just as easily attribute that to last night's rain.

The corporal returned a minute later. "There ain't no body back there, either."

Nolte looked over Payne like he was executing a sobriety test on a driver. "So, you're the man tracker...you wanna tell me where these three dead guys went? I mean, let's assume for a minute that the shootout went down like you said, but you only wounded these guys." He waved a hand at the tree line. "I'm just not seeing any obvious trails that they limped away."

"Like I already told you: two of 'em had their brains spilled out from .223 rounds, while the guy at the rear had his head slammed into my back door and busted his neck on the way down. The fourth guy took a round in the arm, then ran off into the woods."

Payne glanced at the soil by the tree line and then up the pathway leading to the woodshed. "Must've been a mop-up crew who came in and hauled off the bodies, then scrubbed the scene, raking the tracks clear and tossing all this debris around my place." He pointed to the fresh leaf litter and unbroken twigs on the ground along the trail. "None of this was here before, and the ground was covered in blood and bone fragments."

The two troopers gave each other sideways glances before Hicks spoke up. "This is the same guy you said found all the tracks out at Birch Lake?"

Nolte pursed his lips and sighed, pacing around the front of the cabin. "Payne, you struck me as impressive as hell yesterday, but now I don't know what to make of it all. Fortunately for you, Gus thinks you're shit-hot, but this story about a hit team coming for the girl, then magically disappearing into the storm is more like something I'd expect from those mushroom lovers down in Homer."

Payne gestured to the dense trees to the left. "Give me some time, and I'll turn up their tracks out there."

"Maybe later. For now, let's go to the lodge so I can talk to the girl." Nolte extended a hand towards the trail, indicating Payne should walk in front of them. Whatever faith the trooper had had in Payne the day before was eroding away quickly.

He kept his .38 pistol concealed under his shirt and watched the forest on the left with a predator's eyes. Payne had witnessed scrubbed crime scenes in urban environments before. Hell, he had even been involved in performing several himself, but nothing like this.

*This was a reasonably professional crew of hitters and with some resources to do a cover-up.*

He could understand last night's deluge washing away the blood and some of the tracks, but removing the bodies of three adult men was no small feat. Since there were no obvious ATV or vehicle tracks, he assumed the wounded man had returned with a small group of guys who hauled out the corpses on foot. Somewhere in the forest beyond his place, there would be prints or drag marks or depressions from the weight displacement.

Payne heard a raven in the fir trees, wishing he had the bird's aerial perspective right now. Of course, what he really wanted was to enjoy the remainder of his stay in the region before departing on his motorcycle next week.

Now, with each step, he felt like his boots were caked with twenty pounds of mud, and he had suddenly gone from a reliable asset assisting a friend to someone interfering with a criminal investigation—in a case that was growing more nebulous with each passing hour.

————

HATCH FELT something hard nudging him in the shoulder. He awoke from his nightmare, wondering if the devil had finally come to drag him off, but only saw Groh in the driver's seat.

The man was sipping on a sixty-four-ounce cup of iced Coke, his usual breakfast. He wasn't even sure when Groh had stopped along the highway to buy the drink. It must have been in one of the small towns in the Kenai Peninsula, since they had been heading towards Homer.

"Go take a piss and get some food in you. We move on the next target in two hours."

Hatch rubbed his eyes and arched his back. From the pullout along Highway 1, he stared at the welcoming waters of Kenai Lake just west of the town of Cooper Landing. He exited the rig and walked to the porta-potty at the edge of the gravel parking lot to relieve himself.

When he was done, he returned to the vehicle and dug through the cooler in the back seat, removing a prepackaged ham sandwich and an energy drink.

As he ate, Groh moved up alongside him and leaned on the rear bumper. "We'll drop the next target like we did that Jenkins lady in Fairbanks last week. I've got a substitute for her meds that will be a lethal cocktail once she gets a few drinks in her."

"I'm not setting foot in a bar again."

"Relax, you won't have to. You'll hold her while I get the tequila and pills down her throat."

"What's the story on the woman—or don't I want to know?"

Groh shrugged. "Sixty-two-year-old. Lives alone. Worked as an archivist up in Fairbanks and still does some freelance jobs at the state capitol."

"I thought archivists were anti-government?"

Groh shot him a puzzled look for a second. "You're thinking of anarchists, dumbass. Archivists analyze and preserve old documents and photos and shit like that."

"Whatever." Hatch turned, watching a family walking along the mud flats below. The parents were carrying colorful plastic pails while their three kids gathered stones and tossed them inside. "Ever wonder what it's like—having a normal childhood?"

"You mean Little League baseball and family game nights —fuck that. I'd take living in the bush full time any day."

"Easy for you to say: your dad was the Jedi master of hunters. I had to learn from whatever drunken uncle on my mom's side would take me out, until I met you and Packard."

"My father also grew up in the Siberian wilderness and later came to Alaska before it became a state in '59, back when the laws and people were few and far between, and prodding wildlife officers sometimes went missing."

"Your contact said that that old bastard Gus Freed was part of the initial team that went to Birch Lake. Ain't he the one who put your dad away fifteen years ago?" Hatch left the sentence hanging as he finished off his sandwich.

"Fifteen years next month to be exact. And fifteen years too many for Gus Freed to still be enjoying his life. But he'll get what's due after we're done with this current assignment." Groh kicked a pine cone over the edge of the parking lot. "Like my father used to say: patience is bitter, but its fruit is very sweet."

# CHAPTER 16

Payne found himself on the flight back to Saxon, though he hadn't intended to go. Their story about the cabin attack had raised Nolte's suspicions about the girl and, by extension, about Payne himself. He felt compelled to ensure she was treated fairly and to see what, if anything, they'd discovered about the wounded man with the chin beard.

The ride from the docks in Saxon to the state troopers' post already had a different feel than yesterday's visit, partly due to Payne and Micah sitting in the prisoner-containment unit at the back of the cruiser, and the fact that there were dozens of news vans and rental cars parked outside Nolte's building.

"When did these maggots arrive?" Nolte barked as he accelerated, taking a hard left turn around the other side of the building to employee parking. He came to a halt in his designated spot and then got out, walking around to the rear hatch and opening it. He removed two black rain jackets and walked to the middle door, passing them to Micah and Payne. "Put those hoods on and keep your heads low while you walk to the side exit with me. I don't need your faces all over the news."

They complied and slipped out of the vehicle, sandwiched between Hicks and the lieutenant. Once inside, they continued past the other rooms and into the employee lounge. Nolte shut the door and slid down the blinds, then gestured for his two guests to sit.

The disembodied voice of Nolte's secretary emanated from the front lobby. "Lieutenant, you've got a visitor."

"Not now," he snapped back.

"She's already waiting in your office."

"Goddammit, Carlie, what'd I tell you about letting people in there? We've got a lobby for a reason."

"And your lobby smells like a nightclub," said a brunette woman in a gray suit who stepped around the corner, holding up her badge. She looked no more than thirty, and her outfit didn't have a wrinkle on it. "Detective Emma Cartwright out of Anchorage. I messaged you earlier."

Nolte gave an unenthusiastic handshake. "You did?"

"I emailed a few hours ago about driving up this morning."

"I don't recall placing a request for help with Anchorage PD."

"The governor asked me to assist, given the nature of the slayings at Birch Lake."

Payne saw Nolte's right fist partially clench. "That right? The governor sent you."

"He thought you might need help containing the public response along with lending some of my insights into the recent case, and it would be a goodwill effort between the state troopers and Anchorage PD."

"Any other bullshit reasons you wanna pitch?"

She shrugged. "I can think of more."

"You a profiler or something, because I already rolled up

the psychopath behind the killings." Nolte raised a hand, cutting off her reply. "All the governor cares about is controlling his image and the tourism dollars flowing into this region of Alaska during peak season, and I don't need your or anyone else's help from the big city for that."

"Whoa. Relax, LT. I'm not here to step all over your investigation. I know of your reputation for getting things done."

Payne saw the man ball his fist tighter. "And what the hell reputation is that, *Detective*?"

"That came out the wrong way. I've only ever heard you're a pit bull when tackling a case. Or you used to be." She averted her eyes.

"Well, here in Backwater, Alaska, we got everything under control, so you can tell your boss in his three-story mansion that things are nearly wrapped up, so you can be on your way back home."

"I already checked into a motel. I'm here to stay until my orders say otherwise."

Nolte glanced at Payne and Micah, then back towards Cartwright, looking like he was standing on a tightrope. He scrutinized the woman and let his fist relax. "I know most of the detectives in Anchorage, men and women with decades of experience. You wanna tell me why the governor sent you specifically?"

"Because I used to be Jimmy Dean's case manager when he was in juvie."

# CHAPTER 17

Nolte motioned for the detective to follow him into his office. He closed the door to the employee lounge and locked it, without providing an explanation, and Payne figured from the trooper's looks that he felt like his grasp on things was beginning to spiral beyond his control.

Payne stood and headed to the small kitchen counter. "You wanna mug of coffee, or you already awake enough?"

"Hook me up," said Micah. "I think it's going to be a long day." She slouched back, pulling the rain-jacket hood down over the bridge of her nose. "I'm tired of hearing how Jimmy was behind this. That's such bullshit, and I can prove it."

"Your word against the mountain of evidence it sounds like they found at Dean's place is going to be a tough slog."

"I have evidence of my own—a video of the two killers— if I can just get back out to Birch Lake and find my damn phone."

Payne put her coffee mug on the table. "How did Nolte react to that?"

She smirked. "You're the first person I've told. I don't trust cops or anyone claiming they're sworn to uphold the law and protect others." She clawed out air quotes at the latter terms.

Payne glanced at the woman-child on the couch. *She's tough, I'll give her that, but tough only gets you so far against men like the ones last night.*

He thought of how he could spend his remaining days in Alaska before catching his scheduled ferry south to Washington. Halibut fishing in world-class waters had been his only priority, but now he felt odd about packing his bike and taking off.

*But it's not my job to solve those murders. And tactically, getting involved deeper is stupid. I'm one man with a .38 snubbie and borrowed rifles against an organized crew with resources to scrub crime scenes. They've got surveillance, multiple shooters, and God knows what else. Smart money says finish out my arrangement with Gus, then get on my bike and say adios.*

*Yet here I am, playing bodyguard to a runaway with a target on her back. She's not my responsibility. I did my part—kept her alive last night, got her to Nolte. But those eyes…Christ, she reminds me of kids from refugee camps. The ones who've seen too much. And if I walk away now and she ends up like her friends at Birch Lake— could I live with that?*

He sighed, watching the diminutive teen huddled on the couch. *If her phone really has evidence, she might be the only thing standing between Jimmy Dean and a murder conviction he doesn't deserve. Do I care about some kid I've never met? Not really. But I want her to make it out of this alive. And Gus took a huge risk harboring us last night. His business is hanging by a thread. If I bolt and something happens to the girl that connects her back to Wolf Lake Lodge, the media attention could destroy everything he's built.*

He cradled his coffee mug. *Dammit. I can give her and Gus a few more days.*

She stood and paced around the room. "How long will I be here?"

"Not sure. You'll have to give your official statement on what you witnessed at the lake, and then who knows? I'm not a cop."

"You sure?"

"First, you said I was an inbred mo-fo, and now you think I'm a cop. Which one is it?"

"The two are not mutually exclusive."

Payne sipped his coffee, staring into her eyes the whole time. "By the way you talked about Jimmy last night and those scars on your hands, I'd say you knew him from juvie."

"Aren't you observant? Yet you can't explain what happened to those goons at your cabin."

"You also like to draw attention back to your questioner. That's actually my habit of responding to people, but I had to work at it, and you do it like it's second nature. So what gives?"

"Why'd you have to work at it?"

He chuckled. "Nice. Answering a question with a question. You're good."

"Good, bad, we're not philosophers."

"And interjecting nonsense when you're unsure what to say."

"You trying to cozy up to me, Payne, making it seem like you know me? Were you a hard case who grew up on the mean streets, too, and bounced around a dozen homes by the time you were fifteen?" She waved her hand in the air. "You been in the shit and just wanna offer up your wisdom, is that it?"

He knew she was a scared kid who had witnessed too much abuse in life, and probably not just in the past thirty-six hours. He wasn't about to debate with someone as slippery as she was, although a nod of appreciation for helping her would be welcome.

"It was a simple question: did you know Jimmy Dean personally? Because if you did, that detective in the next room is filling Nolte in on everything about Jimmy right now, which may differ from your story of him, and I'd really like to know if he was actually capable of killing all those people at Birch Lake, or if there's something larger going on here. If Jimmy is your friend, then I think you'd want to help him."

She put her mug down and slid back her hood. She steepled her fingers and stared at Payne, her blue eyes unflinching like he had just stepped into the ring with a boxer. The terror he'd seen previously in her was now replaced with a fierceness, and he hoped he'd pressed the right buttons.

She was about to speak when Payne held a finger to his lips. They canted their heads, hearing Nolte and Cartwright raising their voices in the next room. When the two were done arguing and the detective explained Dean's overly aggressive nature in juvie, Micah's eyes had suddenly grown wider.

"But that's not the guy I knew. Jimmy wasn't belligerent. He used to look out for the other kids around him."

"People can change, especially when living around violence on a daily basis."

She shook her head. "Jimmy isn't the killer. I already told you there were two big guys who hacked up everyone. And with what you saw happen last night, you have to believe me. They want to shut me up so Dean can take the fall."

"I'm afraid my credibility may have slipped away since the three bodies from my cabin vanished."

"Then I'll prove it myself. If I can find my phone, I can show Nolte the video I took."

"Maybe you should have told me this last night."

She rubbed her arms. "I wasn't sure I could trust you."

"And you do now, after all your bullshit retorts?"

"What's a 'retort'?" she asked with a grin.

————

AFTER CARTWRIGHT LEFT THE STATION, Nolte unlocked the door to the lounge and entered, closing it behind him and tossing his tablet on the counter. He leaned against the wall, rubbing the back of his neck, then glancing at the two inquisitive faces across from him.

"Payne, your story and Micah's matched up word for word, but that's all it is for now, a story. Without any evidence of what you claim happened at your cabin, I have no actionable information to work with."

Micah leaned forward. "What about the guy Payne shot in the arm? He sounded exactly like the creep who picked me up yesterday and was going to keep me locked up in his house. The dude had an ugly chin beard and looked like Gandalf on meth. Shouldn't be hard to find."

"Agreed. Not to mention his right arm is probably missing some flesh," said Payne. "Find him and you'll find out what happened to those three stiffs."

The lieutenant folded his arms. It looked like his head was about to explode, and Payne could see he was no longer the even-keeled guy he'd met yesterday. "The little help I have is combing through Dean's cabin and property. I don't have the time or manpower to scour the boonies for every redneck with a beard. Two days from now, that might change, but right now, you're free to go, Payne."

He immediately pointed at Micah. "Not you, though. You're a minor and will be staying here until your case worker and parents arrive."

Micah shot him a smug grin. "*Was* a minor. I turned eighteen today, so I'm outta here, too."

Nolte narrowed his eyes, then yanked his tablet off the counter. After a few minutes of stabbing the screen, he lowered it by his side. "Well, happy fucking birthday, Ms. Brezny. However, I have to ask you again about your timeline for arriving at Wolf Lake Lodge—you said it was after that stolen ATV ran out of gas, is that right?"

She sat up, giving the man a perplexed look. "Yep. Got to the property sometime before sundown and hid in that toolshed until Payne showed up. Why?"

"I received a notice early this morning from the Department of Social Services about a runaway teen from Anchorage who was spotted in Saxon last night, possibly inebriated or on drugs," Nolte said. "You match her description."

Payne thought about the implications: the attackers at his cabin were there to grab the girl and tie up loose ends from Birch Lake. A loose end they never expected since Micah wasn't on the official camping permit. *Now, they're trying to present her as a troubled teenager with a habit.*

"Get a lot of runaway kids lingering around the streets of Saxon in the rain?" he asked the trooper.

"Not in the time I've been here," Nolte replied.

"Does it say on the notice when the report came in about that teenager?" asked Payne.

Nolte gave him an irritated look, then glanced at his tablet again. "Eleven p.m. A couple saw the teen heading into the forest after hearing the girl argue with her mother on her phone in the diner."

"No way it was me, then," said Micah. "And my oxygen thief of a foster mom was probably passed out on the kitchen floor by sundown."

"Interesting timeline, though," said Payne.

"How so?" inquired Nolte.

"If my memory is correct, most of Saxon shuts down around nine p.m., including the two restaurants; and that string-bean I shot in the arm hobbled into the woods sometime around nine thirty to ten. It would have taken him a while to get out of the immediate area on foot and patch himself up."

Nolte raised an eyebrow. "And you seriously think that guy then decided to call social services with a concocted story about a doped-up kid in Saxon?"

"Not that bush rat—whoever he works for," said Payne. "Whoever is behind the murders at Birch Lake is desperately trying to button things up, and now that means launching a verbal campaign against their intended target to weaken her credibility in your eyes. Coupled with the lack of dead guys at my cabin and this latest report, it must be turning some gears in your head about our statements, Lieutenant."

Nolte pressed his fingers into his left temple. "The only thing going on in my head is a fucking headache—and I've got a beauty right now. And it's only going to get worse sorting through conspiracy theories."

Nolte set the tablet on the counter again and shifted his gaze towards Micah. "As I would advise any material witness connected to a criminal case of this nature, you are required to remain in the borough until further notice."

"Staying where?" she inquired.

Nolte replied, "The department will spring for a room at the Caribou Inn on the far side of town. It should be off the radar of the media since the establishment is going through partial renovations."

She shot him a penetrating gaze. "I overheard some of what that detective said about Jimmy Dean. She sounds certain it was him, but it wasn't."

"You already explained that you thought there were two

killers at Birch Lake, as did Payne. I have my people looking for an accomplice, but the physical evidence at Dean's place doesn't support that."

She and Payne exchanged looks. "What if I could get some proof of who those two men were?" she asked.

Nolte put a hand on his hip. "I'm listening."

# CHAPTER 18

After explaining the plan to retrace Micah's escape route from the campsite, Payne stood. "I'll contact Gus and see if he can pick us up at the dock in town here and fly us out to Birch Lake. And if the video on Micah's phone pans out, then it sounds like it should provide critical evidence of who the real attackers are."

Nolte gave a reluctant nod.

He could see the man wrestling with the idea. Right now, it seemed like he had a slam-dunk case against Dean. The only thing in his way was the girl and, now, her potential video of the supposed killers.

It would be easy to bury that story since that was all it was: an unsupported account. From the physical evidence, Dean was the murderer. The governor and Cartwright would be happy with that verdict and so would the locals whose livelihoods depended on Saxon having a postcard image. In a few days, the media crews would dissipate, having satiated themselves with the tale of a former juvenile killer who couldn't control his demons. And Nolte could go back to citing speeding drivers.

Except none of this sat well with Payne, and he figured if Nolte was the man of integrity he seemed, then he wouldn't be getting much peace knowing he sent an innocent guy like Dean to prison while the real murderers roamed free.

Nolte ruffled out a long exhale and alternated his gaze between Payne and Micah. "The campsites have already been processed and the bodies sent to the coroner's office in Anchorage. A grid search was done of the immediate area, and you'll see the crime scene tape extending around the three tent sites, so stay out of those spots. The rest of the forensics teams are still out at Dean's place, and I'll have the preliminary report on his cabin tomorrow afternoon. Following that, I'll probably have enough to make a state-ment to the press."

*So we have twenty-four hours to present actual evidence supporting Micah's story and Dean's defense* was what Payne heard.

"You still want that room at the Caribou Inn?" asked Nolte as he glanced at them both.

"Sure," Payne said without consulting Micah, who shot him a nervous glance.

"I'll have Carlie up front arrange it. I've gotta get on the horn with the governor since he's left four messages already." He exited as quickly as he'd entered.

"I hope you're going to ask for separate motel rooms," said Micah.

"Just one will do since we won't be spending any time there."

"What? Why not?"

"Because word's probably going to get out that you're staying there, seeing how someone seems to know your whereabouts, and I plan to use that to our advantage."

"'Our advantage'...Look, I appreciate your help, but I don't need a bodyguard, Payne."

"The three dead guys at my cabin say otherwise. Besides, those rat bastards violated my friend Gus' place, and they would have killed me, too, and I plan to find out exactly who they are."

————

AN HOUR LATER, once Micah had finished recounting the events of the past thirty-six hours to the secretary, who video-taped her statement, Micah and Payne got a ride across town from Corporal Hicks, who drove a circuitous route around Saxon to avoid any reporters.

Saxon's downtown stretched along four blocks that could be walked end to end in five minutes, its weathered diner, general store, outfitter shop, and hand-painted signs reflecting the unhurried pace of a community that swelled from 1,200 year-round residents to nearly triple that during peak hunting season each fall. All of the storefronts and neighboring motels had a rustic log and cedar-shake appearance, giving the town an authentic frontier feel that both tourists and termites found appealing.

After passing through several small neighborhoods to the east, Hicks dropped them in the parking lot of Andy's General Store a block from the motel.

From the faded photo on the wall in the lobby, Payne figured Andy was the original founder back in 1948. The man was wearing an old fleece-collared leather bomber jacket, which made Payne think he had served on a B-24 flight crew or something similar in World War II.

The store only had ten aisles, and there wasn't an empty space on any shelf in the entire place. There also wasn't much organization, and the cereal aisle had shelves lined with boxes of ammo, which were next to stacks of diapers and a smattering of offerings from Kellogg's. Everything from home repair to hunting and fishing, to beer and canned goods and auto repair items were jammed into wherever an inch of space allowed.

While Micah filled a hand tote with chips and soda, Payne headed to what could be called the personal security section and perused the video cameras he'd seen before on a previous visit. He grabbed a packet of two USB chargers with embedded security cams.

When he was done, he meandered around the store, gathering some snacks, locally made moose jerky, and bananas. The fruit was a rare but pricey treat since it was shipped up from Seattle.

He glanced at Micah's tote as she came up beside him. "Cheetos and Mountain Dew…is that your usual lunch?"

"I usually add in peanut butter and crackers, too."

"That'll change in a few years when your stomach finally rebels."

"Spoken with regret. An old-timer like you must miss his carefree days."

"You have no idea."

"How ancient are you, anyway? I figured about forty-five when I first saw you, but by the way you got up from the couch in that lounge, maybe it's more like sixty-five."

He frowned. "You're funny, kid. I get around just fine."

She hunched forward, shuffling an inch at a time and chuckling. "Like I said, you seem prehistoric."

"Had a few injuries over the years is all, and they catch up with me on occasion when I'm sitting for too long."

"Is that why you're hanging out at the lodge with that guy Gus? You two run a retreat center for senior citizens?"

"Well, at least I didn't just graduate from using a sippy cup for my drinks."

She laughed. "Ooh, so the old guy does have a sense of humor. I was beginning to wonder if that had shriveled up like your face." She walked beside him as they headed to the cashier.

"You sure like to push people's buttons. You always have a need to test the waters with everyone you meet?"

"Nah, some people are just easy targets. Like you, with those droopy puppy eyes."

"I could accuse you of elder abuse."

"Ha, see—you admit you're an old dog, after all."

Payne set the items on the counter and looked at the thirty-something female cashier, canting his head towards Micah. "My friend here will be paying for everything."

Micah's smile froze for a second. She reached in her back pocket and pulled out a bunch of folded bills and tossed $60 on the counter.

Payne shot her a surprised look, then started bagging the items. They exited the store and sat on a picnic table around the back, digging into their brunch.

"Where'd you get the cash from? And don't tell me you had it in your pockets when I found you at the woodshed."

Micah tore open the Cheetos and began eating. "The withered secretary who works for Nolte—she had it in her purse, so I liberated some when she went to the bathroom."

Payne paused in mid-bite of his jerky. "You stole from the gatekeeper who works for the guy you want on your side? Not only is that wrong, but that lobby had cameras in it."

"Two cameras spaced eight feet apart on the same wall, so I stayed in the blind spot. How pathetic is it when you can actually rob someone in a law-enforcement building?"

"Was that all you took of hers?"

She nodded, then swigged down a mouthful of Mountain Dew. "She had, like, three hundred bucks in cash on her; taking a sliver of that won't raise her hackles."

"Steal anything of mine at the cabin?"

Micah smirked. "Like what? You live like a Buddhist monk."

"Look, kid, I get that you've had to develop a unique skill set to survive over the years, but Carlie's a good person…she uses all of her hard-earned money to feed the four orphans she takes care of."

Micah set down the pop bottle, lowering her eyes. "Ah, shit, really?"

Payne fought back a grin as he chewed on the jerky. "Just messin' with you. But don't pull that shit again."

She flicked a Cheeto at him. "Whatever you say, old man."

"And I'm twenty-eight, by the way."

"Bullshit. I'd say ten years past that, give or take a year."

He had to admit she was as sharp as she was resourceful. Her assessment and street smarts were things he had to work at in his line of work, but they came naturally to her. Or were born out of a necessity that he couldn't imagine needing to acquire so young.

One thing was certain: her childhood had been short, and for someone like her, trust in others would be seen as a weakness, a detriment to survival.

Maybe that was their common ground.

# CHAPTER 19

After their hasty meal, they walked one block over to the Caribou Inn. The owner was expecting them. A forty-something woman with red hair pulled back in a tight ponytail and with more freckles on her face than Payne had ever seen on a person.

She relayed the conversation with Nolte and how the lieutenant had stressed anonymity and privacy. She handed Payne the key for the last room at the end of the L-shaped motel.

Since it was almost noon, the other patrons hadn't checked in yet, and the latter half of the wing had units under various stages of renovation, so Payne and Micah would have considerable space from others.

They strolled across the empty parking lot and went into their room. The motel looked like it had been built in the '60s and had a brown brick front with faded green trim around the windows and doors.

Heading inside, Payne noticed the faint odor of cigarette smoke cloaked with Lysol. The carpet and faux paneling were new, but the two sagging beds and chipped furniture looked like they had been acquired at secondhand stores.

"Bed bug central," said Micah, plunking down on a padded leather chair and shoving her grocery bag on a corner table. She grabbed the complimentary lotion and shampoo and put them in her jacket. "Look, I appreciate everything you've done for me, and you don't come across as a perv, but sleeping in a bed next to you ain't gonna happen."

Payne was examining the wall sockets and rearranged the table and chairs. "Like I said before, we're not going to be staying here."

She gave him a surprised look. "You planning to head back to the lodge?"

He tossed her the two mini-cams. "Remove the packaging. We're going to turn this place into an information-gathering center and record whoever enters tonight."

"You think they'll have balls enough to come right into Saxon this time?"

"These are people with resources and manpower, given their efforts to remove their dead pals at my cabin and their ability to track you there in the first place. Not to mention setting up Dean to be the patsy—that last part took some advanced planning."

He sat on the bed, drinking from his bottled water. "When I was assisting Nolte at Birch Lake, I noticed the two other victims were there alone. One looked to be in his early forties and had a bunch of high-end photography gear; the other was older, maybe mid-fifties. His canoe and camping gear looked pretty new, but nothing unusual stood out about either of those guys."

"So?"

"The efforts the goons at the cabin were taking to locate and abduct you meant that they needed to keep a tight lid on their story about Dean being the killer. But why? And why kill all those people, who don't appear to have any connections to one another?" He scratched his thick beard.

"I saw that photographer snapping off pics of a beaver in the lake when we first arrived. If he'd been out in the wilds for a while like us, then maybe he captured some images of something he wasn't supposed to," she said.

"Did you talk to him?"

"No, just the older guy at the north end when we were both gathering firewood. He was a super-nice dude, actually. Said he was a history professor out of Anchorage...Ian something. I don't remember his last name. Said it was his third trip on the lakes this summer."

"So, a professor, a nature photographer, and three seasoned outdoor explorers. Just doesn't make sense. Why would Dean, or any criminal for that matter, venture out that far to a wilderness region to go on a murder spree?"

"Especially since there are dozens of campgrounds and RV sites around Saxon," said Micah, who put her boots on the bed.

The sound of a vehicle pulling up caused Payne to hop up. He removed the .38 from under his shirt and moved to the curtain, pulling it back slightly and peering out.

"You're packing a weapon. I thought you gave up all the goods to Nolte?" she asked.

"This is my own, and just forget you even saw it."

"And with those cop eyes of yours, I figured you to be a law-abiding citizen."

"This is Alaska, not DC. Everyone out here is probably carrying."

"Who's out there?" asked Micah, moving up and peering through the peephole in the door.

"That detective out of Anchorage."

"So much for us being off the radar out here."

Payne tucked the revolver back into his beltline. He

motioned for Micah to duck into the bathroom. He moved to the door and opened it just as Cartwright was about to knock.

"Pardon the intrusion, but I saw you and Ms. Brezny at the station earlier and wanted to ask you both a few questions."

"Maybe later. I was just heading out."

She glanced at the empty parking lot. "Where to?"

"Just got some business to take care of and should be back before sundown," said Payne. He stepped outside, closing the door.

"You, no doubt, heard Lieutenant Nolte and I discussing the Dean case. I just had a few questions for Ms. Brezny about her relationship to the prime suspect."

Payne decided to feign ignorance to see what her angle was. "I didn't think there was one. She was from Anchorage, and Dean lived north of here."

"The lieutenant mentioned that Ms. Brezny indicated Dean couldn't have done the killings and that there were two men involved. The former comment implies previous history with the prime suspect, and I'd really like to know what that entails."

Payne didn't have time for this. He needed to finish bugging the room and meet Gus at the dock so he could fly them out to Birch Lake. "She took off to God knows where. I'm not even sure she's going to be back, to be honest."

Cartwright seemed irritated. She stepped back, glancing over Payne. "And how are you connected to all of this, exactly?"

"Entangled is a better word. I got dragged down to Birch Lake by my boss, Gus, who thought I could assist since I've done some man tracking in the past."

"You former military?"

"No. I never had the distinction of serving. My father's a

game warden in the Great Lakes region, and I grew up tracking in the woods."

"Tracking animals seems a far cry from tracking down criminals."

"Hardly. It's all about detecting things out of place and following the trail until it leads you to your prey or the lost child or the poacher on the other end."

"And what did you find out at Birch Lake?"

"Surely, Nolte must have gone over the case already?"

She folded her arms. "I'd like to hear your take."

"Alright. From the little I know about Dean, I don't think he did it. There were two killers, wearing boots with identical tread patterns."

"What does that prove? Dean could have doubled back over his tracks."

"Let me ask you something first: you indicated you were Dean's case officer. So how tall is he?"

She pursed her lips. "Five feet six, I believe. Short guy, for sure."

"There were two different strides evident at the campsites, both of which were typical of big, tall guys, probably six-foot-four dudes, maybe taller, but not by much."

Cartwright sighed. "This is all fascinating, but it's not conclusive and certainly not empirical evidence that can be used in court."

He was so shocked by her naïve comment that he wondered how much time she'd actually spent on field assignments outside of the office. "Well, the FBI, US Marshals, and thousands of wildlife conservation officers would beg to differ, Detective. The results gleaned from man-tracking evidence has been used in countless federal cases over the past forty years and has been responsible for apprehending plenty of fugitives. And Nolte has my account on record, which will clearly show that the two strides of the attackers don't match up with someone of Dean's size."

She leaned against the hood of her Lincoln Town Car. "I'll admit, my time over the years has been focused on more of an urban setting than what goes on in places like Saxon." She dragged out the last few words like they were stuck in her throat. "If you and Nolte have evidence that could exonerate Dean, then I'm more than happy to re-examine my position, but when I heard that he had been arrested by Nolte as the main suspect in the slayings, I wasn't surprised."

She pulled out her car keys and walked to the driver's side, opening the door. "I'm not sure how what you discovered on the ground at Birch Lake fits into all of this, but I'm willing to bet that boy had a hand in this, and no amount of stride stuff and boot soles is going to change that."

# CHAPTER 20

The float plane's pontoons carved white lines across Birch Lake's surface as Gus brought the Cessna 206 in for a landing. As the plane approached the cove nearest the campsites, he throttled down the engine and let the pontoons ease onto the sandy beach. The late morning sun glimmered across the water, making the place resemble something far from the crime scene it had become in recent days.

Payne scanned the shoreline through the passenger window, noting the yellow tape still fluttering at the three campsites. The tents, bodies, and canoes had all been removed like Nolte had indicated. A murder of crows and a lone coyote digging in the ground by Ryan's former tent location were the only other occupants.

"You've got ninety minutes before I start getting nervous," Gus said through the headset.

"Copy that." Payne checked his Ruger .375, ensuring a round was chambered. He'd also brought a can of bear spray in a holster for Micah, figuring she would feel better being armed, not to mention the actual danger of coming across bears, which would be drawn to the blood still lingering around the sites.

Micah hadn't spoken during the flight, her face looking frostbitten as they exited the plane. Now, as she and Payne walked along the shoreline, she finally broke her silence.

"The place where April and I...it's on the south side. Maybe two hundred yards from where we pitched our tents."

"Take your time," Payne said.

He kept the rifle at low ready while Micah oriented herself. The familiar surroundings seemed to awaken something in her. The teen's posture straightened as they walked beside the crime-scene tape by the last campsite where Payne had last seen her friend Ryan. The girl averted her eyes, brushing back tears, then pushed on along the beach.

She pointed to a large spruce tree forty feet away. "That's where we were when we saw Ryan get attacked."

It was the same location Payne had previously identified as the primitive latrine.

"This way." At the end of the yellow tape, she veered into the forest, leading him along trampled vegetation where the forensics team must have been.

"After Ryan was...after it happened, April and I ran through the woods towards this little swamp. We were almost to the cattails, but April took a fall and mangled her ankle." She pressed her hands into her sides as her lips trembled. "I tried to help her, but...it was...it was too late. She..." Micah kneeled and began sobbing.

Payne shuffled closer, resting a hand on her shoulder. This time, she didn't pull away but leaned slightly into his leg as the tears flowed freely.

A minute later, she dragged a sleeve across her wet cheeks and stood. Micah stomped on a branch, then kicked the shattered pieces into the swamp ahead. "Those fuckers. I'll kill those guys if I see them again."

"Finding your phone will be the first step in getting some justice for your friends and the others out here." He pointed the muzzle of his rifle towards the ground. "Does this look like the area you were in when you filmed them?"

Micah pushed aside vegetation, walking towards the swamp. The marshy area extended into the lake to the right, thick with reeds and cattails that could hide a person—or a phone.

"After the guy was done with April, both men started circling around. That's actually when I realized there were two of them. I dove to the ground and crawled into the mud near the edge of the swamp. Then I took out my phone and started filming them." Her eyes were glazed over as she stared into the cattails. "It felt like hours before they left, but when I thought it was clear, I crawled out and started making my way along the other side of the swamp."

She bent down, searching the transition zone between the forest and the swamp. "It must have fallen out around here. Or maybe when I was climbing under some fallen trees up ahead."

Payne divided his attention between watching Micah search and scanning the tree line.

"Got it!" Micah pulled her dirty iPhone from between two rocks. "Please work, please work." She pressed the power button. The screen flickered to life. "Yes. It's still got twelve percent battery."

"And the video…is it clear?"

Her fingers flew across the screen. "It's here. Look—" She held it up, showing grainy footage of two men in plaid shirts, both of them with thick beards and carrying bloody knives. Despite the poor quality, neither matched Jimmy Dean's description, like she'd indicated.

"Good job. Now let's get that over to Nolte," said Payne.

They retraced their steps, heading towards the lake. The

chattering of boreal chickadees had stopped, and there was the faint odor of fuel in the air, prickling Payne's combat instincts.

The sound reached him a millisecond before his conscious mind processed it—the rumble of an engine throttling up across the cove on the other side of the marsh. The boat must have been nestled in the thick cattail grove where the swamp met the lake, fifty yards away. A small vessel emerged from a hidden inlet, four armed figures visible as it accelerated toward them. The motorboat's engine screamed as the driver beached it hard, all of the men leaping out with assault rifles.

"Run!" Payne grabbed Micah's arm, pulling her toward the forest as the first shots cracked across the woods. Bullets whined past, shredding cattails and tree bark.

They sprinted for a fallen log, Payne pushing Micah ahead of him. More shots chewed up dirt at their heels.

"This way." Payne veered left into denser forest, remembering something from their aerial approach—another marshy area that would slow down their pursuers.

Behind them, branches snapped as the gunmen crashed through the underbrush.

The ground turned spongy underfoot, then outright swampy. Moss-covered logs created a treacherous obstacle course ahead. Payne heard one pursuer curse as he stepped into deep muck.

"Keep the phone dry," he told Micah, then pulled her behind a massive cedar stump. "Stay here."

He scurried away from her position, intentionally snapping twigs to draw attention. When he heard footsteps adjusting to follow his movement, he circled back around the outer half of the small marsh. He hooked around his pursuer in a wide arc, then found suitable cover behind a spruce tree and got into sniping position.

The first thug appeared twenty yards away, a bald man with an AK-47.

Payne leaned out slightly from behind the tree, slowly squeezing the heavy trigger. The Ruger boomed in the confined space. The .375 round from the bear rifle caught the guy center mass, spinning him into the murky swamp water.

His partner reacted instantly, spraying automatic fire in Payne's direction.

Payne was already moving, low-crawling through ferns as bullets shredded trees overhead. He worked his way to a rotting log, using it for concealment.

The second shooter was younger and smarter. He didn't charge forward but took cover, trying to flank Payne's position, disappearing out of sight. Payne heard a splash to his right after the shooter stepped into deeper water.

Seizing the moment, Payne rolled left and came up shooting. The Ruger barked once. The round caught the man in the shoulder, twisting him towards the swamp. Payne racked another round and fired, the second bullet punching through the guy's right pec. He toppled backward into the black water and didn't resurface.

As Payne stood, he heard the sickening sound of a branch cracking behind him.

"Drop your weapon, or I drop you," said a gravelly voice.

Payne lowered the Ruger onto the ground and turned slowly. The man with a wispy chin-beard and one arm in a sling was pointing his 1911 at Payne's chest as he emitted a smug grin. With the sizable space between them, Payne knew a disarm was out of the question.

"Where's the girl and her phone?" the thug asked.

"How could you possibly know about the phone?"

"This is bigger than you and that bitch." He stepped forward, thrusting his pistol out. "Where, dammit?"

"Probably climbing back in the plane about now. I was merely here to slow you guys down."

The man's eyes shifted to the left as the fourth henchman emerged from a thick stand of birch trees. "Head to the lake and take out that plane."

The stout figure with greasy black hair nodded, then trotted back into the forest. Anemic Gandalf lowered his pistol, aiming at Payne's right knee. "Now, a little payback for last night."

"So did you and your goons already deposit those dead idiots at my cabin in a nearby swamp?"

"Something like that." The man trailed his index finger down to the trigger.

Payne heard the hiss of discharge and saw a brilliant stream of red fluid launch from the shrubs on the right. Micah held the bottle of bear spray like a pistol, unleashing the full contents, which struck the guy in the side of his face. He recoiled, gagging and firing wildly into the trees. Payne grabbed a rock and hurled it, hitting the thug in the forehead. The guy staggered to the side and fell to one knee, dropping the weapon as he pawed at his face.

Payne rushed up, sending a stomp kick into the man's ribs and driving him to the ground. Payne grabbed the 1911 and did a partial chamber check before stepping back, while the man furiously rubbed his jacket sleeves along his face.

"Micah," Payne called out.

She emerged from the thicket and tossed the empty canister aside. She came up beside him, sending her boot into the writhing man's leg. "You piece of garbage. Tell me who killed my friends."

"We don't have time for this. I need to cut off the other shooter before he gets to Gus." He gestured in the direction of the lake. "See if you can pick up his trail."

When she was out of sight, Payne glanced down at the

retching figure. "You tried to kill me and the girl twice now. You don't get another chance." He squeezed off two rounds into the guy's chest, then bent down and searched his pockets, pulling out an iPhone and a vintage Zippo lighter.

Payne grabbed his Ruger rifle and trotted off, quickly catching up with Micah.

"Did you kill him?"

"Yeah."

"Jesus, you're definitely not like a cop."

He pushed past her, following the other set of fresh tracks from the big man heading to the plane. Payne caught a sliver of movement near the lakeshore, a hundred yards ahead. The guy was just rounding the bend near Micah's former campsite, which would put him in shooting range of the float plane.

Payne picked up his pace, going from a trot to an all-out sprint as he hopped over logs and swerved around bushes. The man had stopped and was leveling his AK in the direction of the nearby beach.

Payne came to a sudden halt, pressing his left shoulder against a tree trunk for stability. He aimed the Ruger and fixed the crude iron sights on the center of the goon's torso, then steadied his breathing and squeezed the trigger.

The thug's arms trembled, and he staggered to the side before collapsing to his knees. He dropped his weapon and clutched the crimson hole in his ribs, then fell face-first into the lake.

Payne glanced back at a stand of young poplars as they parted, and Micah emerged. "Please tell me that wasn't the old man getting gunned down."

He shook his head. "Far from it, but Nolte's forensics team is going to be working a lot of overtime."

Payne led them away from the lake and followed a wide arc back toward the first cove where Gus waited with the plane. Though he hoped there had only been four shooters, he knew there could be more out here on foot, and started scrutinizing the shadows.

After several minutes of careful movement, they finally spotted sunlight dancing on water through the trees. The float plane sat peacefully in the cove with Gus visible in the cockpit, but his head was slumped back.

Payne felt his gut twist and raced towards the Cessna. Splashing through the water, he climbed onto the left float and flung open the door.

Gus sat up with a wild look in his eyes and pulled off his headset. "Scared the hell outta me, kid."

"So you were napping this whole time?" asked Payne.

"Possibly. Why? What happened?" Gus asked, glancing at their muddy clothes and grim expressions.

"A repeat performance of last night."

Gus canted his head, staring at the shoreline and finally settling his gaze on the lifeless figure floating in the distance. "Damn, Kyle. How many this time?"

"Four, including the ringleader of the crew who assaulted my cabin." Payne gestured for Micah to climb inside while he pushed the plane free from the sand and hopped onto the float before getting in.

Micah tugged on Gus' sleeve. "Can we go, please?"

Gus started the engine and prepared for takeoff. "Where to?"

Payne considered their options. Going back to Nolte seemed risky—someone had leaked their location and knew about the phone. But they needed help, and the video evidence required official handling.

"Back to your place briefly. Can I borrow that old Jeep you have behind the woodshed? I need to piece things together and figure out the next move, and I'd rather not do that back at your property."

Gus gave a thumbs-up, then slid his headset back on as he turned the plane around. A few minutes later, they were airborne again.

As Birch Lake receded below them, Payne wondered how many more bodies would pile up before this was over. Whoever wanted Micah silenced had resources and someone on the inside in Nolte's department. But now they had proof of the two attackers—video evidence that could expose the real killers.

The question was: who could they trust with it?

The float plane banked north, leaving the killing grounds behind. But Payne knew the hunt was far from over. If anything, recovering the evidence had only raised the stakes. The real battle—discovering why four innocent people had died and why Micah was being targeted—was just beginning.

# CHAPTER 21

Payne was loading the cargo area of the Jeep with his backpack and some food from the lodge kitchen when Gus came up alongside him. He handed him an empty leather holster and a box of .45 ACP ammo. "Here are the goods for that newly acquired pistol of yours."

"Thanks, Gus. I sure appreciate it. I'd also appreciate it if you could give us an hour before calling Nolte about what happened at Birch Lake."

The older man nodded and tossed him the keys to the vehicle.

"I hope to get this resolved and then get back here and finish out my contract."

Gus patted him on the shoulder. "Just take care of the girl for now and watch your own hide, too. Whoever these bastards are, they ain't foolin' around. This is some kind of criminal enterprise, and they don't like loose ends, it seems."

Payne nodded. He leaned around the bumper after hearing footfalls as Micah approached. "Show Gus the video. Maybe he'll recognize 'em."

The girl pulled out her phone and clicked on the footage.

Gus' eyes narrowed as he watched the grainy image. He grabbed the device and fumbled with his thick fingers to enhance the video. "Damn, can't be."

"You know them?" she asked.

"One of 'em. Maybe. Not entirely sure—looks like someone I helped put behind bars for killing a state trooper nearly fifteen years ago. Yancey Groh."

"Could he have been released already?" asked Payne.

Gus stared at the image. "Impossible. He died a few years ago, and I'm sure that not even Satan himself wanted that murdering trash back."

Payne and Micah shot each other nervous glances. "Who, then?" asked the girl.

The older man returned the phone to her. "Yancey had a seventeen-year-old son, Andre. But I don't see how it could possibly be him. He disappeared into the woods and was believed to have died a few weeks after his father was arrested." Gus leaned over and glanced at the still image again. "But, God, that sure looks like Groh."

"What's the story on his disappearance?" asked Payne.

"I had been trying to nab Yancey for poaching for years. After our little task force cornered him at one of his trapping cabins east of Talkeetna, he shot one of the troopers who was with us before taking a round in the leg. After he was arrested, I figured that was the end of it, but his son, Andre, came after the people on that task force. He started with my partner, Marty Pearce, ambushing him near a trailhead northwest of Saxon. Marty still walks with a limp to this day, but he managed to get off a round from his service pistol and hit Andre in the shoulder."

Gus gave Micah a concerned look. "That guy you described with the chin beard…that sounds like Ernie

Packard. He was a known associate of the older Groh. It was believed that's where Andre headed after he was wounded, but me and the other troopers never turned up anything at Packard's place during our search."

Gus sat on the tailgate. "I never truly thought Andre died. He was cut from the same cloth as his old man. Groh senior was a helluva skilled poacher and had grown up in the Siberian wilderness before immigrating over here in his twenties. He knew traps and snares that I had never seen before and was great at covering his tracks. Took us two years to finally nail that son of a bitch. I remember stories floating around afterwards about a young poacher killing bears in Alaska and the Yukon for their gallbladders. Sounded a lot like Andre, but whoever it was, was a damn ghost and wouldn't stay in one area of operation for long."

"I've known a few poachers back home, and those types are always extreme loners," said Payne. "If this is the same guy who killed everyone at Birch Lake and sent his thugs after Micah, he has to be on someone's payroll. Someone who is calling the shots."

"But who, and for what purpose?" asked Micah, tucking her phone in her pocket.

Payne smacked a mosquito on his arm. "That idiot with the pistol on me at Birch Lake said, 'This is bigger than you and that bitch.'"

"The hell does that mean?" asked Gus, who stood up.

Payne slammed the tailgate shut and looked at Micah. "That's what we're hopefully going to find out in Anchorage."

"Why there? I thought we needed to get this video to Nolte," she said.

"In time we might, once I can be sure he's not the leak. For now, the trail leads to the University of Alaska, and you and your long-lost uncle are going to tour the campus today."

She frowned. "Hard pass. I have no desire to act like a college puke, and you're no uncle—more like a poor man's John Wick with dandruff."

Gus chuckled. "I can't wait to hear how this road trip goes."

# CHAPTER 22

Nolte exited the float plane and hopped off the pontoon, walking along the gravel pathway that led up to Wolf Lake Lodge. Trailing behind him was Emma Cartwright. The detective had insisted on coming along despite Nolte's objections. He only yielded because he knew his chances of maintaining a grip on his case, and his town, was going to slip away and be turned over to the state if he didn't have something definitive to present to his superiors in the next twenty-four hours.

Gus was waiting at the top of the ridge above the beach. All of them exchanged handshakes, with Cartwright stressing her role in Saxon was at the governor's behest.

"So Payne and the Brezny girl are gone?" Nolte asked.

"Yep. Drove out of here shortly after we got back from Birch Lake."

"When was that?" asked Cartwright.

"Not long after I called the lieutenant."

"But what time was that was my question," said the detective.

"Hell, I don't know, probably eleven thirty." 'He waved a

beefy hand at their surroundings. "Not like I keep track of the exact time out here."

"Payne indicate where they were going?" inquired Nolte.

"Anchorage. Said he had a hunch he was following, something connected with the college down there."

"Say what his hunch was about?" asked Cartwright.

Gus shook his head.

"Alaska Pacific University or University of Alaska?" she asked.

The older man shrugged, then looked at Nolte. "You didn't come all the way out here to ask me about this, though. What's on your mind, Lieutenant?"

"A lot of bodies have been stacking up around these parts lately, and a number of those are connected to Payne and the girl. My crew is back out at Birch Lake again and found the four dead guys you mentioned Payne taking down, but I wanted to get a look around his place here again."

Gus gestured towards the trail heading to the caretaker's cabin. "Follow me."

They walked along the meadow, passing the woodshed and then heading down the trail through the forest. While the two men slogged through the muddy patches, Cartwright skirted around them, avoiding getting her boots and gray dress slacks blemished.

"You haven't asked me the most important question yet," said Gus as he shot a glance back at the sheriff. "About the phone, I mean."

"I actually wasn't hopeful about them finding it and, if they did, of it being intact," said Nolte.

Gus paused outside the porch of the cabin. "She found it alright and showed me the video. It was a little grainy, but there were two guys, just like she said. Big men with gutting blades."

"The same weapon the Dean boy used to butcher his father," said Cartwright.

"Could you make out their faces?" Nolte asked Gus.

"Enough. Pretty sure one of them was Andre Groh, the son of a notorious poacher."

"That's a lot to glean from a hastily made video," said Cartwright. "How can you be so sure on the ID?"

"Because I helped put away the old man years ago. His teenage son, Andre, fled into the woods later, taking a shot at my partner and nearly crippling him." He stepped closer to Nolte. "I don't know how that Dean kid is involved, or if he was involved at all, but you need to put out an APB for Andre Groh. He, and whoever he was with at Birch Lake, are looking like the real killers."

Nolte folded his arms. "I remember the Groh story being all over the news back then because they never found evidence of what happened to his son. Andre was rumored to have disappeared into the bush and was living off the land and being helped out by the locals. For a few years after, people would attribute any unsolved break-ins or thefts at their cabins around Alaska to the Groh kid."

"No offense, but this sounds like a ghost story," said Cartwright. "A mysterious poacher who became a local legend with the rednecks."

"Call it what you want, but I'm pretty sure that was Andre Groh in Micah's video."

Cartwright threw up both hands. "But she didn't leave you with the phone. She and that guy Payne just took off and are running their own investigation with critical evidence… evidence that could, by the way, exonerate her friend Dean and help provide a lead on the murders of her two friends at the lake, but she didn't turn it over to us."

Nolte narrowed his eyes. "What do you mean 'her friend Dean'? You saying she knows him?"

Cartwright gave a hearty nod. "I saw the cagey look on her face in your lounge when I mentioned I had been Dean's case manager. I think they might have been neighbors or gone to the same school at some point when they were kids, or even been in juvie together."

Nolte replied, "That doesn't prove anything. And juvie is segregated, so it's not like she would have crossed paths with him in the hallway. You should know that."

"In case you forgot about all the blood and the actual murder weapon being found at Dean's place, his signature is all over those killings. He might have teamed up with a few other guys who left him to hang for it, but bringing an old folk tale about a mysterious poacher into the story might be what this Brezny girl intended with her video."

"And what about the four dead men at Birch Lake who came to kill Payne and the girl today?" said Gus, giving her a hard stare.

"Guys that you stated you didn't see," said Cartwright. "Nor did you see what unfolded between Payne and those four people. Is that right?" She flung her hand at the cabin while glaring at Nolte. "And now we're here, wasting valuable time, looking for more evidence of Payne's handiwork when he could even be connected to what's going on."

She pivoted towards Nolte. "I mean, did you even do a deep dive to see if Payne and Dean have any past history? It seems kind of odd that this drifter, who also just so happens to have some man-tracking skills to interpret crime scenes, shows up at the same time the Dean kid goes on a murder spree."

Nolte licked his lip. "You seem to have it all figured out, Detective. Maybe you should've been a prosecutor instead. But you're right about one thing: my time is valuable, and I didn't come here to argue a court case. Something hasn't been sitting right with me about this whole thing since that first morning at Birch Lake, and I have no intention of pinning the entire case on the Dean kid without more substantial information, especially since there appears to have been a coordinated attack to silence the girl." He gestured towards the lake. "So you can either assist me with my efforts here or go wait with the pilot in the plane until I'm finished."

She removed a satellite phone from her jacket. "I actually have to call the governor for an update about your supposed progress, so I'll return when I'm done."

The two men watched her walk off towards the woodshed before Gus spoke. "She's a real piece of work. Maybe I should send her into the woods with a jerky necklace."

Nolte chuckled. "Heading into the woods is what I had in mind but minus the bear bait." He pointed to the dense spruce trees to the left. "I'm going to scout around the back of the cabin for a minute, then walk a few hundred yards into the forest…if I were to keep walking though, how long would it take me to reach the dirt road that comes in from Saxon?"

"Twenty minutes or so."

"And let's say I was doing it at night while carrying a dead guy on my back?"

Gus glanced at the forest, then at Nolte. "Depends on how big you are and what shape you're in, but probably three times as long, given you'd have to move slower to avoid busting an ankle, along with the ups and downs between here and the road." He scratched his graying beard. "I'd say an hour since it'd be at night and the ground would've been slick from the rain."

"I'll be back in a little bit." Nolte walked past the porch and skirted to the left of the cabin. "By the way, have you or Jasmine or any of your staff been out here to clean up since the incident?"

"Nope." Gus took a step forward. "You want me to tag along?"

"Nah, just wait here for Velma from *Scooby-Doo Mystery Incorporated* to come back, and tell her where I've gone. I'm gonna check around the back of the cabin first, then head into the woods."

Nolte walked slowly, scanning the damp ground along the left side of the cabin, then made his way onto the rear porch. He donned a pair of latex gloves and opened the screened entry and examined the enclosed space. He headed to the mangled rear door, seeing a broken window. Pushing past the opening, the lieutenant scrutinized the kitchen and living room as the thick odor of woodsmoke wafted over him.

After a cursory look at the Spartan interior, he returned to the rear porch. The sunlight was flitting through the treetops and illuminated part of the wooden floorboards. Nolte kneeled, tilting his head and studying the play of light on the flooring closest to the entrance.

There was a twelve-inch section that was lighter than the rest of the wood. He leaned in closer, smelling the faint odor of bleach. Nolte stood and stepped back to the corner, taking in the entire length of the fifteen-foot porch. The same area with the chemical odor was also the only spot free of broken glass shards.

He stepped closer to the door frame again, his eyes tracing along the damaged window. At first, he thought it was a sliver of white mold growing in the wood. He removed his Buck folding knife and flicked it open and pried out a tooth fragment.

*This corresponds with where Payne said he slammed a guy's head into the door. Is Corporal Hicks really that green? How the hell did he miss this?*

He pulled out a small evidence bag from his jacket and slid the tooth inside, then stepped back towards the exit. He looked at the new details that had somehow been missed during the initial visit.

Nolte moved outside and walked along the tree line, locating some recently trampled ferns. He pushed aside the poplar branches and headed into the forest, following what looked like a faint trail. Whether it was old or new was beyond his comprehension, but it was wider than deer trails he'd seen, and that meant either a bear had come through the area or a handful of people.

Either way, he kept his hand on his service pistol, realizing that a 9mm would do little to a charging bear. But it did help to calm his nerves.

He followed the path for a hundred yards down a muddy slope. At the bottom, he slipped, but caught himself on a small sapling. He uprighted himself, hearing a crunch sound under the rotting birch leaves. Nolte slid aside the debris with his boot, noticing something black protruding from the soil.

Leaning over, he swept the rest of the leaf litter away, his fingers detecting something rigid with straps. He yanked out a device, seeing a military-style night-vision monocle. The lens and housing were cracked, but there were hair strands embedded in the frayed strap.

*So Payne was telling the truth all along. And he not only killed three guys here but four more at Birch Lake. Jesus, what kind of war has descended on Saxon?*

He pulled out a larger evidence bag and slid the mangled NVG inside. *I need to get a hold of Payne and that video. Then maybe I can figure out why someone has gone to so much trouble to hire a hit team to take out the girl, and how Dean is involved in all of this.*

He headed back up the slope and followed his tracks to the cabin, wondering what other details in this investigation had been muddled and who around him could really be trusted.

# CHAPTER 23

As Payne approached Anchorage from the north on the Parks Highway, the ninety-minute drive from Saxon had transitioned during the last few miles from boreal forest to urban sprawl, beginning with strip malls and big-box stores that lined the highway before the road expanded to a multilane freeway near Eagle River.

After passing through several residential areas near Rogers Park, the downtown skyline emerged against the dramatic backdrop of the Chugach Mountains and Cook Inlet.

The organic GPS unit to his right had provided a colorful tour guide's knowledge of the region and now directed her efforts on the high-rises. "That twenty-two-story building is owned by ConocoPhillips—Alaska's tallest structure. Bet you didn't know there was oil in this state," Micah said in a sarcastic tone.

"That other nearby building is the Hotel Captain Cook, named after the celebrity explorer who made it sound like he was the first person to set eyes on this land even though the

Inuit had been here for a few hundred generations. And over behind that gas station is where all the junkies hang out, so steer clear of that place."

It seemed her knowledge of the urban world wasn't limited to architecture, and he sensed she knew these streets in a way that was light-years apart from the average visitor or apartment-dweller.

He exited and drove down Fourth Avenue, stopping at a red light. He motioned to the cluster of homeless under the highway overpass. "That's not something you read about in the travel guides for this city."

"Yeah, major issue. And a lot of gang violence connected with the heroin trade."

"Heroin is the illegal drug of choice here?"

"Black tar heroin, comes in with the Polynesians who arrive here."

"Never would've expected people from a tropical region to migrate to Alaska, of all places."

"Anchorage is a major port city, so we get folks from all over the world here, but especially other coastal countries. It's the funniest thing to see a huge Samoan guy shoveling his driveway in just his shorts and boots. Their body shape is similar to the Inuit, so they must be less bothered by the cold than the rest of us."

Payne chuckled.

"What? It's true," she said, unplugging her phone from the charging cable.

"It's not that. Just that I've come to expect a barrage of sarcasm about someone's appearance whenever you open your mouth and, instead, you come up with something very insightful and observant. You surprise me, is all."

Micah was quiet, staring ahead with a blank look on her face.

Payne wondered when she'd last had a kind word said to her. By her barbed replies since they'd met, he figured she was someone always on guard and ready to run—or fight. Constant stress had become her daily norm. Too many years of that, and it would become ingrained to the point where she wouldn't know how to live any other way and seek out the means, conscious or otherwise, of maintaining that consistent cortisol dump. He'd seen it in colleagues who had stayed downrange for extended periods—and he'd seen it far too often in the eyes of the person in the mirror towards the end of his career in black-ops.

"University of Alaska isn't far from here," she said.

He proceeded through the green light. "I need to find a secondhand store first and get some new clothes—ideally a cheap suit jacket and nice slacks so I don't stand out when I'm strolling across campus. That's where one of the victims from Birch Lake worked at. Professor Ian Zandri."

"Turn right at the next light. A few blocks down is a place called Savers." She turned towards him. "So how did you figure out the dead man was a professor?"

"I saw all the IDs when Nolte was going through the victims' belongings. Zandri was the old guy you said you talked to. I looked him up—he's a longtime faculty member in the history department on campus here. And since the photographer at the other campsite was from Indiana, and I don't have access to his film, he's not much of a help right now."

"What does Zandri have to do with what happened at Birch Lake, though?"

"We're about to find out."

She frowned. "Not me. After we buy new clothes, I'm going back home to check on something and will meet up with you later."

He turned right into the parking lot for Savers and parked

at the back of the lot. "The way you talked before, home sounded like a place to avoid, permanently."

"My foster parents are at work, so it won't be a problem, and I won't be there long."

He turned off the Jeep and swiveled towards her. "Have you spoken with them? Did they call to check on you?"

Micah shrugged. "They're probably lining up another foster kid already so they can get their subsidy check from the state." She pointed to a couple of college-age students leaving the store with used backpacks and sleeping pads. "You know, I didn't even realize that having three meals a day was a thing until I started working on the trail crew when I was fifteen. Saying you were hungry in my house meant you'd get served a knuckle sandwich, so screw my foster family."

"Sorry I brought them up."

"It's just life, man."

"It should've been different. You deserve better. Every kid does. Just don't spend too much of your newfound adult years recovering from your childhood. There's a whole world out there, and it's yours for the taking."

Her rigid cheeks began to soften, and she lightly punched him in the arm. "Careful, or I might take your advice to heart and ride off on that cool motorcycle of yours when you're not looking."

"I said the *world* is yours, not my ride."

"We'll see."

———

THIRTY MINUTES LATER, they left the store with their purchases. Business-casual clothes and shoes for Payne; and new jeans, a T-shirt, and a hoodie for Micah. They changed into their wardrobes in the store.

As they walked back to the Jeep, Micah trailed off to the

left. "Text you in a few hours when you're done playing college boy." She removed a folded piece of paper from her jeans, handing it to Payne. "But here's my number in case you get lost in our big city."

"Alright. Keep your head on a swivel—and be good."

"Whatever you say, *Uncle*."

# CHAPTER 24

After Payne left, Micah returned to the secondhand store and purchased a pair of nurse's scrubs she'd seen in the women's section.

From what she recalled overhearing Nolte say to Cartwright, Jimmy Dean was at Anchorage Memorial Hospital—and that building was only a half mile away from the secondhand store. This might be her only chance to visit him, whether he was conscious or not. She had to figure out a way to see him—to learn what he knew that could help explain what had happened at Birch Lake, and about the people behind it.

When Micah was thirteen, she'd met Jimmy at her third foster home a few years after her parents' deaths. Her foster mother was friends with Jimmy's mom, and the two of them stayed in Micah's foster home for nearly a month the first time Jimmy's mom had fled her abusive husband. It was a pattern that would repeat itself during the following two years until the fateful day Jimmy took a stand against his father after enduring another severe beating.

That day changed Micah forever and her perspective on

adults. It certainly altered the life of the kind-hearted boy who had become like a brother to her. The same boy who had showed her how to whittle, filet a fish, and build a campfire at their fort in the woods. She was moved by his deeply sensitive eyes, which were coupled with a bottomless anguish that she'd only witnessed in a handful of the worst abuse cases in foster care.

*There's just no way he's involved. If anything, he's the patsy like Payne said. He has to be.*

After changing into the scrubs in the store, she left and took the city bus to the hospital. Along the way, she pulled her hair back in a tight ponytail, which always made her look a few years older. Though she didn't know much about the nursing profession, she had a veritable master's degree in conning people to get what she needed.

Micah drew her shoulders back and glanced up at the mirror in the corner of the bus, running through a mental rehearsal for what came next.

———

THE FIVE-FLOOR ANCHORAGE MEMORIAL HOSPITAL rose like a practical structure of concrete, steel, and glass against the backdrop of the Chugach Mountains. Upon entering through the automatic sliding doors, Micah stepped into a large lobby with high ceilings and muted colors of soft blues and greens, which she figured was supposed to be calming. But she was far from calm, and she kept her eyes focused on the tiled floor as she strode by the reception desk, where several volunteers in burgundy vests were trying to describe where the radiology department was to someone with a heavy accent.

Micah walked past a gift shop and a small café, where the rich aroma of coffee temporarily overpowered the building's antiseptic smell. She paused near the elevators, scanning the digital directory for the location of the intensive care unit. *Shouldn't be too hard to locate Jimmy once I'm up in ICU—probably not many patients with a cop outside their door.*

The elevator on the right opened, and she stepped aside as the bustle of orderlies, visitors, and other staff emerged. She moved to the back corner as people flooded inside, filling the small space to capacity. The last figure was a large security guard, who was nearly as wide as the entrance and gave a casual glance at the occupants before facing away. In addition to the others, there were two female CNAs in seafoam scrubs discussing shift schedules beside her; the oldest nursing assistant had graying roots showing through her blonde hair, while the other younger woman had multiple piercings along her ear that glinted off the overhead lighting.

Micah kept an eye on the security guard as she fought to control her breathing. Every floor that passed without someone noticing her was a small victory.

Micah's elbow was nearly pressed into the nearest CNA, and she took advantage of the tight confines to unclip the woman's badge from the bottom hem of her shirt.

Micah's heart hammered in her chest as she exited the third-floor elevator, tugging nervously at the bottom of her green blouse and attaching the new badge to the base of her scrubs. This floor was noticeably quieter than the bustling first level, which helped ease her jangled nerves.

On her way through the hall, she grabbed a clipboard, latex gloves and a catheter bag from a rolling supply cart parked against the wall. Twenty feet ahead was the nurses' station, which appeared to only have one woman working the desk.

Micah paused near the closed door of a patient's room, glancing at the chart on a wall slot beside the room while waiting for the nurse to take a call. Once the woman was occupied, she flowed in behind a janitor passing by with his mop bucket, making a right turn at the next intersection.

Pushing through a set of swinging doors, she kept her eyes down when passing a doctor engaged in a chart review. Through the small window in the final door ahead, Micah spotted her objective and what she'd feared—a police officer seated outside a closed room. The dark-haired man was scrolling on his phone while occasionally glancing up to scan the hallway.

Micah donned the latex gloves and rehearsed the script she'd prepared. She pushed through the doors and pulled her chin up as she walked. She kept her movements purposeful, forcing herself to make direct eye contact as the officer looked up. "I'm here to replace the catheter bag. The one the patient currently has, has a faulty drain tube."

The officer gave her an irritated look, shoving his phone into his shirt pocket. "There was just a nurse in there a while ago. She didn't mention anything about someone else coming down."

Micah brushed her thumb over the photo on her badge. "That's because CNAs are invisible to everyone in a hospital, and why we get all the dirty jobs."

He glanced at her face and smiled. "You're not invisible to me."

"That's very sweet, but unless you want the janitor to be called in to mop up the upcoming biohazard on the floor in that room, I need to change out that bag."

The officer stood and unlocked the door. "He's cuffed to the bed, but just to be safe, don't get too close to his upper body."

"I thought he was unconscious?" She recalled the earlier comment from Nolte about the young man's condition.

"That maniac came out of the coma this afternoon, but he's only up for a few minutes at a time. He's lucky to still be breathing. Guess it was nearly a fatal overdose." He rested a hand on his holstered Taser. "Don't worry, I'll be right here if you need anything." The man waved her inside before returning to his chair, keeping the door open.

"Perfect," Micah replied, her heart pounding beneath her calm exterior.

Inside Jimmy's room, Micah froze momentarily, shocked by the sight of the eighteen-year-old, who was pale and motionless among the tangle of tubes and wires. The rhythmic swoosh of the blood pressure machine activating covered her quiet footsteps as she approached his bedside, positioning herself on the far side where the medical equipment partially shielded her from the hallway.

She set down the clipboard and catheter bag on the bed and tapped Jimmy on the shoulder.

His head slowly moved side to side, his eyes prying open. He blinked hard, then stared at Micah for a moment. His lips trembled as he spoke. "Micah, is it…is it really you?"

She nodded, overlaying her other hand on his arm. "I had to check on you."

"You have to know I didn't kill those people. Tell me you know that, right?"

"Of course I know that, Jimmy." She leaned in closer, whispering, "I don't have much time. I'm trying to figure out what happened and who set you up. Can you tell me anything?"

He squeezed her hand, his eyes watering. Dean glanced at the open door, then back at her. "I'm so glad you're here. They don't believe me. They just keep saying I murdered a bunch of people in the woods, but I…"

"Jimmy—focus. I need you to tell me what you remember about the last few days before you woke up here."

He nodded, lowering his voice until it was barely audible. "There was a couple at the…at the Wolverine Bar with me that night. That night the cops said I killed a bunch of campers. But it wasn't me, Micah."

"I know. I know, but what can you tell me about the couple you were with?"

"We were talking about hockey, and then I…I remember getting really out of it, like I'd had too much to drink, but I was only on my second beer. Next thing I know, I'm cuffed to this fucking bed."

"They must have slipped something in your drink. Do you remember what they looked like?"

"Guy had bad teeth. But the red-headed woman…" He motioned with his cuffed hand towards the pen on her clipboard. She handed it to him, and Dean placed the tip on Micah's right wrist, gently drawing a small crucifix. "She had a tiny tattoo like this."

She glanced at the symbol of the unusual cross with its side arms angled down, vaguely recalling the pattern from somewhere. She heard the guard's chair scrape against the floor in the hallway. "You need to act like you're asleep, or we're both busted. I'll figure this out. I promise."

"But…"

She vigorously shook her head, pulling her hands away. "Now, Jimmy. Close your eyes."

As he complied, she grabbed the lemon Gatorade drink off the rolling bedside tray and poured the contents into the catheter bag, then replaced the cap.

The officer stepped inside, staring at Dean. "Thought I heard him talking."

"He was mumbling something, but his speech slurred," Micah said. "Sounded all Greek to me." She grabbed her clipboard and the catheter bag, following the officer back into the hallway.

"It'll be Russian and gutter English in the prison where he's headed."

"He hasn't been convicted or even tried yet."

The lawman locked the door and slumped down on his seat. "Actually, since this guy's bat-shit crazy, he'll probably end up in a psych ward. Either way, his days of roaming the woods are over."

*Not if I have a say in this.*

# CHAPTER 25

The history department at the University of Alaska was located in Heritage Hall, a striking three-story building perched on the eastern edge of campus with panoramic views of the Chugach Mountains. The exterior featured weathered cedar siding, enormous windows framed in green-tinted copper, and stone accent walls quarried from local granite. The building's curved roof served as both a practical design to shed heavy snow loads, but also embodied the silhouette of traditional Native Alaskan dwellings Payne had seen during his travels around the interior.

The grounds surrounding Heritage Hall included a meditative courtyard with indigenous tree plantings, stone walkways, and sculptures of prominent pioneers and indigenous leaders, with an obvious emphasis on the former figures. Towering fir trees framed the approach to the building, and Payne felt like he was heading up to a cathedral more than an academic building.

Summer semester had ended a week ago, and the few people strolling around campus looked like professors or other faculty preparing for the coming throngs of students following Labor Day.

He strode up the steps and pushed past the glass doors, stepping into the spacious lobby. Natural light flooded in from clerestory windows above. A grand staircase with wooden treads and glass balustrades curved up to the second floor, while a central skylight allowed sunlight to penetrate the building, which he imagined was welcomed during the shortened winter days. In a state that was notorious for alcoholism and depression due to the harsh climate for much of the year, he figured such things were intentional design elements to help mitigate the effects of seasonal affective disorder.

Payne walked past the staircase, examining the exhibits contained in glass showcases down the hallway. Most contained displays of historical artifacts from Alaska's rich past—gold rush memorabilia, traditional Native tools, and early statehood documents sealed in climate-controlled cases. The walls above were lined with life-sized black-and-white photographs of Anchorage from its earliest days as a squalid tent city to its modern skyline.

Down the main corridor were seminar rooms with floor-to-ceiling bookshelves, a cozy student lounge with a fireplace, and the department's administrative offices. He paused to examine the faculty list posted on the wall. It seemed that the entire third floor belonged to the history staff, with the other floors reserved for archives, the folklore department, and Indigenous studies.

He located Zandri's room number, then retraced his steps back to the stairwell and trotted up. The third floor was as silent as a church on a Monday morning, and Payne walked past more exhibits showcasing graduate student projects and a display of weathered mining tools from a bygone era.

Payne approached the secretary's desk, watching her look

up from her laptop with the wary expression of someone who'd fielded too many unwelcome visitors. She looked to be in her fifties with her auburn hair up in a bun and blue-rimmed reading glasses resting on the bridge of her nose.

When he introduced himself and mentioned he was looking into Professor Zandri's death, her fingers stopped moving over the keys entirely. "Are you a reporter?" she asked, her tone defensive.

Payne shook his head and explained he was a freelance consultant working with the Saxon troopers' post. The mention of the law-enforcement agency seemed to shift something in her demeanor. Her shoulders dropped slightly, and she gestured to the chair beside her desk.

"I'm Margaret Beecher," she said, extending her hand. It was the first time in weeks he'd shaken someone's hand that wasn't calloused and rough in this state.

"Kyle Payne. Nice to meet you, though I regret the unfortunate circumstances."

The woman momentarily gripped the edge of her seat like she was preparing for a turbulent flight. "Professor Zandri was such a gentleman. Always brought me coffee in the mornings, and would sit with me for a few minutes, asking about my grandson or the books I was reading. He had this old-world courtesy that you just don't see anymore. That's what makes this so hard to understand, Mr. Payne."

He leaned forward slightly, pulling out a small notebook. "How long had Professor Zandri been with the department?"

Margaret straightened in her chair, seeming to appreciate the official nature of his questions. "Twenty-six years this fall. He was a local boy, actually—grew up right here in Anchorage. Of course, it was much smaller then, and not as much traffic."

"Did he have a specialty—an area of study that he devoted himself to, apart from his colleagues?"

"Ian's love was Alaska's mining history. I used to joke with him that it was his mistress. He was actually working on a book about the early gold rush era when he...when this happened."

Payne made a note and looked up. "What about the canoe trip? Was that something he did regularly?"

"That was unusual for him," Margaret replied, her brow furrowing slightly. "For one thing, it was just him, and he wasn't really a fan of bugs and sleeping on the ground."

"So, any ideas on what led him out to Birch Lake? That's some remote country."

"Something about researching old mining claims." She shifted in her chair. "He seemed excited about it, more so than usual. Said it might be the key to his whole book project."

Payne made another note, then met her eyes directly. "Did he have any enemies or bitter rivals? In twenty-six years, there must have been some conflicts—departmental politics, tenure disputes, that sort of thing?"

Her lips grew flat. "I don't understand—I thought what happened was a killing spree and that a bunch of people were murdered by a deranged madman who is already in custody. At least that's what one news report said."

"That's the working theory, but I'm just trying to gather as much information as possible on the victims since the Saxon post is rather overwhelmed right now, as you might imagine."

She plucked a piece of lint off her sleeve and then brushed the fabric smooth several times. "I see. Professor Zandri ruffled a few feathers once in a while, but never to the point of pushing someone's buttons or angering them. For a scholar, he was a rather humble, unassuming man." She chuckled, glancing up at the ceiling. "And if you're listening, Ian, yes, you were a scholar."

By the way she kept letting his first name slip out and by the lack of a wedding band, he wondered if they had been involved.

"It sounds like work was his life. I had a teacher once who was so into his profession that it couldn't help but rub off on everyone in the class. Those are the best kinds—the ones who light a fire in you instead of just filling your head with facts." He left out the part about it being his sniper-training instructor.

Margaret glanced around the empty hallway, then pulled a set of keys from her desk drawer. "If you really want to understand what kind of man Professor Zandri was, you should see his office—it'll show you just how passionate he was about Alaska's history."

Payne tried to contain his enthusiasm. "Yes, if you have the time."

She stood and walked down the right passage, stopping at the fourth room, which had the man's name spelled in a Papyrus font on the frosted-glass window. Margaret unlocked the door and carefully opened it, staring at the empty chair on the other side of the desk for a moment. She cleared her throat, then stepped inside.

Payne followed. The room smelled musty, and there was a fine layer of dust on the bookshelves on the right. "When's the last time the professor was here?"

She shrugged. "Not sure. He wasn't teaching this summer, so maybe early May after winter semester ended."

Payne wondered if he was standing in a room akin to Indiana Jones. Aside from a handful of academic accolades on the left wall and the dog-eared journals on the oaken desk in the center, the place was full of antique mining equipment propped in every corner or hanging from the floor-to-ceiling bookshelves.

The woman walked to the windows, pulling back the thin

white curtains. Payne moved up beside her, both of them gazing at the stunning view of the snowcapped mountains.

She stepped back, gliding her delicate fingers along the smooth edges of the large desk. "The view he had from here was the best on campus, but he wanted to face away from it so he could focus on his students and not get distracted." She removed a tissue from her pocket and dabbed her cheeks.

Payne moved to the opposite side and gazed at the contents of the desk, which resembled organized chaos: stacks of old newspapers, several antique maps held down by a Klondike gold pan, and an Inuit carved box with a scrimshaw design on the lid depicting a whale hunt.

Payne moved to the left corner near the window, where a worn leather armchair was situated beside a small side table stacked with books flagged with numerous colorful sticky notes.

"When he wasn't advising his grad students, he was often there, reviewing some old report from a century ago. He was a literal gold mine of information on all things Alaska, from Inuit prehistory to the Russian explorers who arrived here in the 1700s, and every pioneer town from here to the Yukon. But his real passion was the effect mining had upon the state. And he knew every story about the early prospectors as well as having interviewed a lot of those old-timers before they passed on."

"Seems like mining, cattle, and timber are the things that shaped much of the history of our country. Of a lot of countries, actually. Only now, it's mining for lithium instead of gold or silver."

She gave a faint chuckle before a deflated look drifted over her face. "Isn't that the truth. It's too bad he's not here, or he would spend all evening talking with you about that."

"I know this must be difficult, but do you know where he was headed on that extended canoe trip west of Saxon?"

"Any trips he took, anywhere, were always connected with uncovering some kernel of history. I think it was related to interviews he'd been doing the summer before with an old-timer in Talkeetna, the next town up from Saxon. I think he was in his nineties."

"A former colleague of his?"

"The individual was an author. Wrote a lot of popular field guides on Alaska. If I recall correctly, the man's father had worked for the big timber company near Talkeetna in the 1960s or so and knew the Saxon area like few others."

The woman walked to the middle shelf along the wall and ran her finger along the leather-bound journals, finally settling on a thin volume with a tasseled bookmark stuck in it. She put it on the desk and flipped through the pages, stopping past the halfway mark and pointing to the entry. "Stanley Hirovicz." Scrawled in pencil below the name was a set of longitude and latitude figures.

Payne removed his iPhone. "Would you mind if I take a picture? This might be of use in my report since it's probably near Birch Lake. I probably won't even need it, but I'd hate to have to come back here and bother you."

She waved at the bookshelf. "Go ahead. This stuff will probably all be packed up and sent God knows where. He didn't have any family, so I'm sure the research materials will be archived in the basement, but the rest will…" She pressed her arms to her sides. "I'm sorry. I just can't believe he's really gone."

Payne snapped the photo before she changed her mind. He stepped aside, extending his hand. "Again, I'm so sorry for your loss."

He headed to the door but paused, pointing to the one new object on a chair near the coatrack. It was an exact match for the large orange backpack Payne had seen at Zandri's campsite, minus the arterial blood spray. "Was Professor Zandri planning a backpacking trip?"

"I highly doubt it. That's probably an extra pack he bought after taking a bunch of field courses this past spring with a local survival school, in case he got in over his head. Raven Survival School is the company. You probably passed the dirt road where it's located, coming into Anchorage."

She followed him to the door, her eyes lingering on the pack. "I found a way to get the university to pay for the training by convincing the dean that it would reduce liability during field trips if the professor had some safety skills." She rested her pale hands on the door handle. "Lot of good that did him, eh?"

———

AFTER HE EXITED, Payne waited around the corner, listening for the door closing to Zandri's office. A second later, the secretary's heels clacked on the tiled floor as she returned to her own office down the hall.

Payne quickly made his way back to Zandri's room, using his credit card to jimmy open the simplistic lock, then slipping inside. He made his way to the middle bookshelf and plucked out the tattered journal he'd just seen. He glanced over at a small wooden barrel near the window, which contained dozens of rolled-up maps.

Payne sifted through them one at a time, examining the handwritten labels in their corners, until he located the fifteen-minute quadrangle maps for the wilderness area west of Saxon.

He spread the map out on the floor and scanned the terrain features, seeing Wolf Lake, Birch Lake, and the adjoining waters in the vast region. Payne folded the map until it would fit into the journal, then tucked the items inside the pocket of his suit.

He returned to the door, cracking it open. Hearing Margaret talking on her phone, he exited and headed in the opposite direction from the secretary before taking another staircase down to the lobby.

As he walked across campus to his vehicle, he tried to piece together the new information but still had too many blank spots.

*A history professor who was a fanatic about mining and a discovery of something in the lake systems near Birch Lake. That must mean Zandri discovered gold or silver—that would certainly be worth killing for.*

# CHAPTER 26

A traveler driving up the winding road to the posh mansion on the hillside would think they had been transported to someplace in Austria.

As the CEO of Frontier Mining Technologies, Sean Klurman had designed his fourteen-thousand-square-foot timber and stone estate to resemble a conqueror's monument on the rocky promontory overlooking Turnagain Arm Bay, eighteen miles southeast of Anchorage.

The meticulously manicured grounds sprawled across thirty acres of prime Alaskan real estate, featuring terraced stone gardens and a gated perimeter, while a separate seven-car garage housed Klurman's collection of vintage automobiles. A helicopter pad for a Bell 429 sat carved into the hillside behind the main house, allowing him to come and go without using the main access road.

On the estate's south wing, an enclosed Olympic-sized swimming pool complex featured floor-to-ceiling windows overlooking the bay, complete with an adjoining Finnish sauna and a state-of-the-art gymnasium, where Klurman maintained the physical conditioning necessary for his big-game hunting expeditions around the world.

Inside, Klurman's trophy room dominated the western wing—a two-story cathedral to his hunting prowess on every continent. Mounted heads stared with glass eyes from every wall: record-sized grizzlies, rare snow leopards, and an albino Cape buffalo whose acquisition had cost two Kenyan rangers their lives.

Above the taxidermied heads hung a framed quote in elegant script: "Some men collect things. Real men collect power." For Klurman, he collected both, and during his sixty-two years on this planet, his sole focus had been to claw his way to the top of whatever business pursuit stood in his way.

His latest endeavor in the wilderness west of Saxon was no different, though it had become far more chaotic than he originally envisioned. Today's meeting with Andre Groh would hopefully rectify that.

For the past thirty years, Klurman's heavy-equipment company had dominated the North American market as the largest supplier of construction machinery and mining excavators for major corporations in the US, Canada, and Mexico.

But despite his networking efforts, he was still unable to establish lucrative partnerships with Chinese state-owned enterprises that would catapult him to the top of the mining industry, providing billions of dollars' worth of hydraulic shovels, bulldozers, and mineral-extraction systems to fuel China's infrastructure boom.

Now, all of that was about to change. With the recent discovery of gold west of Saxon, along with the critical players who originally pinpointed the gold being eliminated, Klurman would have the wealth he needed to expand his empire into every region of the globe.

Klurman's fingers drummed impatiently against his

mahogany desk as he reviewed quarterly earnings that would make other CEOs weep with joy, yet all he felt was the creeping anxiety that somewhere, someone was gaining ground on him.

In quiet moments between deals and conquests, when the phones stopped ringing and the sycophants retreated, Klurman caught glimpses of himself in windows—a hollow-eyed predator who had consumed everything within reach yet remained fundamentally empty, sustained only by the next hunt.

But this current hunt wasn't for trophy animals or race cars. It was for a mineral treasure he'd thought lost since first hearing about it in his youth. Finally, it seemed within his reach.

He stood and walked outside to the second-floor balcony of his home office, watching a muddy 4x4 truck drive up the snaky asphalt road that wound through a half mile of his wooded property. After parking below the veranda, Andre Groh and another man exited, heading through the front doors.

Klurman's servant escorted the visitors upstairs. The usual smell of woodsmoke laced with sweat flowed in behind Groh and the other man. Klurman didn't mind. In fact, he preferred it over the expensive cologne his corporate clients were usually drenched in.

*A man should smell like a man.*

He met Groh in the middle of the room, both men shaking hands, then Klurman pulling him in for a hug. "Good to see you, Andre."

"Likewise, sir." The man gestured towards his accomplice. "This is Karl Hatch. He's been working for me since we began this new operation."

Klurman gave Hatch a hearty handshake. The business mogul was always thrilled being in the presence of profes-sional hunters, and in this case, the killers of those who stood in Klurman's way. "Welcome, Karl." He waved towards the wet bar in the corner. "Pour yourself a drink if you're inclined."

"I'm good, sir, thank you." Hatch stood a foot back from Groh, averting his eyes like an obedient hound.

Klurman walked around the other side of his desk and sat down.

Groh took a seat across from him, glancing at the animal mounts above the fireplace on the right, his eyes settling on the head of a jungle cat with yellow eyes of glass. "I see you finally added that endangered black jaguar we tracked down in Brazil last winter."

"It took a while to smuggle back into this country, but, fortunately, our mutual friend Lee worked his usual wonders at his taxidermy shop. I'd say this is his finest work."

"He's an artist. Few have his patience and skill."

Hatch was tapping his fingers nervously on the armrest until Groh gave him a hard stare. "Karl, why don't you get some fresh air while Mr. Klurman and I go over some business details."

"Will do." Hatch eagerly made for the door like a rope was tugging at his waist.

Klurman chuckled. "Ah, I love your breed. Being indoors too long makes you guys insane."

"I don't think his surroundings have anything to do with that. He was born a little off his rocker."

"Has that been a problem?"

Groh shook his head. "No, Karl is reliable, and if that changes, then I'll handle him." He leaned forward, rubbing his leathery hands. "But what has become an issue is a newcomer in Saxon. Some guy named Kyle Payne. He's inserted himself into the criminal investigation at Birch Lake and has come between my guys and the lone survivor, that girl Micah Brezny I told you about on the phone."

"Payne's a cop? If that's the case, then get me his price or his jelly spot, and I'll make him go away."

"Not a cop, sir. Not sure…ex-military most likely, though nothing showed up in the usual databases. So far, he's taken out seven of my guys, including Ernie Packard."

Klurman let out a heavy sigh. "Shit. I'm sorry to hear that. I know how close you and Ernie were. I'll never forget what he did for you after your father died."

"You mean what you both did for me back then, sir. I wouldn't be the person I am today without you two helping me out, financially and otherwise."

Klurman glanced at the mounts on the wall. "It's been a two-way street, my friend." He interlaced his fingers. "So this guy Payne—what's his angle? Is he freelancing for the state troopers' post?"

"I have no idea. My contact in Saxon said he appeared out of nowhere almost a month ago, doing some kind of work-trade with my old nemesis Gus Freed out at his lodge. That's where the girl appeared after she fled Birch Lake. Now, he seems to be helping her out of his own accord."

"Freed—that crusty old fucker."

"You know him?"

"I had my firm approach him two years ago about buying his property. That would make a great hunting lodge once I got rid of all his mothballed shacks, but he likes his poverty-with-a-view lifestyle too much."

"Well, he's also tied up in this since he's been providing sanctuary to the girl, and he flew her and Payne back to Birch Lake so she could look for her phone—a phone that apparently has video evidence of me and Hatch on it."

Klurman sat up straighter. "Dammit. I thought you said murdering Zandri and the others would be straightforward, especially given how isolated that campground is."

"Everything went as planned until the Brezny girl slipped

away from us. She was more resourceful and experienced in the woods than I expected. Frankly, she'd be at the bottom of a swamp by now if Payne hadn't gotten involved."

"It sounds like everything keeps circling back to this outsider. I need this wrapped up so I can start the next phase of my operation. If you need more funds or more people…"

"It's not that. I have more crews. But this is going to get ugly and could involve collateral damage with locals in Anchorage, where Payne and Brezny are currently at. I need to know how far you're willing to go with this, because the gloves will need to come off further. This is no longer simply a murder spree we can pin on Jimmy Dean. The whole story has to be reworked now."

"But you didn't mention anything about that video footage getting out—why not? If this girl has such critical evidence that could alter the investigation, why hasn't it been leaked to the press or handed over to Nolte?"

"Good question."

"Unless she and Payne are going to use it as leverage, figuring they can track down who was behind the killings. That has to be it—they're going to hold on to it for a hefty payday, which means they must think they're getting closer to discovering who was behind the killings, beyond just you and Hatch."

"There's absolutely no trace back to you. And barely to me, since, from what I'm told, the video footage is spotty and in low light, so reliable facial recognition might not be possible."

"Time to draw Payne out—corner him, cut off his exits, and make sure he doesn't walk away this time, before he completely fucks up my timeline."

Groh gave a hearty nod. "I know just the guys to handle this."

# CHAPTER 27

After leaving the university, Payne still hadn't heard from Micah, so he stopped at a brewery a few blocks from downtown. The parking area was full, and he drove back onto the side street and pulled into an elevated lot behind the brewery, next to an old warehouse.

He exited the Jeep. A second later, the street behind him rumbled, and four Harleys rolled in. By the way they made an immediate beeline for Payne, he figured they weren't heading to the brewery for happy hour.

His first instinct was to hop in his vehicle and hightail it back to the side street, but these guys had something else in mind. The bearded driver at the front veered off and drove to the left, parking a few feet from the back of the Jeep.

Payne glanced at the brewery lot below, but it was a ten-foot drop, and he wasn't about to risk busting an ankle. By the speed and surprise of their approach, he figured they must have had a spotter or two following him from the university.

*But who knew I was even in Anchorage?*

There would be time for determining that later. These

guys were only here for one thing. The four men disembarked their Harleys and pulled out collapsible batons, and Payne had never felt so backed into a corner.

Standing with his boot on the precipice of the cement wall, he reached around for his 1911 in the holster at his four o'clock.

"I wouldn't do that," said the bearded guy, gesturing to the area below.

Payne flicked his head for a second, seeing a tall guy in a leather vest, holding a sawed-off shotgun.

"Boss man said to bring you to him alive," said the bearded leader.

"Didn't know they had rent-a-thugs this far down south," said Payne, assessing the four cretins.

"There's a sweet bounty on your and Micah Brezny's heads," said the leader as he moved past the Jeep's bumper.

The two other guys were inching to his right. One had a long black goatee with bone beads in it, and the other looked Polynesian with a red snake tattoo on his neck and a miniscule ponytail. The last man was short with a shaved head.

This wasn't a weekend-warrior group who toured the coast on pricey rides. These looked like some battle-hardened ex-cons who probably lived on the fringes of the city in some burnt-out building where they peddled dope and stolen goods.

They were ten feet away now, fanning out in a half-circle. The only potential room Payne had was if he could get over the hood of the Jeep to the other side and get behind a dumpster a few feet away so his pistol could do the fighting.

The goateed biker with bone beads moved first, rushing Payne with his baton raised high. Payne had no choice but to meet him head-on, stepping inside the swing and driving his fist into the man's throat. The biker let out a muffled snort, dropping his weapon and clutching his damaged windpipe with both hands.

But the Polynesian guy rushed in before Payne could get off a shot. Payne spun just as Snake-tattoo's baton whistled toward his head. He caught the man's wrist with both hands and slid in closer, using the thug's momentum to execute a hip throw and sending him slamming into the bald goon. Snake-tattoo hit the other man hard, then crashed to the ground, his shoulder cracking on the pavement and a sliver of bone piercing the skin.

The bearded leader was charging now, and Payne knew he had seconds before the other two could get back in the fight. He feinted right, then dove across the hood of his Jeep just as the metal weapon cracked against the surface. Payne snatched up a jagged piece of broken bottle near the edge of the drop-off, its green glass catching the late afternoon light.

The goateed guy came around the front of the Jeep while the bearded alpha dog circled the back. Payne slashed with the glass shard, catching goatee across the forearm and drawing a line of blood. The man cursed and swung his baton in a vicious arc. Payne ducked but not quite fast enough—the tip caught him across the shoulder, sending what felt like flames down his arm.

Using his momentum, Payne spun and drove his opposite elbow into the bald guy's jaw. The man lurched to the side, gasping, and Payne grabbed his wrist, twisting until the baton clattered to the ground, then kicking the guy in the quadriceps and toppling him over.

But the leader was already on him, his weapon whistling through the air. Payne threw himself sideways, the baton missing his skull by inches and striking sparks off the dumpster's metal edge.

The bearded guy had circled around now. "You're just

making this harder on yourself," he growled, advancing with his baton raised.

Payne's hand closed around a length of rusty rebar protruding from a pile of construction debris. He yanked it free just as the leader lunged again. The baton cracked against the rebar with a metallic clang; then he swung it down onto the guy's bicep. The leader's arm bent at an awkward angle as he groaned, and Payne sent a swift shin kick into the guy's groin, dropping him.

But the bald man to the left was already swinging. The baton caught Payne across the ribs, doubling him over as pain exploded through his torso. Stars skipped around in his vision as he stumbled backward, gasping for air. The thug pressed his advantage, bringing the baton down in an overhead strike aimed at Payne's skull.

Payne sidestepped, the weapon striking the side of the dumpster. Chunks of metal slivers sprayed his face as he spun around, swinging the rebar like a baseball bat. It connected with the bald guy's knee with a crack that resembled a branch breaking. The man screamed and toppled sideways, clutching his leg.

The goateed idiot had recovered and was charging again, blood still flowing from his arm. Payne shuffled to the right, clotheslining him with the rebar, sending the biker crashing into a stack of empty paint cans.

A gunshot cracked through the humid air. The tall dude with the shotgun was trotting up an angled path that connected the two lots.

Payne grabbed a chunk of broken concrete from the edge and hurled it with everything he had. It spun end over end, catching the gunman in the chest. He staggered backward, the shotgun discharging into the sky as he toppled over the side and landed on a row of metal trash barrels.

The bearded leader was gasping for air, using the side of

the dumpster for support. The goateed biker was groaning among the paint cans, clutching his throat where the rebar had caught him. Payne heard the other two bikers moaning in agony from their injuries, both of them lying on their sides.

Payne's ribs felt like they were on fire, and his shoulder throbbed where the baton had caught him, but he needed to get going in case there were reinforcements coming.

He walked up to each bike and grabbed their ignition keys. While leaning over the alpha dog's Harley, Payne noticed a GPS device mounted to the handlebars. He yanked it free, staring at the screen, which showed their location and a red dot. Payne enhanced the latter symbol, seeing the Jeep indicated.

*Someone's been on me since leaving Saxon.*

He needed to get a few blocks between him and the five gorillas before he could sweep the vehicle for a bug. He headed to the Jeep and fired up the engine.

In his rearview mirror, he could see the bikers slowly picking themselves up from the asphalt as he drove away.

# CHAPTER 28

Three miles later, Payne pulled into a self-serve car-wash bay, figuring the overhead cover would buy him some time to locate the tracker. It took less than a minute to find a magnetized device under the rear bumper. He did a complete sweep of the entire vehicle, then walked to the trash bin outside. He rummaged around, pulling out a crumpled piece of aluminum wrapper from a burger joint along with a mini Coke can.

Payne returned to the Jeep, grabbing the tracker and folding the dime-sized device in the wrapper, then slid it inside the empty pop can, unsure what use he would put the tracker to but not wanting to discard a potentially useful electronic tool that had his enemy's signature on it.

When Payne was done, he drove out of the car wash. Micah had just texted her address, and he followed the GPS on his phone to the east side of Anchorage. Cookie-cutter brick homes with a token sapling planted along the curb and the occasional flower garden in front of the porch. Except the address Micah had given him was for a dwelling that looked twenty years older than the rest, with flaking white paint on the trim, a severely dented garage door and a front lawn that had succumbed to weeds.

He pulled up by the curb. Micah was nowhere in sight. He exited the Jeep and was heading to the porch when he heard yelling around the right side of the house. Micah and an older man were exchanging curses he'd thought he'd only hear in the military.

As he rounded the corner, a huge man in a black Steelers T-shirt was clutching Micah's arm and shouting inches from her face. Behind him was a folding chair and crushed beer cans.

"You ungrateful little princess," he slurred out. "You owe me rent since you're supposedly an adult now. You're lucky I don't call the cops after getting contacted by social services last night about you peddling drugs in Saxon."

"You're full of shit, Davey. And I'm done living here. I only came back to check on the other kids and say goodbye." She tried to pull free, but the man's giant hand kept a firm grip on the back of her arm. The street-tough kid Payne had seen before was replaced with someone terrified.

"Let her go," shouted Payne as he stepped closer.

"And who's this—your boyfriend?" The man released Micah, his bloodshot eyes fixed on Payne with instant hostility. "Get off my property before I teach you some fuckin' manners."

Payne waved a hand. "Sir, I really have no desire to fight anyone else right now."

"That's 'cause you're a pussy. My daughter never did have good taste in guys."

"Must be the male figure in her life."

Her foster father advanced, swaying dangerously but still managing to look menacing in his drunken rage.

Payne instinctively pushed Micah behind him.

"Think you're tough?" the man snarled, jabbing a finger toward Payne's chest. "I'm gonna crucify your ass."

The stench of alcohol was overpowering, and Payne found himself staring up at the six-foot-six man who was as wide as a refrigerator.

Micah grabbed her pack off the ground and ran to the corner.

The first punch came fast but sloppy, a wild right hook that Payne easily ducked. The foster father's momentum carried him forward, and Payne simply stepped aside, letting the drunken idiot stumble past him onto the grass. The same dance repeated itself two more times as the men moved towards the front lawn.

"Stand still and fight me," the man roared, throwing another haymaker that Payne avoided by leaning back.

Payne would have liked nothing more than to send a right hook across the man's jaw, but a further display of violence in front of an already traumatized Micah was the last thing she needed. Instead, Payne caught the man's wrist and used his forward motion to send him spinning sideways, where he tripped over his own feet and nearly fell again.

By now, neighbors were emerging on their porches to witness the spectacle. After three more wild swings that hit nothing but air, the foster father was gasping and red-faced, his shirt soaked with sweat.

The man's eyes darted at the other porches; then he backed up. "This ain't over," he muttered, but the fight had gone out of him completely. He staggered around the other side of his house, and Payne heard the door slam.

He didn't need to stick around in case the alcohol-riddled moron returned with a gun.

The girl followed him to the Jeep, both of them getting inside. Payne drove off, noticing she kept her misty eyes on the mountains ahead as they sped towards the highway.

A few minutes later, she wiped her cheeks and leaned back. "Thank you."

"I just happened to walk up then. You would have handled it."

She glanced at his red knuckles. "Thought you didn't hit him."

"I didn't. This is from someone else. Actually, a few people."

She shook her head. "Do I wanna know?"

"Nope."

# CHAPTER 29

The dirt road to the Raven Survival School wound through dense national forest for nearly eight miles, finally arriving at a dead-end turnout onto private property.

Payne downshifted the borrowed Jeep as they crested a small hill and saw the school spread before them in a natural clearing. He drove a hundred yards down the road and parked beside a green Ford F-150 with the school's logo on it.

He and Micah stepped out of the Jeep, studying the layout: ahead and to the right were a cluster of weathered canvas yurts arranged in a horseshoe pattern around a stone fire ring where split logs served as classroom seating. Beyond that lay a training area marked by bark shelters and dozens of practice knots hanging from horizontal poles like some primitive art installation.

At the far end of the property sat a modest silver travel trailer, its awning extended over a wooden deck with Adirondack chairs, where Payne pictured a grizzled instructor cleaning fish or sharpening knives after hours.

Micah leaned against the Jeep. "Sure you got the right location for where Zandri learned his backcountry skills? I'm waiting for some emo chick in a tie-dye skirt to walk up and offer me a joint."

Payne gestured towards the muscular guy with a high-and-tight haircut who just emerged from the travel trailer. "That looks like the owner I saw on the website, so your hippy commune theory just went down the drain."

"I'm Neil Burke. You Kyle Payne?" asked the man as he walked up and offered his hand to both of the visitors.

Micah simply introduced herself by her first name and allowed Payne to do the talking, as they'd agreed.

"This looks like a nice setup you've got out here," said Payne.

"It fits the bill for now. I'm hoping to expand to offering fly-in trips…like castaway survival courses where students get dropped off on a small island and have to fend for themselves for a week. Of course, that'll be for advanced students."

"I saw from your website that you were a former SERE instructor. You ever spend time at Camp Mackall?" Payne asked, referencing the military's premier survival and resistance training center nestled within Fort Bragg in North Carolina.

He gave Payne a surprised look. "Oh, yeah, everyone gets over to Mackall eventually and even Fort Rucker in Alabama. I started with the Air Force at Fairchild outside Spokane, originally, but logged some teaching time at Mackall during an exchange program with our instructor cadre before being sent up here my last two years and finished things out at Cool School, the military's Arctic survival center." He glanced over Payne. "Were you in SF, then?" he asked, referring to Army special forces.

Payne shook his head. "Nah, just had some buddies who went through SERE at Mackall. Back then it was known as 'Camp Slappy' since the psy-ops guys during the capture phase were known to slap people around. Now, it's all verbal abuse."

"Sounds like my first marriage."

Payne laughed.

"You said on the phone that you had some questions about the training I did for one of my students—an Ian Zandri. I'm not in the habit of discussing individuals in my courses, but I can fill you in on the skills and focus of the particular course he was in."

"That'd be great, but anything else you could share about the man might help give me an idea on what he was doing out near Birch Lake before he died."

"And you said earlier, you're assisting with the investigation, is that right? You wanna tell me what that means, exactly. Are you officially working with the state troopers?"

"There's nothing official about any of this, and if you want to stop talking with us right now, then I'll understand. I was at Birch Lake with the lead trooper, examining the bodies and providing track interpretation. Something about the scene didn't sit right with me—the boot tread evidence and the wound patterns on the victims. This didn't strike me as a random murder spree—it was organized." He glanced at Micah. "And we can't let it go, so we thought we'd do some digging around on our own."

"Well, like I said, I'm not going to divulge personal information on my clients, but I'm happy to answer other questions about the training I provide, but let's get into the shade." He motioned for them to follow him to the instructional area, which was a large green parachute suspended by a center pole and rope fanning out from the sides of the silk fabric to the trees.

They sat on stumps across from each other around the firepit. After a long moment of silence, Burke chuckled and nodded at the charred logs. "Every time I sit down with people here, they all stare at the logs like there's flames dancing around. It's so woven into our DNA that nobody has ever failed to do it."

"I'm guessing it's that kind of approach to teaching that makes your lectures come alive in a way that they just can't inside a regular classroom," said Payne.

Burke leaned back, his eyes taking on the distant look of someone remembering hard-won lessons. "You know, when I started offering this survival course to civilians, it was all about the basics of how to make fire, build leaf shelters, make traps and so on, but I like to think I provide something more than that compared to other schools."

He gestured toward the woods. "What I'm really teaching isn't just how to survive in the woods—it's how to survive in life. How to think when everything goes wrong, how to stay calm when panic wants to take over, how to find solutions when there don't seem to be any."

"It's all about being self-reliant and being able to improvise, whether it's in the city or the wilds," said Payne in agreement. "A mindset that seems to have faded in the modern world."

Burke nodded, picking up a worn piece of rope from the ground, absently working it between his thick fingers. "See, real survival isn't about the gear you carry or the techniques you memorize. It's about the person you become when everything's stripped away. When you're cold, hungry, lost, and scared—that's when you discover who you really are. I want my students to meet that person before they have to in a real crisis. Because if you've never been truly uncomfortable, never had to dig deep and find that inner strength, you're not prepared for what life's going to throw at you."

Payne glanced over at Micah, who must have been wondering if Burke was specifically directing his lecture at her.

Burke's expression shifted, his instructor's passion giving way to something more guarded. "But I have a feeling you two didn't drive all the way out here to listen to my philosophy on character building."

He set the rope down and fixed a steady stare on both Payne and Micah. "So let's cut through the pleasantries and tell me what you're really after since Ian Zandri, in addition to being a regular student of mine, was also a friend."

Payne rested a hand on Micah's shoulder. "It's okay. Why don't you tell him what happened, if you're up to it?"

She clutched both hands as she stared into the firepit. "What did you hear on the news about what happened at Birch Lake?"

"Four fatalities related to a murderer who went on a stabbing spree. The authorities down there are still piecing things together but seemed sure they have a prime suspect."

Her voice was barely audible when she replied, "There were actually five of us camped on the lake. And Ian Zandri was the second person to die that night."

There was a pregnant pause, and it felt like time had stopped for Payne as he glanced around the teaching area. Micah seemed transfixed on the charred logs, so he continued for her, "I was assisting with the investigation and was called in because of my man-tracking experience. Since that night, there have been two more attempts on Micah's life, and we think the slaughter at that lake was a cover-up for something else—Ian Zandri's death in particular. I think he knew something about that region that was worth killing for, and we're just trying to get to the bottom of who was responsible."

Burke arched up, fixing his gaze on the trail leading up from the driveway, then out to the woods. "If this is all true, then what makes you think these guys didn't follow you right to my fucking doorstep?"

"They didn't. I know a few things about counter-surveillance and made two go-arounds before I pulled onto the road leading here."

"Counter-surveillance, man tracking, knowledge of Camp Mackall. You former Delta, since those guys shared ground near my compadres at Fort Bragg?"

"Like I said, I had friends that attended SERE there. The survival training I went through was on a similar level but wasn't military. It was run by Ground Branch out of Langley."

"So you're a spook? Really?"

"Was. I got out of that line of work, and I find it's usually best not to introduce myself to strangers by mentioning my former employer. I figure you would understand. It's not like saying I was former SF or a Marine, which can be easily verified."

"What does he mean you're a 'spook'? And what the hell is Langley?" asked Micah.

Burke chuckled. "She doesn't know? You're trying to help her out, and she doesn't even know who she's hitched to, assuming you're even telling the truth?" He leaned in towards Micah. "If he's not yanking both our chains, your buddy here used to be with some heavy hitters with the CIA."

"That explains a few things, actually," said Micah.

"This is all beside the point…is there anything you can tell us about what Zandri was doing here? His secretary at the university said he didn't really enjoy the outdoors. If that's the case, then why would he suddenly undertake your training?"

Burke stood, pointing to the driveway. "Time for you two to leave. I don't appreciate being deceived and not sure either of you are even who you say you are."

Micah pulled out her iPhone and unlocked the screen. "Click on the last video."

Burke reluctantly took the phone. He stepped back a few feet, casting a glance between Payne and Micah, then examined the video. Micah's frantic breathing on the audio was enough to cause goosebumps on her forearms, and she covered her ears for the last few seconds.

When the horror show stopped, Burke stared blankly at the screen.

Payne stood. "Micah watched everyone at that campsite get gutted and managed to escape. If anyone embodies the skills of surviving you teach here and knows firsthand how to evade crazed pursuers, it's her. And she's been through hell since then just trying to figure out who killed her friends. All we're asking for is a little of your time to find out what could have possibly led to those poor souls being murdered. I think it's connected with whatever Zandri was doing on that trip and might make all the difference in getting justice for him— and this brave woman who watched it all unfold."

# CHAPTER 30

Burke handed Micah her phone. "Ian was a good man, and I sure enjoyed our conversations. I'm not sure what you're hoping to learn, but I'll answer what I can. First, I need to get my dinner out of the oven in my trailer."

Burke led them to the wooden deck attached to his travel trailer, where three camp chairs surrounded a small firepit. He motioned for them to sit and asked if one of them could start a fire. Micah volunteered and got busy while Burke headed inside and grabbed the meal he had been preparing, adding in a few more servings.

Twenty minutes later, the flames danced in the evening breeze as Burke served up plates of grilled salmon and wild rice, the kind of meal that tasted infinitely better when eaten outdoors after a long day.

"So, you done with government service for good or just on hiatus?" asked Burke in between bites of his meal.

Payne leaned back. "Unemployed and seeing what the open road brings next. A good friend and I had this grand plan to travel the US on our motorcycles and see our own country for a change, but fate had other plans for him, it seemed, so I'm taking it in for both of us."

"Ever miss it—the adrenaline and the frenetic pace that goes with your former lifestyle?" asked Burke while Micah alternated her gaze between both men as she ate.

"What you described defines my past week. And, no, I don't miss it one bit. You?"

Burke put his half-empty plate on the small table. "Sometimes. I miss the camaraderie. And the training schools we went to over the years were awesome." He shook his head. "But when you hit a point when you start questioning every mission and the agenda behind it, it eats away at morale, both yours and everyone's on your team, and that kind of thinking is what causes screwups in the field. Don't get me wrong: I love my country, but the US government's main business is war and spreading unrest around the world, and that is best done to people in third-world nations without a voice. That part got old real fast—seeing the gaunt faces of kids in these shattered villages who probably won't make it to their fifteenth birthday. But that shit never makes the headlines."

Payne felt like someone had pressed Play on his own mental tape, and the grizzled former SERE instructor had crystallized some things he had been mulling over since leaving the agency.

"Neither of you guys should ever work as recruiters," said Micah, finishing her last forkful of salmon.

The two men chuckled.

Payne sipped his glass of cold apple cider and watched a chickadee flitting on the branches above them. He turned towards Burke. "So tell me about Professor Zandri's training."

Burke paused, wiping his mouth with a sleeve, his expression thoughtful. "That's what was unusual about Ian. Most of my clients want basic wilderness safety, but not Ian. After completing my introductory course, he specifically requested what I call my 'advanced evasion' curriculum."

"Which is what?" Micah asked, though Payne could already guess where this was heading.

"Techniques for moving through terrain without leaving obvious signs. How to camouflage your presence, create false trails, make concealment shelters, and cover your tracks." Burke set down his utensils and leaned forward. "The kind of skills you'd need if you thought someone might be following you."

"Escape and evasion skills that normally only a soldier would need if he were on the run and avoiding capture," said Payne. "Not something your average backpacker would ever call upon."

Payne felt pieces clicking into place. "So he knew his research had attracted dangerous attention."

Burke nodded. "Given what you've told me and what I recall about Ian from our conversations, he was pretty intent to learn those skills, and nobody requests counter-surveillance training for a casual canoe trip." He gestured toward his training area in the growing dusk. "We spent two days just on track discipline—how to step on rocks instead of soft ground, how to use streams to break up your trail, how to create dummy paths that lead nowhere."

"Did he say why he needed those skills?" Micah asked.

"Claimed it was for his book research; said he wanted to understand how the old-time prospectors avoided claim jumpers and thieves. But I've trained enough people to recognize when someone's really worried about their safety."

Payne thought about the meticulous way Zandri had prepared for his backcountry trip. The professor hadn't been planning a simple research expedition—he'd been preparing for something that might require him to disappear into the wilderness for a while if things went wrong, or how to elude someone who was after him.

"Was it just him, or did he ever come out with other people?" Payne asked.

"Mostly him, but it varied. Hang on." Burke stood and walked into his trailer, returning with a weathered photo album. "I keep pictures of all my classes for insurance purposes and promotional materials."

He flipped through several pages before finding what he was looking for. "Here we go. Zandri's group from this past spring. Originally, he attended a basic course with a dozen other folks from different parts of Alaska, but the advanced course two weeks later was just him and five other people."

Payne studied the photograph showing students in outdoor gear standing around Burke's firepit under the parachute. Professor Zandri was easily recognizable in the center, his academic bearing obvious even in wilderness clothing. But it was the man standing beside him that made Payne's breath catch.

"That's TJ Reynolds," he said, pointing to a bearded figure in his thirties. "The missing geologist from Saxon."

Burke leaned over to look at the photo more closely. "You're right. I'd forgotten his name, but yeah, that's the rock guy, as we called him. Quiet fellow."

"I remember seeing a flyer of that guy at the troopers' post in Saxon," said Micah. "So Zandri and Reynolds must have been training together for whatever they were planning."

Burke nodded. "Those two spent hours talking about a pet project of theirs during breaks. Never got specifics, and I figured it was some university research they were discussing."

Payne studied the other faces in the photograph. "What about the rest of the group? Were they part of this project too?"

"Not that I recall. The other two guys were park rangers involved with search-and-rescue, and the woman was an avid hiker. She, Ian, and Reynolds all knew each other but not sure how."

"What was her name?" asked Payne.

"Rebecca Jenkins—from Fairbanks, I think. She was a genealogist, or at least knew a helluva lot about genealogy."

"Did any of them seem worried about specific threats?" Payne asked. "Or mention names or organizations they were concerned about?"

Burke shook his head. "They were careful not to discuss details in front of the other students. Frankly, if I get creepy vibes from people about why they're undertaking my evasion training, then I will send them on their way. Like, I got a few guys last summer who wanted that specific training, and as the course progressed, it became clear these dudes were probably dope growers, so I sent 'em packing. But I didn't get that feeling from Ian and his friends."

Payne stared into the fire, his mind working through the implications of Zandri's background and the specialized training, along with the harrowing events of the past couple of days. The coordinated attacks, surveillance, and the resources needed to orchestrate everything from the Birch Lake murders to the attempted hits on Micah—it all pointed to someone with serious money and connections.

"Given Zandri's and Reynolds' backgrounds and research, this has to somehow be connected with a gold mine in the backcountry," said Payne.

"Wouldn't be the first time people have been killed in these parts for yellow fever," said Burke.

Payne rubbed the mosquito bites on the back of his neck. "The question is who has that kind of power in Alaska, and how did they find out about Zandri's research in the first place?"

Burke added another log to the fire, sending sparks spiraling into the darkening sky. "In my experience, the people with that kind of reach are usually the ones who've been around long enough to build networks throughout the state. Old families with connections in government, business, law enforcement—not too different from what I witnessed overseas during deployments."

"Except this is someone or some group who can track mining claims, monitor research permits, maybe even surveil people inside the university system," Payne said. *And definitely someone with enough pull to keep tabs on law enforcement investigations.*

As the fire burned lower and darkness settled over the training camp, Payne felt they were getting closer to understanding the scope of what they were dealing with. The professor and his colleagues had known they were walking into danger, had trained specifically for evasion and survival, but it hadn't been enough. The enemy had found them anyway, tracked Zandri to his remote campsite and slaughtered him with cold efficiency along with several seemingly innocent bystanders.

*But why? Why not dispatch Zandri near his house or in a parking lot? Why have him brutally slain in the backcountry?*

He didn't have the answers. Not yet. He glanced over at Micah, her face aglow in the firelight. Whoever was behind the Birch Lake massacre had made one mistake—they'd let Micah escape.

And now their carefully constructed cover story was unraveling, one thread at a time, and Payne was going to keep pulling until it all unraveled.

———

AFTER ANOTHER HOUR around the campfire, Burke offered them a yurt to stay in rather than driving back to Saxon. He walked them past the classroom to their accommodations for the night.

The canvas yurt was rustic: a sixteen-foot-diameter structure anchored to a wood deck in the woods a hundred yards from Burke's travel trailer. In the middle of the yurt was a woodstove whose pipe vented in an insulated barrier in the large skylight. Four cots lined the lattice-work walls along with a small table and two chairs against the back.

A few shelves were adorned with coffee mugs, aluminum pots, utensils, and several hanging solar lanterns suspended from thin chains.

After Burke left, Payne sat on the edge of his cot, staring at the floorboards. "There's one thing I can't figure out: since you arrived at Wolf Lake Lodge, someone has known our every move. First, they knew exactly where to direct those four goons who came to my cabin. They didn't attack the lodge itself, just my place. Then they managed to remove the bodies of the three dead guys, which means they knew Nolte wasn't going to be coming out that night. And someone clearly knew we'd be at Birch Lake, not to mention the one caveman with the chin beard specifically asking about your phone."

"You think Nolte is in on this?" She kicked off her boots and leaned back on her cot.

"My gut says no. He would have already pushed ahead with the press conference implicating Dean for the murders, and he strikes me as a competent, if jaded, trooper."

"That leaves that woman detective who could use a hairbrush, Corporal Hicks with the porn mustache, the giddy secretary with wads of cash in her purse, and, sorry to say, your buddy Gus."

"Gus isn't involved."

"He was conveniently asleep in his plane when the shootings went down at Birch Lake."

"It's not Gus. I know people well enough to tell when they're stone-cold killers, and he's not one of them. Plus, why would he ID the shooter in the video?"

She shrugged. "People put on all kinds of masks to get what they want in life, no matter how likable and innocent they seem. And the more they want something, the greater the façade, until, one day, the mask slips and their fangs come out."

"It's not Gus. And Detective Cartwright seems like a ladder-climber, trying to make the governor happy. But Hicks was pretty cavalier in his hasty search around my cabin, and I overheard him say his wife was eight months pregnant."

"So how's having a screaming gargoyle on the way an issue?"

Payne chuckled. "If you want to turn someone to your cause, then exploit their desires or needs. In the case of Hicks, his income as a small town trooper is probably only a few bucks more an hour than that clerk at the general store. He would be an easy target to bribe. So would Nolte's secretary, for that matter."

She blew a strand of blonde hair off her nose. "I just want this to be over. I don't want to keep thinking about it, and having everyone staring at me like I'm a criminal."

"I know. With what I've learned today from Burke and Zandri's assistant, we're moving closer to understanding what this is about."

She flung her hands up. "Oh, really? You care to share that with me, because a treasure hunt for gold seems pretty far out."

He reached in his jacket and removed the map and journal. He unfolded the former document and spread it on the floor, then turned up the lantern. "Got this from Zandri's office. Pretty sure it's connected with what took him out beyond Birch Lake."

"You stole stuff from a dead guy's office?"

He tossed her the journal. "You gonna help me or just condemn me with your eyes?"

"I can do both."

"Open up that book to where I folded a corner page and slowly read me the first line for the longitude." He knelt over the map, tracing his finger along the side as she followed his request. He opened the woodstove door and removed a tiny piece of charcoal and marked a slash on the map for the first set of coordinates. Next, he pinpointed her readings for the latitude, making another slash.

"Now what?" she inquired, thumbing through the journal.

Payne tapped on his X mark. "This spot is deep in the forest by the confluence of two small rivers. It's six lakes farther west from where you and your friends camped, just a half mile past Pickerel Lake."

"That's a few days of hard paddling and portaging, trust me."

"To be honest, I'm not sure what it means, but since Zandri's specialty was mining history and he had been on several extended trips beyond Birch Lake, I can only guess this is connected with a gold vein or an old mine shaft. Maybe that's how Reynolds was involved. He would have known how to locate such things."

"I'm just not sure, Payne—if you grew up here, you'd hear dozens of stories about lost gold. Each year there are tons of cheechakos who come up from the lower forty-eight to try to find some gold deposit they read about online. Half of those dumbasses get lost and are never heard from again."

"Except Zandri was a history expert and had this spot flagged for a reason, and in my experience in other parts of the world, people are willing to kill for gold and other natural resources." He looked up at her, noticing her eyes beginning to tear and knew this conversation needed to wrap up. "Just one more thing: did you notice anything unusual about the professor…did he mention anything about what he was doing on the trip, or something cool he came across?"

"No, it was just small talk about the weather and how both of us couldn't wait to have pizza." She chewed on her lip. "Pizza…I remember he smelled like an Italian restaurant, which I thought was weird, being in bear country. I mentioned that, asking him if he'd just made dinner and telling him how to stow his food in one of the bear boxes. He said he'd had an MRE of beef stroganoff before the last portage."

Payne's face soured. "Those meals actually repel bears."

He thought back to his youth in the wilds of northern Michigan. "I once tried out all manner of natural insect repellents to see if they would work against mosquitoes—everything from consuming garlic to B12 to brewer's yeast, but I smelled so bad I couldn't even stand myself. And none of it even worked. Do you think Zandri was on some natural regimen like that?"

She shook her head. "He was spraying himself with repellent just before I left. And this wasn't a garlic odor. It was more like when you're cutting up an onion."

He sat cross-legged, staring at the map. "There's one more person to talk to who might help figure out what Zandri was doing by Pickerel Lake. Assuming he's still alive."

"You think the guys after me got to him already?"

"I'm more worried about his deck of cards being played out. He's in his nineties."

Micah slid the journal on the floor towards him. "So I'm going to be surrounded by more old people like you."

"And hopefully absorb some much-needed wisdom."

He folded up the map and slid it back in the journal, then

dimmed the light. He returned to his cot and lay on top of the sleeping bag while she did the same.

"Was all that stuff about you bein' in the CIA true?"

He stared up at the stars through the skylight, realizing it had been over a year since he resigned. Now, it felt like a decade ago. "Almost fifteen years, but it was time to move on."

"To what, being a drifter? I mean, no offense, but it sounds like all you do is move around on your motorcycle every few weeks. Not much of a life, if you ask me."

"I didn't ask, but since you feel it necessary to hurl your opinions at whoever is in your crosshairs, I'll tell you: the open road has its appeal for now, especially after being told where to go and what to do for so many years." He turned toward her. "What about you…ever want to get out of Alaska?"

"Yeah, of course. I've always wanted to go to the jungle. Some place like Costa Rica, where it's warm all year and the people aren't so uptight, and life's about sandals instead of boots."

He perked up at the latter comment. He'd never thought about such lifestyle things. Each environment was evaluated from a tactical or survival standpoint: what were the choke-points for setting up ambushes; where were the rebels, vipers, or landmines; and where to set up extraction points to get the hell back home after the deed was done. Practical not philo-sophical. He wondered if he could ever retrain himself to think more like her and less like a hunter of other humans.

"Lots more bugs down there than here," he said.

"You've been to the tropics?" She propped up on one elbow, his standing seeming to have moved up a notch in her eyes.

"Did some training in Belize years ago, similar to what Burke does here, only it involved surviving on the run while locals chased us. Eventually, we were captured and then went through the interrogation phase. I liked the first part better."

"See any monkeys? I love monkeys and chimpanzees. I've read every book on them and watched all the Jane Goodall shows since I was little. Bet you didn't know that most old-world monkeys have tails and new-world monkeys don't."

"I did not know that, actually. And, yeah, they're everywhere. They're the jungle alarm clocks when dawn strikes." Payne decided to leave out the part about roasting a monkey over the campfire that his group had snared during the survival phase.

"There's an eco-preserve in Costa Rica that offers internships. They do rehab work with injured and orphaned white-faced capuchin monkeys. You can live in a treehouse on the property, and there's this huge waterfall nearby for bathing in, and there are mango trees everywhere, so you can eat as much fruit as you want."

Though the lighting was dim, this was the most animated he'd seen her since they met. She went on for another ten minutes about the birds, snakes, cultures, and edible plants.

"Too bad you don't speak Spanish…you could get a job working for the tourism bureau down there."

"I've been learning some Spanish. I bought the Rosetta Stone language program last summer with the money I saved from working on the trail crew, but I suck at comprehension."

"You gotta be immersed in the culture for a few months or more to get the basics down; then it'll come, especially if you're living with a family who won't speak to you in English."

"You speak Spanish or any languages?"

"Some Espanol. Russian and Arabic were, you could say, work requirements for the places I was sent, so we received extensive training in those languages, not to mention years of practical application."

Micah grew quiet for several minutes, and he suddenly felt a solemn tone in the air. "Does the horror ever go away—of seeing someone dead—someone you cared about?" The exuberant voice of the young woman was gone, replaced by something soft and childlike.

He sat up. "I'd be lying if I said yes, but it does hurt less with time, Micah. Someone once told me that where there is great love, there is also great pain. I've learned that you have to focus on the first part if you ever want the second part to lose its grip on you."

She was silent for a long while, then spoke in a whisper. "Thanks for helping me, Payne. You're okay, even if you were with the government."

He leaned back on his pillow. "Good night, kid."

She turned on her other side, her voice trailing off. "Buenos noches."

# CHAPTER 31

It was just after sunrise when Nolte threw his pack in the back seat of his SUV, watching the crowd of reporters camped out on the other side of the police tape at the far end of his parking lot.

He was about to climb inside his vehicle when a woman's voice emerged near the back door of his building. Emma Cartwright was trotting towards him.

*Shit, what's she want now?*

"Lieutenant, glad I caught you. I just got in, and Carlie told me you were heading to Anchorage to check on Jimmy Dean. I'd like to tag along, if you don't mind."

Nolte ruffled out an exhale as she stood across from him. "Wanna make sure I conduct a proper interview?"

She rested her hands on her hips. "Look, I can see we got off on the wrong foot. That's my fault, and I came on a little too strong."

"Just a 'little'?"

"The governor was breathing down my neck and hasn't let up, and I let that trickle down into my work here. I apologize if I stepped on your toes."

*Why the sudden change of heart? She must be getting even more pressure from her boss and decided on a change of tactics. Well, let's see where this goes. A softer Detective Cartwright might be less of a fucking thorn in my side.*

Nolte motioned to the vehicle as he opened the driver's door and got inside. She scampered around and hopped in. He headed onto Main Street, driving south on Highway 3 along all four blocks of downtown Saxon, which hadn't woken up yet.

"Any word from that fella Payne or the girl?" asked Cartwright.

"Nope, and it's starting to really piss me off. Guy inserts himself into my investigation and becomes a magnet for violence, then drops off the radar."

"I talked to him yesterday at the Caribou Inn. He was pretty elusive about the girl and seems protective of her. Sure there's no prior connection between the two?"

He yielded at a stop sign, disinterested in coming to a complete rest, then sped off. "I looked into him—he's got a clean record and had previously worked as a risk-management consultant overseas, providing training in how to avoid getting kidnapped and other high-risk shit. He struck me as a solid guy. And his story about his father being a game warden in Michigan checks out as well, which leads me to trust what he said about the tracks at the first crime scene."

"I discovered the same thing, but it still doesn't mean that he wasn't spinning the interpretation of the tracks at Birch Lake to his own advantage. Let's face it: how many people can read the ground like that anymore—this is different than following a wounded moose, which leaves a trail like an elephant. He could have said whatever he wanted, and who was going to challenge him?"

"You a hunter?"

"Who isn't in this state?" She glanced out the window as

the south side of Saxon transitioned to grassy fields and then forest. "I have an uncle who took me hunting a lot when I was a kid. You?"

"I have a freezer full of salmon and halibut but not much into big-game hunting anymore, or killing animals in general. I get the whole notion of ethical hunting and all that, but I moved here to get away from pulling a trigger."

"You know, when I said yesterday morning that you had a reputation...I meant that with all due respect. Your work in homicide around Anchorage is still talked about around the department. Shame you left the fringes of our city."

"You trying to butter me up still?"

"Maybe, a little." She folded her arms. "I guess I get it. If I had seen what you had during twenty years of dealing with bodies being dumped in the ditches outside of Anchorage, I'd want to escape to a place like Saxon. Heck, maybe I'll be doing the same in a few years, myself."

"Well, when you find yourself reaching for Tums constantly instead of your coffee, you'll know it's time."

———

AFTER FINISHING a bowl of oatmeal on the deck at Burke's travel trailer, Payne removed the Zippo lighter he'd found on the dead man at Birch Lake. He flipped it around in his hand, examining the image etched on the front, which showed two bears standing and facing off with each other with their outstretched paws.

"You a smoker?" asked Micah.

"No. Found this on Mr. Wizard." He slid it across to her. "I saw this same image on a taxidermy shop outside of Anchorage on our drive down here."

Burke leaned over, examining the Zippo. "Norwood Taxidermy. Sleazebag operation owned by Lee Norwood. Pretty sure he keeps his business afloat by dealing in more than just stuffed animals, since his brother heads up a biker gang who's been busted a bunch of times for possession." He slid the lighter to Payne. "You think they're somehow connected with what happened at Birch Lake?"

Payne could feel his bruised ribs every time he turned. "Before you said 'biker gang,' I would have said I was unsure. Now, not so much, but I have an idea for finding out and hopefully learning who the big fish in the pond are."

———

As NOLTE DROVE through the bustling traffic at the north end of Anchorage, his phone rang. He didn't recognize the number and put it on speaker.

"Lieutenant—got a minute?" asked Payne.

He and Cartwright shot tense glances at each other.

"Go ahead," said Nolte.

"I was greeted by quite a welcoming committee in Anchorage yesterday. Some bikers who said there was a bounty on me and Micah. Heard anything about that?"

"Can't say I have. Does this mean there's a few more bodies in the morgue?" He pulled off on the second exit for downtown.

"No, but the physical therapists in town will probably be getting some new clients, and I'm pretty sure those meat-heads were connected with Ernie Packard. I'm going to follow a lead at a place called Norwood Taxidermy, so I'll let you know what I find."

He glanced at Cartwright again, seeing her face rigid and wondering why she wasn't piping in with her usual blitzkrieg of questions.

"Not a good idea," said Nolte. "I'll look into it. Just get

back to Saxon, and we can talk. Plus, I really want that goddammed video."

"It'll be on your desk by nightfall, but first I gotta make a stop at the Alaska Museum of Science to inquire about some geology specimens."

"One more thing…" Stopping at a red light, he noticed the screen had turned off. "Son of a bitch just hung up on me."

"He's a wild card, sir. I'm not surprised." Cartwright was busy staring at her own phone and suddenly looked up, jabbing a finger at a four-story building ahead. "Can you drop me at the precinct—I've got some business to take care of and will find my own way back to Saxon later."

Nolte scrunched his eyebrows together. "Thought you came on this little trip to talk with Dean?"

She glanced at the screen of her iPhone again. "Something came up. I need to report to my boss."

"Your CO, or the other guy up in the governor's mansion?"

"Seems like one and the same person these days."

"Anything you want me to know about Dean—or to ask him since you were his case officer years ago? I was hoping to get your insights on him, especially once he saw you in the room."

Cartwright was quiet for a long moment. When she finally spoke, her voice carried the careful tone of someone choosing her words deliberately. "Jimmy was always a paradox—he had this uncanny ability to become whoever he needed to be depending on who was sitting across from him, to the point where sometimes I wondered if he remembered who he really was underneath it all."

"He was barely a teenager when he killed his old man in self-defense. Not sure he knew who he really was—hell, I know plenty of folks in their twenties who don't even know that."

Cartwright paused, rubbing her temple. "Don't let him make you feel like you're having a conversation with an old friend—that's his greatest weapon—he's a master manipulator."

He made a right turn near 6th Avenue, pulling to the curb by the Anchorage Police Department. Nolte swiveled towards her. "I don't get you, Detective. You seem hell-bent on seeing Dean go down for those murders, yet you can't take twenty minutes to be in that room while I question him?"

She unbuckled, grabbing her small shoulder bag and stepping out. "There's something urgent I have to handle. If things shake out quickly with my boss, then I'll come down to the hospital." She slammed the door and walked at a brisk pace to the front doors of the building.

Nolte gripped the steering wheel with both hands, wishing he could've seen the flurry of texts she'd received in the past few minutes to know who was really pulling her strings.

# CHAPTER 32

Payne finished talking to Nolte and put his phone away, resuming looking through his binoculars as he studied the Norwood Taxidermy shop below. From his vantage point on a treed ridgeline three hundred yards away, he had a good field of vision for any vehicles coming and going from the tiny parking lot.

"Are we really going to the museum back in Anchorage?" asked Micah, who was lying prone to his right.

"Heck no. I just needed to draw away the apes inside that place so I can have a friendly chat with the owner."

"Other than that lighter with the matching logo, what makes you think the owner is connected to all of this?"

"My bruised shoulder. Those bikes down there belong to the same cabbage heads who came for me at the brewery downtown yesterday." He removed the GPS unit from his pack and slid it toward her. "Keep an eye on the red blip and let me know when it's ten miles out."

"Is that why you went below to put trackers on their bikes?"

"A tracker—same one that was on the Jeep yesterday."

A second later, the steel door at the rear opened, and four men in leather jackets emerged. Three of them had black-and-blue faces while the fourth with the thick beard moved with a limp. All of them headed to their motorcycles and quickly peeled out of the lot.

"Jesus, those guys looked like they were beat with a lead pipe."

"Aircraft aluminum. Collapsible baton. Less bone breakage and skull fractures."

She flared an eyebrow. "Thanks for that clarification."

Payne watched the bikers drive south and disappear around the bend in the highway. He waited for Micah's mileage report, then stood, shaking out his stiff legs. "Stay here. Call me if those goons or anyone else pulls up."

"I'm not waiting—"

"Yeah, you are, actually. What I need to do will only take a few minutes. You still got that new bottle of bear spray?"

She patted her jacket. "Yep."

He tossed her the keys to the Jeep. "Just in case something goes sideways."

He headed down the slope, making his way to the road, then followed the shoulder back to the parking lot. Payne made a beeline to the front door, pulling his ball cap low and heading inside.

The stagnant air was a mix of cigarette smoke and tanning solvents, which he was sure had to be some kind of fire code violation.

Eight shoulder-high aisles of supplies lined the front of the place, while dusty glass showcases with small-game specimens filled the remaining section before the counter. Behind it was a forty-something guy with wispy black hair, who was applying paste wax with a buffing pad to a salmon specimen attached to a plaque.

There was barely a blank spot on each of the four walls,

which were covered with the heads of large and small game mammals, fish, waterfowl, and a lone musk ox. Oddly, a stuffed orange tabby cat was given an overwatch position behind the register, staring at the front door with green glass eyes.

"Help ya?" said the man without looking up, a half-spent cigarette tucked in the corner of his mouth.

"Yeah, I got a fox in my truck that I want to see about getting processed and wondered what you'd charge."

"What kind?"

"Pardon?" He hadn't heard anyone in the back room, but he still wasn't sure and didn't need any surprises.

"Fox—what kind is it?"

"Gray?"

The man stopped polishing, setting the rag down. He pried the cigarette from his dry lips and dropped it into a water glass next to him. "Ain't no gray fox in Alaska."

"I thought the red fox had a gray color phase?"

"It's the other way around—gray foxes have a red color phase, but grays ain't found in Alaska. We only got reds and Arctic foxes."

Feeling confident no one else was in the place, Payne shot this thumb towards the door. "Well, maybe you could take a look. It's in the back of my rig."

"Yeah, sure. Hang on a second." He grabbed his iPhone off the desk behind him, scrolling through it. The man's index finger and thumb enhanced something on the screen; then he glanced up at Payne, his yellow teeth accentuated by his pale cheeks. The guy's right hand was shaking slightly as he set the phone down, but Payne was sure he caught a glimpse of his own face on the screen.

The taxidermist's left hand began sliding towards his untucked shirt. Payne lunged forward, reaching over the counter and grabbing the owner's shirt collar and slamming his head down onto the surface hard enough to break his nose. Payne dragged the man over the top and shoved the sinewy figure onto the floor, stomping his boot onto the thug's right wrist, which buckled and snapped.

With the owner shrieking and clutching his damaged hand, Payne pulled out a concealed 1911 pistol with a customized pearl grip. "God, everyone carries .45s up here. I love it."

"The fuck you want?" said Lee Norwood.

"Who's pulling your strings—since you're associated with the bikers who came after me yesterday?"

"I don't know what the hell you're talking about."

Payne grabbed Norwood by the ankle and dragged him along the floor to the back room, shoving aside the floor-length curtain. The walls were covered with nude women holding rifles, while the lone workbench in the corner was neatly organized with tanning and skinning implements, stitching tools, and an array of chemical preservatives.

Payne released his grip on the guy and grabbed a roll of duct tape, then secured his ankles together while keeping the .45 fixed on his head.

"Who just sent that crew of bikers on their way?"

The guy shook his head, leaning against the workbench. "They don't report to me, man. I have no idea where they're going."

Payne grabbed a bottle of chromium solution off the shelf. "As I recall, this is used for breaking down the collagen in animal hides so they soften up. Pretty caustic stuff if used in its concentrated form, though." He squirted a stream onto the guy's shirt. "Next round will be a little higher, so think about how important your eyesight is to your line of work."

"You're fucking insane. You'll never—"

Payne pointed the bottle at the guy's face.

"Stop, alright. Just stop," the man shouted. "There's a hit

out on you and the girl. Ten K for each of you. We just got a text about you heading to the museum of science in Anchorage, so I figured that was gonna be the end of you two."

"Sent by who?"

"Someone at the Saxon post—that place is bugged. You've pissed off some powerful people, and now they want your heads."

"Andre Groh?"

The man's cheeks quivered. "Andre's a scary motherfucker and always gets what he's hunting, but he's the least of your worries."

Payne unleashed a flurry of fluid onto the photos on the wall, then doused a partially completed head of a bobcat on the workbench.

"He'll kill me if I say any more."

"You're already looking at one boot in the grave." Payne sent another stream of fluid onto the man's lap.

Norwood frantically waved his good hand. "Don't know who it is, but everyone answers to him—me, Packard, Andre. He's the one who had me drug that Jimmy Dean kid at the bar."

"To what end?"

"I don't know that side of things. I was just told there'd be a big payday coming over the next few months once his little venture got underway." He rested his head back, staring at the ceiling. "If only that little bitch hadn't gotten in the way."

"That girl has more backbone and character than you'll ever muster."

"I lost a lot of my good friends at that cabin of yours and at Birch Lake. When Andre gets a hold of you, he said he's gonna skin you alive."

"Hard to do once I put a hollow point through his head."

"You'll never even see him coming. The man's spent his entire life living like a ghost."

Payne squirted the remaining liquid onto the floor around Norwood. Then grabbed the gallon container of chromium from the workbench and unscrewed the lid. He stepped outside the room and flung the fluid onto the counter and nearby shelves.

Returning to the workshop, he pulled out Packard's Zippo. "If you can crawl to the back exit by the time I get to the front door, you might have half a chance to avoid becoming a melted fixture in here."

"Wait, no!"

Payne maneuvered past the puddles of chromium, the vapors beginning to burn his nose. He shoved open the front entrance, igniting the Zippo and flinging it back into the store.

---

THE FIREBALL in the Jeep's rearview mirror diminished with each passing mile as Payne and Micah drove north back to Saxon. Whether Lee Norwood had made it out was unknown. Frankly, Payne didn't care. He'd shown more mercy than he should have.

The same wouldn't be said for Groh—and whoever was leaking information inside the Alaska State Troopers.

# CHAPTER 33

Nolte sat in his SUV outside the hospital, fingers slowly drumming the steering wheel as he stared at the stark white building through the windshield. He had one more essential stop to make before returning to Saxon, but his head was still swirling from recent revelations that confirmed his suspicions.

*Jimmy Dean should be dead—and not by his own hand.*

That much was clear from the medical report Nolte had reviewed before entering the hospital room and hearing the kid's story. The cocktail of drugs in Dean's system— Rohypnol and trace elements of fentanyl—were enough to kill a horse. The doc said it was a fluke of biology, some genetic quirk that enabled Dean to process opioids differently.

The eighteen-year-old's eyes had been bloodshot and unfocused, pupils still dilated from the chemical cocktail working its way out of his system. When Nolte had asked him about the night of the murders, Dean's response had been genuinely confused and almost childlike.

"I just don't remember," Dean had whispered, his voice

barely audible above the medical equipment. "I was at the Wolverine Bar and only had two beers with a couple. Then his lady friend with a cross tattoo on her wrist started flirting with me, which was weird. After that…" He'd shaken his head helplessly. "I wake up here with nurses telling me I almost died and my hands cuffed to the bed because I'm… I'm a mass murderer."

Someone had targeted Dean specifically—a nobody without a family, no friends, and no one who'd miss him or ask questions. They'd drugged him into unconsciousness, committed four brutal murders, then planted evidence around his cabin before dumping his body on the couch with enough poison in his veins to ensure he'd never wake up to tell his side of the story.

The perfect patsy: a dead junkie with the victims' blood on his clothes and the murder weapon on his kitchen counter. Case closed. No trial, no testimony, no inconvenient questions about a blackout doper.

Except Dean had survived. So had Micah. And now the woods around Saxon were alive with monsters wanting to clean things up.

Driving out of the hospital parking lot, Nolte felt his anger burn bright. His mind was churning through the implications and the leak he suspected in his own post. He thought back to how Corporal Hicks had so easily dismissed Payne's statements after the cabin attack, and how the trooper had conveniently overlooked the evidence on the back porch and the path of trampled vegetation leading into the woods.

*And Payne said someone knew exactly where he was in Anchorage. Hicks drove Payne and Micah to the Caribou Inn and could have planted a tracker on them, and he also knew that I gave the green light for Gus to fly them to Birch Lake to search for Micah's lost phone.*

Nolte slammed a fist on the armrest. Dean's survival was

a miracle, but it was also a liability. The real killers knew their patsy was still breathing—still able to potentially remember fragments of that night.

*And now Micah and Payne are beginning to unravel the mystery.*

The real killers would be desperate in ways that made Nolte feel like there was a growing bullseye on his own back as well.

He needed help from someone outside the system, an ally who couldn't be bought or threatened. A person who, like him, understood how predators operated when they were cornered.

Now, all he needed to do was locate Payne and convince him they were on the same side.

# CHAPTER 34

It was a single-story log home with a wraparound driveway of crushed gravel. Lush stands of paper birch enveloped the place, and numerous bird feeders hung out front, which seemed to be feeding the chipmunk population more than the winged members of the forest. The logs were flat and hewn, reflecting the older skill of axmanship and practical know-how, which was in stark contrast to the machine-milled cabin kits with their varnished exteriors.

Payne had called ahead of time, getting the caregiver for Stanley Hirovicz, who arranged a time to meet given the ninety-two-year-old's limited stamina. Micah remained in the back of the vehicle, playing a video game on her phone though Payne was sure she'd be fast asleep once he was out of sight.

Payne walked up the drive, inhaling the rich aroma of the wilds. From what the nurse had described on the phone, Hirovicz's place was situated down seven miles of torturous dirt road and surrounded by thousands of acres of state land. The nurse had jokingly mentioned trying to convince the older man to move to a senior center in town, but he refused, having been born in this very spot nearly a century ago.

The screen door opened, and a forty-something woman stepped out, waving. "You must be Kyle. I'm Maribel."

He shook her hand. "Yes, ma'am."

She led him inside. The place was roughly thirty by thirty with a dining area and kitchen on the right near the wood-stove, and a small hallway on the left with a bedroom, den, and bathroom. The place had the rich aroma of cedar wood smoke. For a minute, Payne envisioned himself living here, spending his days fishing and exploring, and severing his few ties with the modern world. He'd experienced the same thing about the caretaker cabin at Gus' place, and it left him wondering if his Indian motorcycle was capable of feeling betrayal.

"Thanks again for arranging to have me out on such short notice."

"That's all his doing. He loves having visitors and talking about Alaska. He's usually good for an hour and then needs to rest."

"Gotcha. I'll get right to the point with him, then. I just had some questions about local mining history."

She frowned. "You're the second person to drop by in the past month, wanting to talk about that. Usually, people want to know about the famous explorers or pioneers."

He followed her inside, pausing in the small foyer. "Who was the other individual?"

She glanced at him. "Young fella with a beard, about your age. JT Reynolds...or maybe it was TJ Reynolds."

"TJ—the geologist who went missing."

"Heard about that. Such a nice man." Maribel pointed down the hall to the second room on the right. "He's waiting for you."

Payne walked past dozens of old photos showing

Hirovicz receiving different literary awards or teaching before a classroom full of students.

He knocked on the open door and stepped inside the den. The room was lined with floor-to-ceiling bookshelves, each of which was peppered with indigenous handcrafts from baskets to snowshoes to sinew-backed bows hanging from their sides.

*Yeah, I could definitely live here.*

In the right corner was Hirovicz, sitting on a rocking chair with a blue and green quilt over his legs. He was wearing a thick fleece robe patterned with black bears. He didn't stand, but his warm smile was welcoming enough, and Payne closed the distance, eagerly extending a hand.

"Nice to make your acquaintance, Carl."

"It's Kyle, actually, Mr. Hirovicz."

"Ah, damn hearing aids aren't turned up all the way. You can call me Stan, by the way." His bony fingers fidgeted with the two devices in his ears; then he waved towards the other rocking chair across from him. The man had a full head of white hair and a lean face that was as furrowed as a piece of driftwood, reminding him of a lot of the woodsmen he grew up around.

"By your accent, you're not from Alaska…Midwest, maybe?"

Payne sat. "That's pretty good. Born and raised in the Upper Peninsula of Michigan."

"The UP—that's some rugged country up there, comparable to what we have here, so I'll sort of count you as one of us."

"I'm grateful, sir."

For the next ten minutes, the man spoke about his travels around the Alaskan interior during his youth. And teenage years working for a timber company as a cruiser in two-man teams, exploring the forests and mapping out the regions where the lumbermen's saws would cut. It was another era before satellite imagery replaced fieldwork that required an array of bushcraft skills seldom used by modern outdoorsmen. He filled Payne's head with stories of deadly encounters with wolves, bears, hypothermia, and wildfires, and Payne was sure he would need a few weeks to soak up what this sage could reveal about the backcountry.

When he was done, Payne glanced at the man's books on the shelf behind him. "I see you've written on many facets of Alaskan wilderness and wildlife, but I don't see a biography in there."

"It's the places and the people I've always written about, and those stories are far more meaningful than anything that could be written about me." He pulled the collar of his robe up around his neck. "So, Maribel said you had some questions about local mining history?"

"What can you tell me about gold prospecting by Pickerel Lake?"

Hirovicz sat up, stroking his fingers along the quilt on his lap as if he were clearing away a layer of dust. "Hell, I thought you were going to ask me about the mining industry itself. Sure seems like the lost gold by Pickerel Lake has piqued people's interests again. Always does every coupla years when some news article gets recirculated on the internet or in some magazine."

"Maribel said TJ Reynolds had also been inquiring."

The man nodded, lowering his eyes. "And I heard he went missing, too. Hope it's not connected with that damn lost gold. It's cost enough people their lives over the years, probably including my old friend Ian Zandri."

The man was staring straight at Payne and, by his expression, must have noted Payne's surprise.

"You oughta tell me right now, son, before we continue— who you working for, 'cause this doesn't seem like just a personal-interest thing, especially by the way you lit up when I mentioned Ian's name."

"Actually, it's become a personal matter, but I'm not on anyone's payroll—just trying to help someone out and keep them safe, and I think whatever happened to Professor Zandri at Birch Lake is connected with him trying to locate a gold deposit."

The old man clutched the arms of the rocking chair and leaned forward. "Keep talking."

Payne recounted the harrowing events of the past few days, beginning with his involvement in man tracking at the crime scene to the attempts on Micah's life and his subsequent findings at Zandri's office and Burke's place.

When he finished, Hirovicz sat back, his slippered feet pushing lightly off the floor as he rocked back and forth while remaining quiet for a few moments. "I told Ian to keep things bottled up about that lost gold, but he must have told someone about what he was doing at Pickerel Lake."

"Who would want to kill him over an old legend?"

The man studied him, and Payne could see the gears turning behind his eyes. Finally, he replied, "The legend was just that until last summer, when Ian uncovered something new. As to your other question, I can tell you exactly who orchestrated the murders at Birch Lake."

# CHAPTER 35

When Payne heard the name Sean Klurman, he recalled seeing ads for the man's mining firm on billboards, benches and the sides of buildings during his travels around Alaska. All of them featured the business mogul with his arms folded and a toothy grin, standing beside an image of a massive drilling platform. "How does a guy like Klurman figure into all of this?"

"His family goes way back in this region of Alaska. Sean's grandfather started out as a prospector back in the 1940s. He was a smart one, though—used what money he had after finding a low-yield gold deposit to buy up other parcels rumored to have potential gold veins on them. At first it was him and his younger brothers working the land, but eventually they realized there was more money to be made in selling tools to starry-eyed arrivals from the lower forty-eight than from getting their hands in the mud."

Hirovicz glanced at the activity at the bird feeder outside the window. "Over time, he sold his holdings and expanded his supply company around the Kenai Peninsula to towns along the coast and then up into the interior. Eventually,

Klurman went into larger-scale extraction equipment used by mining corporations. Later, when Exxon Mobil and other companies began their oil operations on the North Slope back in '68, he won the contract for supplying drilling equipment."

"How does this relate back to Zandri and Pickerel Lake?"

"I'm getting to that. Just hold your damn horses."

Maribel stepped into the room, scrutinizing Payne, then the old man, who looked agitated. "Everything alright?" she inquired.

"Fine. Fine." Hirovicz waved her off and continued, "My dad worked for the Guardian Timber Company when I was growing up. That's how I later got a job as a timber cruiser, 'cause I knew all those guys and the owner.

"When I was fourteen, I started accompanying my father on surveying trips west of Saxon via canoe. We'd be out there for weeks at a time, living off the land while mapping out new forests. One fall, we came across this old homesteader living way back in the bush, beyond Pickerel Lake. Name was Clyde Jenkins. We got to know him over several timber-cruising trips out there during the years, and we became… well…friends would be a stretch, but he and my dad had a lot of good conversations while we stayed overnight at his cabin."

He scrunched the folds of his quilt, then ironed them flat. "For a miner back then, he was surprisingly educated, and he and my dad both spoke Russian, which wasn't a big surprise then given all the immigrants. On later visits, my dad always brought him some books in Russian, and they often discussed their love of Tolstoy. And on the rare occasions Jenkins ventured into Saxon for supplies, he would drop by this very cabin and spend the night, leaving in the morning with a new book he swapped out with my father."

He lifted the water glass on the small table beside him and drank like he'd run a marathon. "Now, don't get me wrong:

Jenkins was an ornery son of a bitch and a paranoid one, too. Nearly shot us when we first approached his cabin, thinking we were there to steal from him, which my dad said probably meant Jenkins was working an active vein nearby."

"So he was mining?"

"Somewhere—who knows exactly where. Never did find that out. But I'd see him come into Saxon a few times a year when he canoed out to get provisions and his mail."

"Wow, and I feel pretty shut off from civilization after a week of camping."

"That's 'cause you come from a generation of narcissists, always snapping photos of yourselves and your fancy gear to broadcast on Instagram."

Payne had come to learn in his brief time in this state that Alaskans sure loved to insult outsiders.

"Anyway, one fall we ended up having to spend a few nights at Jenkins' cabin when an early snowstorm rolled in. When things cleared and we were getting ready to leave, I walked down to the little creek behind his cabin to replenish our canteens. Jenkins had built this ingenious little channel that funneled cold creek water into a small basin surrounded by thick mesh that acted as a sort of water purifier. He had even built a wooden frame around it to prevent the mud and debris from seeping in. I pulled off the lid, and while I was filling my canteens, I saw about a dozen terra-cotta jugs nestled in the sand. Their mouths were just above the water line, and I figured he was using the chilly water to refrigerate his homemade wine or moonshine."

There was an air of silence in the room as the weight of the years seemed to press down upon both men.

"So his gold nuggets were stashed there?" Payne asked.

The old man let out a wolfish grin as his eyes gleamed. "He must have amassed a fortune. And it all probably came from a chunk of land on one of the surrounding parcels, which used to be owned by the Klurmans, though they probably didn't know it at the time, since they got out of that low-yield type of prospecting years ago."

"Did Jenkins know you knew about the jugs?"

Hirovicz shook his head. "We'd have gotten bullets in our brains if he suspected." He let out a heavy sigh. "Three years later, his body was found south of Wolf Lake. His belongings had been stolen, and the only thing left was the copy of the Tolstoy book that he was probably coming to return to my father on his resupply trip to Saxon. My father didn't go into great detail about what happened, but I found out later that Jenkins had clearly been tortured. Sounded like someone had skinned him alive. My guess is Sean Klurman's old man was behind it, figuring he was entitled to the gold because his family had once held the surrounding parcels."

"And those jugs in the spring?"

"I was running my own timber surveys in other parts of Alaska after high school and didn't make it back out to Pickerel Lake for about four years. His cabin was gone, burned down in a forest fire that obliterated that entire wilderness region, and the creek was so flooded that I couldn't even tell where his cache had been. Eventually, the timber company was bought out by a larger firm that was relying more on aerial surveys than boots on the ground, so I left after another year and went to college down in Montana."

"But somehow Zandri discovered where the gold was—because of his background as a historian and your experiences?"

Hirovicz removed his quilt and stood, ambling over to a bookcase by Payne and pulling down a tattered volume of *Resurrection*. "Ironic that this is the last book Tolstoy wrote and also the last one Jenkins read before he died." He brushed his fingers along the faded cover, then handed it to Payne before returning to his rocking chair.

"That's been with me all these years. I haven't read it since my youth, but I couldn't bear to part with it. Last summer when I was retelling this story to Ian, he flipped through the book and noticed something." The old man pointed a gnarly finger at the paperback. "Page 97. You won't understand it unless you speak Russian, though."

Payne's eyes floated over the barely visible sentences written in pencil. Below it were a few droplets of dried blood, and Payne figured these were literally Jenkins' last words. He uttered the three sentences in fluent Russian, then spoke in English.

*"My dear friend, the gold is hidden in water in its own separate current. Take it before K does. My hat goes off to you."*

Payne felt like he had been teleported back with Hirovicz to the wilds of Pickerel Lake and a mystery shrouded by the passage of time. A mystery that had clawed its way back to the present with murderous vengeance.

"My son and I went out to that region a few times over the years, but my maps from the old timber company were all gone by then, and my memory of the exact location of that old creek was too sketchy." He lowered his eyes. "And my son passed on four years ago next month."

"I'm sorry to hear that, sir." He handed the old book back to the old man. "But Zandri was able to piece it together with this information and what he knew about locating old mines?"

"Yes. He was actually coming here after his canoe trip to show me what he'd found. He called me on his satellite phone and left a message a few days before leaving Pickerel Lake, saying he'd finally discovered the spring's location, and the ceramic jugs were still there. He apologized in advance for smelling like a spice factory—said he had to dig through patches of wild onions to get to the spring's source, and that he was going to bring a few nuggets and then return to Pickerel Lake after resupplying on food."

Payne thought about Micah's comments about Zandri smelling like an Italian restaurant. *The wild onions left their signature on the man.*

"So, one last thing, sir: how is TJ Reynolds involved in all of this?"

"Only Ian could have told you that. Those two started working together a few months ago. Talk about a meeting of great minds."

Maribel stuck her head in the room and gave Payne the "time's up" look.

He nodded and reached out his hand, both men shaking. "I can't thank you enough. This has been enlightening, to say the least."

Hirovicz wrapped the quilt around his bony shoulders and stood by the window. "I have a bad feeling about Reynolds, so you watch yourself, young man."

# CHAPTER 36

An hour later, Payne and Micah were staked out in the Jeep, the vehicle concealed on the other side of a thin row of trees between the Caribou Inn and a derelict gas station.

"How long we going to wait here?" asked Micah, finishing a hamburger they'd picked up on the drive back to Saxon.

"Few more minutes. Just wanna make sure there's no surveillance."

Her head flicked to the left, gazing past Payne to a man and little boy who'd just left the convenience store across Main Street. The guy was stout, with an immense belly hanging out below his shirt and a patchy black beard.

"They say you should treat your body like a temple, but his looks more like a haunted house," Micah muttered.

Payne diverted his attention from their motel room for a second to study the portly figure. "Says the girl who thinks Cheetos and Mountain Dew are main courses."

He swiveled back in his seat towards the inn. "You should cut people some slack. That guy could have bad knees and can't get around well, or is just going through a bad bout of luck in his life and is dealing with depression."

"Good and bad luck is all bullshit. So is karma. You have to kick life in the gonads and make it do what you want."

"You read that on a bumper sticker somewhere?"

She frowned. "You of all people believe in luck? I'm not buying it. I've seen what you can do, and that kind of skill only comes from hard work, same way I picked up being on the trail crew for three summers—sweat, long hours, and no whining."

"Then you've developed an admirable work ethic and outlook that will take you far, but it doesn't mean other people's lows in life equates to them being deemed losers."

"What are you, a Buddhist?"

"A recovering cynic who spent too many years seeing only the negative side of things."

"Sounds like a You problem."

"It'll become a You problem for you too, one day, if you remain a pessimist. I'm not saying you should start seeing the world filled with sunshine and butterflies, but just don't let your anger at the people in your past consume you."

She chuckled. "Damn, Payne, you should be making up your own bumper stickers and selling them to the artists in Homer." She balled up the empty hamburger wrapper and tossed it in back. "I get what you're trying to do, and I appreciate it. Well, sort of. I just want this to all be over so I can get on with my life. So I can actually start my life." Micah flung her hands in the air. "I mean, I never imagined spending my afternoon on a stakeout with…with whatever you are."

Payne narrowed his eyes, staring at the approaching vehicle through the trees as it pulled into the last parking spot by their motel room. "Looks like our stakeout is nearly over, but I wasn't expecting Nolte to show up. Be back in a coupla minutes," he said, quietly exiting the Jeep and stalking through the trees, removing the 1911 pistol from his jacket.

A second later, he came up behind the trooper's vehicle just as Nolte was stepping out. Payne kept his body angled so the pistol wasn't visible by his leg.

"Is this a social visit?" asked Payne.

Nolte was clearly surprised and pivoted around, pressing his back to the vehicle's open door and resting a hand on his service weapon. "Damnit, Payne. Don't ever come up on me like that again." The man glanced towards Payne's concealed right hand. "You planning to draw down on me?"

Payne gazed around the parking lot, then towards the corner of the motel. "Just a little paranoid, you could say. Especially given my experience at that taxidermist outside of Anchorage. Funny how those boys knew I was supposed to be heading to the museum."

"And you think I had something to do with that?"

"Ever since the murders at Birch Lake, someone has known precisely where Micah or I were going to be: first the assault at my cabin, then the hillbilly militia at Birch Lake, and yesterday when a group of bikers came at me. So you tell me, Lieutenant."

Nolte licked his lip. "Damn, this is much bigger than I thought. I'll admit that I was skeptical about the attack at your cabin, so I went back there and walked around. Found a set of night-vision goggles in the woods and a broken tooth in your door frame where you smashed a guy's head, like you said. Someone clearly wants the girl and her video evidence out of the way. I'm pretty certain Dean wasn't involved in the murders. He seems more and more like he's…"

"A patsy."

Nolte smirked. "Not the main suspect. I spoke with him at the hospital earlier and then had an interesting conversation with someone at the prison."

"And does Agent Cartwright share your newfound theory?"

"I'm not sure what she believes or what her real angle is, aside from all that bullshit about simply doing the governor's bidding."

"You think she's in on this?"

"I think she's jockeying for a higher pay grade in her department and is willing to do whatever it takes to make that happen."

"You mean outside of the law?"

Nolte sighed. "Not sure, to be honest. I can't get a firm handle on her."

"Where is she now?"

"Anchorage, I think."

"So why come here?"

"As much as it pains me to say this, I think you're right about there being a leak in my own house. You and Gus are the only two people I trust right now. I actually just got off the phone with him."

"Is Gus going to be joining us?"

Nolte shook his head. "No, but he was very helpful in confirming a few things I discovered interviewing the former cellmate of Andre Groh's father."

# CHAPTER 37

Payne lifted his shirt and tucked away his 1911, while Nolte relaxed his weapon hand, letting it hang by his side. "Any good come of your visit?"

"That's why I'm here. I could use your help. I'm not turning up much on Andre and wanna head out to Yancey Groh's old property northeast of town and see if something turns up."

"But I thought the father died years ago?"

"The place may have sentimental value to Andre. Maybe he's been there. I know it's a long shot, but I'm running out of ideas. Gus provided directions, and it's only about a thirty-minute drive."

Payne's gut instincts were telling him that Nolte could be trusted. From his weary expression and the bags under his eyes, it was clear the man hadn't slept in days and was bent on solving the multiple mysteries associated with the murders at Birch Lake.

He glanced back through the trees, seeing the faint outline of Micah still sitting in the car; then he gestured towards his motel room. "If you can cover me while I get something out of my luxurious suite, then we can head off to Groh's."

Nolte nodded, closing the door of his SUV and following Payne to the end of the motel. Both men leaned on the bricks on either side of the door. After Payne was confident no one was inside, he removed his 1911 again, along with the key in his pocket.

The lieutenant withdrew his service Glock. "Do I wanna know where you got that .45?"

"Found it in a ditch. Damnedest thing I've ever seen."

"Uh-huh."

Payne unlocked the door and rushed inside, sweeping the room and heading to the bathroom, while Nolte covered him.

"Clear."

The lieutenant pointed at the made beds. "Where'd you two stay last night?"

"In a yurt in the woods. Long story."

"Where the hell is Micah, by the way?"

"Next lot over, doling out judgment on the locals." He leaned over the table and removed the USB device, then pulled out the other one beside a nightstand.

"Can't live without your charger?"

Payne removed the mini SD cards from the devices. "Got your tablet in your vehicle?"

"Yep."

"Let's examine the footage on these cards, and I'll also send over Micah's video file since I have a backup."

The two men headed outside. Payne locked the door and followed the man back to his rig. As they sat in the SUV viewing the images of two armed intruders on the tablet, Payne noticed Nolte's eyes fill his face.

"You recognize them?" asked Payne.

Nolte enhanced the lead figure. The man was wearing a black ski mask, but there was a visible scar just above the trachea. "I was reviewing state-wide alerts a few days ago and saw something about a home invasion in Fairbanks where a woman was killed. There was a trail cam nearby used by an ornithology researcher, and it showed two men on a popular trail, carrying pillowcases stuffed with items probably stolen from the house. One of the guys had a scar identical to this in the photo that was distributed around the state."

"Who was the dead lady?"

"Rebecca Jergens—or, wait, no, it was Jenkins."

Payne rubbed his chin. "Damn, that can't be a coincidence —I just spoke to an old-timer out here who recounted a tale of lost gold in the region west of Saxon. It was connected to a prospector named Jenkins who was running a small mine in the '50s. I think Ian Zandri, that fella at the second campsite at Birch Lake, was returning from a successful trip locating that gold."

"Not sure I follow."

"Zandri was a renowned history professor who specialized in mining. I paid his secretary a visit on campus yesterday. She was very receptive to talking about him—not sure if they had a thing or not, but she showed me into his office and pointed me to a journal related to what I believe he was doing on his ill-fated canoe trip."

"So you were inserting yourself into my investigation...again."

He pivoted to face Nolte, deciding not to reveal Zandri's notebook in his jacket. "Look, you and I both know those people weren't murdered in some random fashion by Jimmy Dean. Now, I think Ian Zandri was the target all along. He was closing in on the discovery of a lifetime—a sizable treasure buried in the woods miles beyond Birch Lake, in a place that Zandri, with the help of an author friend familiar with the legend, was able to pinpoint. I have to wonder how the

Jenkins woman was involved—maybe she was helping fund Zandri's efforts—or was trying to re-establish her claim on a relative's land, assuming she's blood-related."

"Gold—that would be ample motive to kill."

"And TJ Reynolds is somehow connected to this."

"The missing geologist—he dropped off the radar a few weeks ago, but his wife said he was mapping a region east of town, not west."

"My digging around indicates that Reynolds was working with Zandri in the weeks leading up to what happened to either of them."

Nolte drummed his finger on the image of the scarred man on his tablet. "Bodies stacking up from here to Fairbanks, and someone at my post selling me out. But who's pulling the strings of these killers?"

"This is gold we're talking about...and there could be far more than just the nuggets at this old prospector's cabin that Zandri had been visiting. Who do you know has the resources, know-how, and funds to extract something like that on a large scale?"

The lieutenant sighed. "Sean Klurman, the guy whose mining firm is plastered on billboards all over the state."

"A local source who's familiar with the legend of the missing gold, and the original prospector told me that the Klurmans used to own all the land around the region Zandri had been at. The professor and Reynolds must have been trying to locate the mother vein, and Klurman found out."

Nolte leaned his head back. "Jesus, Klurman is best friends with the governor."

# CHAPTER 38

The dirt road to Yancey Groh's abandoned homestead was barely more than two parallel ruts carved through dense spruce forest. Nolte's SUV bounced and scraped over fallen branches and washouts that hadn't been maintained in over a decade. The old poacher's cabin lay three miles off the main logging road, hidden in a depression between two ridgelines that had kept it invisible to aerial surveys for years.

"This matches what Dmitri told me," Nolte said, referring to Yancey Groh's former cellmate at Briar Creek Correctional Center. "The Russian immigrant shared a cell with Groh senior for three years and remembered the old man's wild stories about his hideout in the woods, where he taught his son the family trade."

Payne studied the GPS coordinates they'd triangulated from Dmitri's descriptions and Gus' recollections from his wildlife enforcement days. When Nolte had called the lodge owner for additional details, Gus said it sounded like the same place he and his former partner had tried to serve a warrant on Groh, but which led to a fierce shootout, resulting in Yancey's arrest fifteen years earlier.

As they crested a small rise, the forest opened into a clearing that looked like a window into Alaska's frontier past. A dilapidated cabin squatted in the center of the clearing like something from a century-old photograph. Built from hand-hewn logs with notch joints, the structure showed the crafts-manship of someone versed in traditional building tech-niques. The roof was constructed of split cedar shakes, many now missing or askew, creating gaps where burgeoning rodent nests protruded.

"There's the well Dmitri described," Nolte said, pointing to a circle of stacked stones near the cabin's side entrance. The water source was surrounded by moss-covered rocks and fitted with a crude wooden windlass for drawing from the depths below.

The lieutenant parked twenty feet from the cabin. Payne exited, clutching his pistol, while Nolte kept his AR-15 rifle at a low ready.

Payne leaned into the vehicle, glancing at Micah in the back. She held up a hand before he could speak. "I know already—stay put, you'll be back in a minute, blah-blah-blah."

"Seems strange to hear you be so compliant, but, yeah, stay here."

He and Nolte proceeded towards the front porch.

"The vegetation along the road looked like it had been trampled down but not recently," said Payne. "I don't think anyone's been out for a week or two."

As they approached the porch, Payne noted the old deer-hide racks of 2x4s lashed between the trees along with a half-dozen rusty leghold traps in a pile at the base. Not an unusual sight for Alaska except the traps were massive and something Payne figured were once used for bears—or possibly humans.

Nolte stepped through the open door first, followed by

Payne. The cabin's interior was a single room with a stone fireplace, rough-hewn furniture, and shelves lined with rusted snares and skinning tools. Everything was coated with dust and mouse droppings, but Payne's trained eye immediately noticed the disturbances—drag marks in the dirt floor, overturned furniture, and dark stains on the wooden planks near the back wall.

Payne shone a flashlight on a dried splotch of blood on the ground. "This is more than a few days' old."

Nolte pointed the muzzle of his rifle at the fireplace. "By those weeds growing out of the ashes, I'd say they weren't here to stay." He walked to the back door, shoving it open on its creaky hinges and staring at drag marks in the dirt that led to a small outbuilding with plank board walls. "Dmitri said Groh senior used to brag about all the protected species he poached over the years and how he stored the illegal furs out back of his place."

They heard the boards on the front porch creak and swung around, their weapons aimed at Micah as she entered.

"Good way to get yourself shot, kid," snapped Nolte.

"I cleared my throat—guess you guys didn't hear me."

Payne gestured towards the open rear door. "I'd stay here. I gotta feeling things are about to get a lot uglier."

"Sure thing. I'll hang out in the murder cabin with the mouse droppings while you two explore the torture shack."

She went to step forward, but Payne raised his arm, blocking the exit. "There are some things you can't unsee in life, and what's in that shed is probably along those lines."

"And so's seeing your friends sliced to pieces. You guys need to stop babying me."

Nolte smirked and stepped outside. "She can't be much more of a liability than she already is being out here."

"Just stay behind me," Payne said, following the lieutenant as they closed the thirty-yard distance to the primitive structure behind the cabin. The shed was barely eight feet square, built with the same hand-hewn log construction but reinforced with heavier timbers that suggested it had been designed for storing valuable items—or preventing something from getting out.

The shed's heavy wooden door hung open, secured by a hand-forged iron hasp that looked like it belonged in a medieval castle. As they approached, the coppery smell of dried blood mixed with the organic odors of the forest floor wafted over Payne. Flies buzzed in the shadows beyond the doorway.

Payne stood to the left side of the door with his pistol raised, while Nolte grabbed the handle. Micah had taken the men's advice after all, and hung back behind the trunk of a large pine tree near the cabin.

Nolte glanced back at Payne, who gave him a nod; then the lieutenant yanked open the door. Both men lowered their weapons, their mortified expressions nearly mirroring each other.

The windowless outbuilding reeked of rotting meat. Hanging from the ceiling beams were thick chains, their links darkened with crimson stains along with a blood-soaked T-shirt on the ground.

In one corner, a workbench held an assortment of pliers, hammers, and other tools that were also being scoured by greedy flies.

"My God, what's been going on out here?" muttered Nolte, holding a crooked arm up to his nose as he stepped into the structure.

Payne swept his flashlight across the floor, the beam catching small, crescent-shaped objects scattered below the suspended chains. "Fingernails," he said grimly, crouching down without touching them. "Torn out, not cut."

"Not sure how you even know that, but I'll take your word on it," said Nolte. He kicked at a pile of rope in the corner, revealing tiny fragments of what looked like dried skin clinging to the rough fibers. "Jesus Christ. When Dmitri said that the old man used to field-dress things in here, he was talking about wild game, but it looks like Andre has taken things a step further."

Payne spotted the glint of metal half-buried in the dirt near the far wall. He kneeled and carefully brushed away the soil with his gloved hand, revealing a silver pendant of St. Christopher on a broken chain. The inscription on the back was scuffed but legible:

*To TJ – God's protection always*
*Love, Sarah*

"Damn, looks like you were right about Reynolds," Nolte said in an angry tone, pulling out his phone to document the scene.

Payne examined the chains and restraint system. The setup was too sophisticated—someone had prepared this torture chamber with careful planning, and it was located in a region so off the grid that screams would never reach any neighbors.

"Seems like there's a long line of people who possessed information that Klurman and Groh were willing to kill for," said Payne. He moved around the small space, scrutinizing the ground from different angles.

"Probably worked over TJ, then buried him out back." Nolte glanced at Payne. "You said earlier that Reynolds and Zandri were working together—on what, exactly?"

"Zandri had learned about a lost gold cache at a remote lake west of Birch. I can't say for sure what Reynolds' particular involvement was, but since he was a geologist, he must have helped Zandri ID the soil or region the gold was located."

Payne walked to the right wall, examining some blood-dappled maps tacked to the planks. "Look at this."

Nolte moved closer, narrowing his eyes as they gazed at a region circled with red ink. At the bottom was the most prominent topographic feature that the map was named after.

"Seems like all the trails keep pointing to Pickerel Lake—the location of the lost gold," muttered Payne. "I think if you're going to get the answers you need for this investigation, that place is the next step."

"How far are you willing to go with this, Payne? Though I'd welcome the help, you don't owe anyone anything, certainly not me or the girl."

Payne glanced out the door towards Micah in the distance. "I've got four days left until I'm on a ferry to Washington, so I'll see this thing through as far as I can until then. Besides, knowing what you now do, you're probably going to move up on Groh's hit list and could use someone watching your back."

Nolte's lips went flat as they both stepped outside. "Well, shit, when you put it like that."

As they retraced their steps back to Nolte's vehicle, he wondered what other revolting mysteries lay buried in these woods.

# CHAPTER 39

Emma Cartwright was approaching the town of Wasilla when a text came in on her cellphone. She slowed the borrowed police cruiser and pulled onto a gravel shoulder along Highway 3, hearing the faint patter of rain on the windshield.

She glanced at the screen, seeing the government number and wondering if it was the governor himself or just his assistant.

> Need to debrief you on the Saxon situation.
> Meet me at 1247 Turnagain Heights Road.
> Urgent.

She'd already spent much of the day getting reamed by her commanding officer in Anchorage about her lack of progress in nailing down the details for confirming who the media was calling the Birch Lake Butcher, and for not getting Nolte to move forward with pressing the case against Dean. With the threat of demotion hanging over her, she quickly responded to the text.

> Be there in thirty minutes.

She checked her mirrors, then turned the Lincoln around, speeding back towards Anchorage. After getting onto Highway 1 and proceeding to the south side of the city, she followed her GPS onto a secondary road that led through increasingly upscale neighborhoods until she found herself on a winding mountain road with million-dollar views of Cook Inlet. The directions guided her through an ornate gate and up a long driveway that climbed through manicured grounds toward what could only be described as a fortress.

The mansion that emerged from the trees was massive—all timber and stone construction that looked like it belonged in an architectural magazine. As she parked at the left side of the circular drive, Emma felt a growing unease. This wasn't a government building or even a discreet meeting location. This was someone's private estate, and an incredibly expensive one at that.

The sound of gunfire echoed from somewhere behind the house—not the sharp crack of pistols, but the deeper boom of shotguns. Emma followed a flagstone path around the side of the mansion, her hand instinctively checking the position of her service Glock.

She found two men on an elaborate skeet-shooting range carved into the hillside, immediately recognizing the pudgy figure of Governor Thomas Slattery. Beside him was a man in a hunting vest who stood nearly a foot taller.

As she approached the firing line, the men's custom 28-gauge shotguns trained on clay pigeons that launched from mechanical throwers on the right. Governor Slattery gave out a boisterous laugh after his successful shots, his silver hair flitting in the wind. The other man was a stranger—a rugged, predatory-looking figure in his sixties wearing hunting clothes that probably cost more than Emma's monthly salary.

"Ah, Detective Cartwright," the governor called out, lowering his shotgun, "right on time. Allow me to introduce

Sean Klurman, who was gracious enough to have us out here on such short notice."

Klurman robotically extended a hand. "Governor Slattery has told me so much about your work on the Saxon case. Impressive results in such a short timeframe."

"You're the CEO of Frontier Mining, right?" she asked, wondering how the man knew anything about the case, and why he was being so flattering, given her recent ass-chewing at the department.

"The governor said nothing gets by you."

Something in his tone made Emma's detective instincts flare. Klurman's casual interest felt anything but casual, not to mention his eyes lingering on her figure for an uncomfortably long time.

"Thank you, sir. Though I have to say, Lieutenant Nolte deserves most of the credit. He's the one who made the arrest."

"Yes, about that," the governor said, setting his shotgun in a rack. "We need to discuss some concerns that have come to light about his investigation. Specifically about this outsider, Kyle Payne, and his influence on the case."

Emma felt her unease deepening since she'd only just revealed Payne's involvement to her CO a few hours ago. "What kind of concerns?"

Klurman gestured toward a small pavilion overlooking the shooting range, complete with a wet bar and leather seating. "Perhaps we should sit down. This is rather sensitive."

As they walked to the shelter, Emma discreetly activated the voice recording app on her phone, tucking the device into her jacket pocket, where the microphone would still pick up the conversation.

"The truth is," the governor began, "we've been monitoring the Saxon situation very closely. The state's tourism industry can't afford an Alaskan serial killer story dominating the national news, and I'm not going to risk having this murder case bog down our economy because Nolte's caught up in speculation."

Klurman stepped closer, resting his shotgun over his shoulder. "Which is why we were originally so pleased when Lieutenant Nolte identified Jimmy Dean as the perpetrator. Clean, plenty of evidence, case closed."

"But now," the governor continued, "this Payne character has been muddying the waters with wild theories about multiple killers and elaborate conspiracies because of some juvenile delinquent he crossed paths with. This is exactly the kind of sensationalism that could turn this into even more of a media circus than it's become."

Emma studied both men's faces, her cop instincts screaming at her. "With respect, Governor and Mr. Klurman, shouldn't we be more concerned with finding the truth than managing the narrative?"

Klurman's laugh was cold. "Detective, in my experience, truth is often a matter of perspective. What matters is what serves the bigger picture."

"And what serves Alaska's economic interests," the governor added. "We can't have some drifter with a mysterious background destabilizing a solid case just because he wants to play hero."

A faint grin emerged on her face. "You two are joking, right? This isn't the Wild West where you make up your own version of the law as you go." She stared into Slattery's eyes. "I don't know what's going on here, sir, but whatever Klurman has dragged you into, it's not too late to do the right thing, because, contrary to what he says, the truth is not subjective."

Slattery folded his fat fingers across his chest. "I am doing the right thing, Emma. And I assigned you to this case not only because of your prior history with the Dean boy, but because I saw potential in you—the kind that could open doors most people only dream about. There's still time for you to take a more aggressive stance against Nolte and shape the account of events regarding the Birch Lake massacre."

Her mouth hung open, and she wondered if she was in some murky dream as she stared at the two sociopaths with their practiced charm who were masquerading as respectable men. She glanced at the isolated hilltop and suddenly felt like prey that had wandered into the wrong territory, every instinct shouting at her to run.

Klurman took a step forward. "You see, Detective, when the governor first asked you to assist with the Saxon case, we were hoping you'd help guide it toward a clean resolution. Instead, you've allowed this Payne character to complicate things unnecessarily and this juvenile girl to run amok, putting my venture at risk."

Emma's hand moved an inch toward her weapon. "I think there's been a misunderstanding. My job is to investigate crimes, not cover them up."

"Your job," the governor said coldly, "is to serve the people of Alaska. And sometimes that means making difficult choices for the greater good."

She glanced at the two men, recalling Nolte mentioning how someone had been feeding information about Payne's and Micah's movements. Then there was Klurman, who knew every detail about the murder investigation. Emma felt pieces clicking into place with sickening clarity, her stomach coiling in knots.

The sound of tires on gravel interrupted her thoughts. Emma turned to see a green Ford F-250 pulling up to the house. Her eyes widened when two burly men with beards and wearing camouflage jackets stepped out, and she suddenly remembered Payne's chilling description of the guys he'd tracked at Birch Lake.

"Ah, gentlemen," Klurman called out. "Perfect timing."

The older guy remained by the vehicle while the younger man trotted up to the pavilion, a visible scar on his throat just below his black beard. Something about it jarred a memory concerning a home-invasion case in Fairbanks.

Klurman sighed. "The problem with idealistic cops like you, Detective, is that you lack vision. You get so focused on procedural correctness that you lose sight of what really matters, even though our esteemed governor here thought you might be smart enough to get on board with our program."

"Which is?" Emma asked, though she was already rising from her chair and making a move for her pistol.

"Results," Klurman said simply, flipping the shotgun down from his shoulder. "Profitable results."

The discharge from the 28-gauge was deafening in the mountain air. Emma felt the impact like a sledgehammer to her chest, the blast sending her backward down the hillside, her body rolling through shrubs and decorative rocks before coming to rest against a retaining wall.

Pain exploded through her torso as she struggled to breathe, feeling the warm spread of blood soaking through her shirt. Above her, she could hear Klurman's voice, calm and businesslike.

"Toss her in the back of your rig and ditch her in the swamp over by Seward."

Emma's vision was dimming, but she could see the young guy descending the slope toward her, his face pale with shock. "Jesus, I never signed up for killing a cop."

"You signed up the moment you took our money," Klurman replied. "Now clean up the mess."

A moment later, the man kneeled, hoisting her up in a fireman's carry and trudging back up the hill. She felt the energy drain from her legs, the last vestiges of her life force retreating to her core.

He walked past the pavilion as she bobbed helplessly. The older hunter had already lowered the tailgate and lifted the hatch on the truck cap. She was flung inside the bed like a broken doll, coming to rest by the left wheel well.

The darkness pressed in around her as the back was shut. Emma forced herself onto her side, blood pooling beneath her ribs. With fingers that barely obeyed her commands, she found her phone and sent the recording to Nolte. The upload bar crawled forward with agonizing sluggishness, mirroring her own fading pulse as her consciousness slipped away.

# CHAPTER 40

After leaving Groh's cabin of horrors, Payne and Micah drove back with Nolte to the outskirts northwest of Saxon and down a maintained gravel road for three miles.

"You live out here?" asked Micah.

Nolte shook his head. "My wife's a real estate agent, and this is a foreclosed house she's been handling. Owners have been gone for months, so it'll be a good place to hole up for tonight. I spoke with Gus, and he'll fly us out to Pickerel Lake in the morning."

"So your wife kicked you out is more like it," said Micah. "She probably kept telling you not to bring your work home with you anymore, or you're out the front door. And now, it's adios, mi amor."

Nolte gave Payne a puzzled expression. "Is this the shit you've been putting up with all this time? You're tougher than I thought."

"Hurricane Micah cuts quite a path," Payne said with a chuckle.

"My wife is on her way to her sister's place up north. I

don't trust that my home isn't going to become a target for Groh and his thugs."

"Tactically sound," said Payne.

Nolte glanced at the girl in the rearview mirror. "There's still some canned goods inside the house, and the electricity works. It'll be a good place for you to wait out the day tomorrow until we get back from Pickerel Lake."

"Hard pass," said Micah in a resolute tone. "I'm Team Nolte, just like Payne and Gus."

"Absolutely not," Nolte said, shaking his head. "This is a law enforcement operation, not a wilderness camping trip. You're staying out here."

Micah leaned forward. "Lieutenant, there's a detail that was left out about Zandri. I mentioned this to Kyle before, thinking it was nothing, but now, given what he just said about the lost gold cache, I think it's important. That night at Birch Lake, I talked with Zandri for a few minutes while we were both out gathering firewood. He had this overpowering odor like he'd been in an Italian restaurant."

Nolte raised an eyebrow. "Fascinating, so the man stank after being in the bush for a week. Maybe he was eating a lot of dehydrated spaghetti."

"If you'd let me finish, you might actually learn something."

The trooper smirked before making a final turn onto the property. "You're a firecracker, alright, but, please, do go on with your story."

"When I was working the trail crew near Lake Clark last summer, we had a botanist with us, and he taught us a lot about edible plants. One of those was wild onions, which are usually located near freshwater springs and creek beds. In fact, a lot of the settlers used to propagate them, and after that, whenever we came across small creeks, we found wild onions and gathered them up for dinner. All of us reeked—just like Zandri did."

"Interesting, and potentially useful, but you're a civilian and a prime witness in this case, which means you stay here."

She interlaced her tan fingers. "Those plants don't grow everywhere—they're specific to certain soil conditions. I can identify where he was digging based on the plant life around the area. You need me to pinpoint exactly where he found that spring."

"The girl's got a point," Payne interjected. "With the map and coordinates I have, I can locate the general area of where the old prospector's cabin was at, but we could spend hours searching the wrong areas without her knowledge, hoping to find Zandri's last location before Birch Lake."

Nolte looked up from the road, studying her face. "Micah, you're barely eighteen. I can't risk—"

"Those bastards killed my best friend and are trying to frame Jimmy Dean for it," Micah continued, her voice gaining intensity. "I survived two days while those maniacs were hunting me, and multiple attacks since then. I'm not some city kid who'll panic under pressure."

Payne seized the opening, glancing at Nolte. "Sitting in a bedroom out here just makes her a sitting duck for their next attempt. At least out at Pickerel Lake, she's with people who can protect her, and contributing something useful."

The trooper rubbed his temple, clearly wrestling with the decision.

"Lieutenant," Payne said quietly, "you need every advantage you can get out there. She's offering a specialized skill that could trim miles and hours off our efforts."

Nolte parked the vehicle in front of the two-story house. He unbuckled and swiveled around to face Micah. "You follow orders without question from the second we board the float plane, and if things go sideways, you do exactly what I tell you. Understood?"

Micah nodded. "Understood, sir."

Payne was sure he saw the girl holding back a grin, and wondered if it was at the thought of finally convincing the lawman, or that she had used a term of respect, which had to be a first for her.

# CHAPTER 41

At sunrise, Nolte drove them back to the airfield outside of Saxon, where Gus was waiting on the small inlet in his float plane. After boarding, they took off, flying due east for a few miles before banking back to the west.

"You think the ruse to make it look like we're heading in the opposite direction from Pickerel Lake is going to throw off anyone following us?" asked Payne, swiveling back towards Nolte, who was sitting beside Micah in the rear seats.

"Hope so. And the flight plan I filed back at the post indicates we're doing a recon of the area near Yancey Groh's cabin. Plus, Gus said he swept the plane for trackers, so we should be clear."

Payne pivoted around, staring at the scores of lakes that sprawled beneath him like a shattered mirror, the crystalline waters catching the Arctic sun across miles of roadless forest and making him wish he was heading into the backcountry on a relaxing trip.

———

ANDRE GROH WAS in the west side of the furnished basement in Klurman's estate, finishing reassembling his trusty Weatherby rifle, the smell of cleaning solvents hanging over the spacious vault.

Klurman's walk-in armory resembled a military arsenal crossed with a collector's showroom. On the left wall were vintage rifles from both world wars, which stood at attention alongside sleek modern tactical firearms, their polished stocks and matte-black receivers creating a timeline of firearm evolution.

Along the right wall were glass-fronted cabinets housing nearly a hundred pistols arranged by caliber and time period —from ornate Victorian-era revolvers with ivory grips to cutting-edge steel-framed sidearms with suppressors. In mesh cages at the back of the room were rows of grenades, flash-bangs, and thermal scopes along with night-vision headsets comparable to what Tier 1 units carried.

Groh had just slid the freshly oiled bolt back into his Weatherby when he heard someone coming down the steps.

Sean Klurman entered and moved up next to him, patting Groh on the shoulder and handing him an ornate wooden box with a walnut lid and silver clasp.

"I wanted to give you something personal to show my appreciation for everything you've done for me these past few weeks," said Klurman.

Groh set his rifle down on the central table and wiped his hands on a rag. He gazed at the box and lifted the lid. His lips parted, and a slow grin crept over his face. "My God, I don't know what to say, sir. This is exquisite."

He picked up the customized Ruger pistol with Bolivian rosewood grips. It was a limited edition run of a Bisley Hunter in .41 Magnum, and Groh stared at it like it was made of platinum, aware that it probably cost more than some of the hunting rifles on the rack behind him.

"These take a 230-grain flat-nosed bullet, as I recall," said Groh as he flipped open the cylinder.

"I prefer the 210 grain, but you'll have plenty of time to try out different loads next month. I booked us a short trip to the Congo. My government contact there indicates a small presence of western gorillas in an isolated valley that fall outside the protection of the conservation officers."

Groh snapped the revolver back in place and brushed his fingers along the barrel. "Always wanted to do big-game hunting with these revolvers, but couldn't justify the price." He put the weapon back in the box and closed it, sliding it back to Klurman. "But this is too much, sir, especially after all the snafus these past few days."

"We learn and grow from our mistakes, son, and things will be straightened out soon enough."

Andre had always viewed Klurman as a patriarchal figure, a steady presence who'd stepped seamlessly into the void left by his actual father when he was arrested. The businessman had been more than just his father's longtime friend and preferred hunting guide through the Alaskan wilderness —he'd become Andre's protector and mentor, the one who'd smuggled him across borders when the authorities were closing in during those desperate early years after he shot a conservation officer.

Andre had known Klurman since he was a scrawny kid tagging along on hunting expeditions, watching from camp as his father led the wealthy American along bear trails and fishing spots, never imagining that one day the businessman would risk everything to keep that same boy alive—and free.

A wolfish grin crept out over Klurman's face, and he gently pushed the box back toward Andre. "Try it on the range out back first. If you don't want it, I won't be offended."

"I want it, but it seems only proper that you take the first shot with it in the Congo."

The business mogul placed his thick hand gently around Groh's neck. "I can live with that, my boy."

Their banter was interrupted at the sound of rushed footsteps clamoring down the stairs.

Hatch appeared, his puffy face more flushed than usual. "We got a major problem." He tossed an iPhone on the table. "Found that in the back of the truck bed under a tarp when I was washing out that detective's blood. She sent a message to an area code in Saxon. Timestamp shows it was just before we dumped her body."

Klurman snatched the device and jabbed the screen. "Fuck me. She sent an audio file." He hit the play button, the conversation from the pavilion by the skeet range echoing around the vault. Cleverly, she'd mentioned everyone's names.

When the recording stopped, Klurman paced around the room as the two poachers shot nervous glances at one another.

Finally, Klurman threw the phone against the steel wall and leaned his fists on the table, staring at Groh. "Gather up whoever you need, and call your contact in Saxon—I want to know exactly where that pissant trooper Nolte and his band of pathetic misfits are at. This fucking ends today."

———

Gus piloted the Cessna lower, skirting along the edge of Pickerel Lake. Just before he was about to descend, Payne tapped him on the shoulder, pointing to the right. "Can you make a pass along that shoreline to the east?"

The pilot arced the plane towards a strip of thick spruce trees a quarter mile away.

"Those look like ATV tracks coming in from the lake," Payne said into his headset.

Gus nodded. "And by the ruts, they were probably hauling gear trailers. Reminds me of when we used to have mobile outfitter camps delivered via helicopter during radio-telemetry studies on wolves.

"Must have been air-dropped since no boat is going to be able to get that kind of equipment this far out," said Gus.

"Set us down in that cove over there," said Payne, pointing to a curved section of the lake about a mile from the ATV tracks.

The older man gave a thumbs-up, then ascended again, banking to the left, then hooking into the cove in the opposite direction.

Once they had all disembarked and anchored the plane, Payne pulled out Zandri's weathered topo map, tracing his finger from their present location to the supposed gold stash. "This is where Jenkins' old cabin was supposed to be, but I think we need to check out where those ATV tracks go first."

"Why?" asked Nolte, who was slathering himself with mosquito repellent before passing around the bottle. "Could be a forest-service operation or a timber outfit surveying the region for the fall harvest."

"Out of all the places in this wilderness, we just happen to come across signs of someone else not far from the source of what brought Zandri here—I'm not buying it. Plus, I don't want any more surprises."

"I agree with Kyle," said Gus. "As I recall, this is mostly checkerboard land ownership out here, and I've not heard anything about the feds doing work this far out."

Micah shook her head. "Jesus, you guys talk too much."

Nolte gestured for Payne to lead the way. The men all kept their rifles at low ready and trudged along the pebbly shoreline towards the road scar in the distance while Micah trailed up the rear.

A few minutes later, they arrived at the ATV-scarred path. Payne walked inland, keeping a parallel route to the route. It was slow going with thick stands of conifers and numerous fallen trees from windblown storms in recent years.

The lane climbed uphill for a distance of thirty yards, then leveled out for a while before coming to a gentle decline. Payne paused at the rim, concealing himself in the thick foliage while the others did the same.

The sound of men talking below pierced the dense foliage, and Payne could make out two guys sitting on stumps, playing cards around a smoky campfire, while a third snoozed on a folding chair. The rest of their encampment consisted of a large green rain canopy strung between the trees, several tents, four ATVs and trailers, and dozens of crates stacked up against a rock face.

Payne glanced at Nolte, who had an *I told you so* look on his face, and Payne wondered if this really was a contracted crew doing work for a timber company.

Then a fourth man stepped out from the shade, his appearance more unkempt than the others and his face sooty. But it was the shackle and chain around his right ankle clanking along the ground that caused Payne to question what he was seeing.

"TJ Reynolds is alive," Nolte whispered.

"Jesus, what'd they do to that poor guy?" asked Micah.

"Reynolds *is* the work crew out here," said Gus. "They must be forcing him to do a survey for that gold."

Payne chewed on his lip. "Not the gold nuggets Jenkins squirreled away. Reynolds must be searching for the original vein since Jenkins' cabin was nearly a half mile northwest of here."

"This just took an unexpected turn," muttered Nolte. "And I can't exactly call for backup, given I'm not sure who to trust at my own goddammed post."

Payne glanced at his fellow ad hoc team and their weapons. If he were alone, he'd be all for plugging the three captors full of holes, but he knew that'd be a hard sell, and they lacked suppressors to make the job smoother. Plus, he didn't know if there were more thugs in the area.

Nolte gazed at the muddy path leading to the camp. "I'll sneak down and then come into their camp and announce they're under arrest for kidnapping, while you two cover me from here."

"That's a crap shoot, Lieutenant," said Gus, glancing through the scope on his Winchester M70 hunting rifle, the same weapon he'd carried for decades as a conservation officer. "Better off to wait until nightfall and then sneak down there and grab Reynolds."

"Sundown is, like, eleven hours from now," said Nolte in an irritated voice.

"You gotta think this through." Gus pointed to a stack of wooden crates beside one of the flatbed trailers. "From the hazmat symbols on those boxes, I'd say that's dynamite, so we'd better be damn sure this doesn't turn into a gunfight."

Payne thrust his finger down the slope and removed his 1911 pistol. "There's another way that won't involve any shots being exchanged. Just wait until the red mist clears."

"What the hell do you mean?" asked Nolte, clutching his rifle.

Payne focused on the makeshift table beside the firepit and squeezed off a single round that struck the cluster of bear-spray canisters, sending out a red cloud of vapor that engulfed the campsite. The men tumbled off their seats, pawing at their faces and gagging, while Reynolds dove behind a trailer.

Payne reholstered his pistol and grabbed his rifle, making his way down the slope. "Gus, you provide overwatch while Nolte and I deal with these idiots."

The lieutenant followed a parallel path thirty feet to the right, his AR-15 pointed at the thrashing men on the ground.

Payne emerged from the woods to the left and quickly made his way to the nearest guy, sending a boot into his face and rendering him unconscious.

"Really?" asked Nolte, shaking his head. "I have a better idea that involves fewer lawsuits." He removed his cuffs and clasped one end around the other retching figure's wrist and ran it through the side rail of the trailer before attaching the other shackle to the last figure's wrist.

Payne moved around the far side of the second trailer, seeing Reynolds crouched in a fetal position and waving his hands. "Don't hurt me."

Payne lowered his weapon. "We're with the Alaska State Troopers. It's over. We know about them coercing you to find Zandri's gold."

Reynolds stood, his wild eyes darting at Payne, then the lieutenant. "Thank God. I've been living like an animal out here for—"

A look of pure terror spread across Reynolds' face as he glanced beyond Payne's shoulder.

Before Payne could turn, he heard the distinctive metallic click of a rifle being racked. He slowly pivoted, seeing a camouflaged figure emerging from the dense undergrowth twenty yards away, his AK-47 fixed on Payne's chest.

The gunman's finger tightened on the trigger, a cold glare coming over his eyes.

The rifle shot cracked the air, causing Payne to stagger back, a heavy bullet catching the would-be killer in the chest and spinning him backward into the ferns before he could complete his shot. The man's weapon discharged into the canopy as his body crumpled, and Payne swiveled to the right, seeing Gus up on the ridge, working his bolt with practiced efficiency.

Payne forced out a breath, grateful for the old conservation officer's steady hands.

# CHAPTER 42

Nolte knelt beside Reynolds, examining the geologist's battered body with the practiced eye of someone who'd seen plenty of violence, while Gus removed the ankle shackle with the guard's key. Reynolds' face was a patchwork of yellowing bruises and fresh cuts, three of his toes wrapped with gauze where the nails had been removed, and his frame gaunt from inadequate food.

"Easy there," Nolte said, offering water from his canteen while checking Reynolds' pulse. "When you're up to it, I'd sure like to hear how you got here."

The man accepted the water gratefully, his hands shaking in between sips, as he mentioned hearing about the murders at Birch Lake and the loss of Zandri from the guys secured to the trailer. When he was done drinking, Reynolds recounted how he'd been conducting a routine geological survey east of Saxon when Andre Groh and another man had ambushed him.

"They dragged me to some old shed in the woods," he whispered, his voice hoarse. "Groh wanted to know everything about my work for Rebecca Jenkins, about her claims on her great-uncle's property out here, and who else was involved in locating his gold. When I wouldn't talk at first, he..." Reynolds shuddered, pulling his torn shirt tighter around his shoulders. "He enjoyed every minute of it. Said he learned his techniques from his father in that very shed."

"Someone like that's not even human," said Payne as he and Nolte exchanged knowing glances.

"My wife—I have to call my wife. She and my little boy must think I'm dead."

Nolte pulled out his phone and gazed at the screen. "I've had some problems with reception lately. We'll get you to the plane and fly back to Saxon. You'll see them soon—I promise."

Micah leaned in, handing him a Snickers bar she produced from a pocket.

He greedily tore into the sweet, smiling up at her.

"We were actually coming out here to locate Zandri's camp near an old prospector's cabin. Know anything about that?" asked Payne.

"Rebecca Jenkins had tracked down genealogical information on her great-uncle Clyde Jenkins, who had once mined throughout this region back in the '50s or so. She contacted Zandri to validate her family stories about Clyde's supposed lost fortune. To strengthen her inheritance claims, she hired me to conduct scientific surveys proving gold deposits existed in the areas described in their oral histories. Once Rebecca got the reports from myself and Zandri, she was going to file formal inheritance claims backed by Zandri's historical research and my geological findings."

He glanced up at a passing cumulus cloud. "That was such a fun time. I felt like Indiana Jones, and all of us took a survival class together so we would be prepared for any contingencies."

Reynolds licked the candy wrapper clean. "I've had a lot

of time out here to think about things, and I believe our combined research must have triggered legal reviews of land ownership and mineral rights in the Pickerel Lake region by someone high up in the state's surveying division."

Nolte crushed a pine cone under his boot. "That bastard Klurman probably learned of all the activity through his network of lawyers and land-acquisition specialists."

"And someone from the governor's office must have been monitoring inheritance cases that could affect mineral rights since those types of things are run through archivists at the capitol," said Reynolds.

Payne thought back to his meeting with the professor's secretary. "Zandri was murdered at Birch Lake to eliminate his academic expertise and prevent his publication, which would have brought historical preservation groups into the fold. Without Zandri's validation, Rebecca Jenkins' inheritance claims would lose credibility, and no governmental agencies would be alerted to challenge Klurman's mineral rights when he tried to purchase the land."

"Seems like Klurman getting the Jenkins lady out of the picture would have solved his problem," said Micah. "So why go and kill everyone at Birch Lake?"

"The single murder of a mining history expert might have pointed investigators directly toward anyone with mining interests in the region, namely Klurman," said Nolte. "But a random massacre in the wilderness points to a deranged killer, not a corporate conspiracy." He glanced at Micah. "The other unfortunate victims happened to be in the wrong place —perfect cover for making Zandri's death look like bad luck instead of a targeted assassination."

"You have to understand something—this is gold on an epic scale," said Reynolds, waving towards the rock piles in the distance as the three pepper-sprayed thugs listened in. "Even I'm surprised at what's out here. If the Klurmans had the capability of ground-penetrating radar decades ago, they never would have sold their parcels to Clyde Jenkins back in the day. And since they never discovered his lost treasure, they must have figured he had located a quirk—a one-off deposit."

He leaned back, rubbing his bruised ankle where the shackle had been. "Once they forced me to start doing surveys out here and realized that Rebecca Jenkins was going to inherit a massive gold payout on Clyde's old land—land that had once belonged to the Klurmans, Sean put his plan in motion to kill anyone who could interfere with reacquiring his family's former holdings."

Payne nodded. "Klurman wants his claws in it all and has been slowly eliminating anyone who presents even a minor threat to his efforts. What I don't get is why they didn't kill Stanley Hirovicz, since he was the origin of the entire legend and helped Zandri piece things together."

"The murder of a beloved Alaskan author would have been scrutinized more carefully than random campers," said Gus.

"And the old man would be more useful alive as a potential source of additional details than dead and drawing unwanted attention," said Nolte.

They heard the sound of a radio crackling. Payne hopped up and searched for the static. He walked to the other side of the first ATV and pulled out a two-way radio in a leather holster dangling off the handlebars.

"Steve, we'll be at your location in thirty minutes. Looks like there's a bird on the lake. Seen anyone?"

Payne moved closer to the others and clicked on the radio. "We've saved a spot around the campfire for you, Andre—or is this Sean Klurman?"

A long pause followed before the man replied, "Andre,

and it's Payne, right? You've been an eternal thorn in my side," said Groh.

"That'll become a jagged splinter in your neck soon."

The sound of a single rifle shot blared out through the speaker. An explosion to the south followed a second later. "Your lifeline back to civilization just evaporated. With your plane gone, you're out here on my terms now."

Payne glanced at his surroundings. "All these crates of dynamite are going to create a helluva mess for your boss, not to mention sending an immense mushroom cloud up that'll be seen by every forest service lookout in the region. I think civilization isn't going to be that far off once I light things up here."

An older man's voice broke in. "What's your price, Payne?"

Reynolds mouthed the word *Klurman* while the others shot nervous glances at each other.

The mining tycoon continued, "You never turned in that girl's video, and you've been carefully eliminating my men, so who the hell are you working for—a competitor of mine—is that what this is: corporate espionage and a big payday for you?"

"This has nothing to do with business. It's personal. You crossed the line when you sent your misfits to my cabin to take out Micah, and you've put a lot of innocent people in the ground. In my experience, guys like you and your lap dog, Andre, need to be put down like rabid coyotes."

The hum of the plane's engine grew evident above the treetops. "Sounds like you've got it all figured out," said Klurman. "I'd just like to know one thing: who's the slowest runner in your group? I'm guessing it's that old fossil, Gus Freed."

Payne heard several thunks on the ground somewhere in the forest behind him. He hopped up on the trailer's wheel well, his eyes flaring as he stared at two bundles of dynamite, whose fuses were hissing to their conclusion.

"I can dig out of anything you throw my way," said Klurman. "You're a dead man, Payne. Nobody fucks with me."

Payne leaped down, waving at the others to run. The plane circled, and Payne heard two more thunks, with one landing close to the dynamite crates by the rock face.

"I think he just called your bluff," quipped Micah.

"No shit." They sprinted alongside each other, moving as fast as they could with Gus and Reynolds possessing matching hobbles, while Nolte brought up the rear. Behind him, Payne heard the three bound henchmen shouting for help.

"Go for those boulders ahead," yelled Reynolds.

The explosion hit Payne in the back like a bat, the dynamite detonating in a chain reaction that sent shockwaves rippling through the ground beneath their feet. He threw himself behind the granite boulder just as the campsite erupted, pulling Micah down beside him as rock shards and tree splinters whistled overhead.

A choking cloud of dust rolled over them, turning daytime to twilight for a few minutes. When the rumbling finally subsided and the debris stopped falling, Payne raised his head to survey the devastation—where the mining camp had stood moments before, only scattered craters and twisted metal remained, while body parts of Klurman's three henchmen decorated the surrounding trees like macabre ornaments.

Nolte shot Payne an angry glance. "You need to take a fucking communications class to learn how to talk to other people."

"Wouldn't have mattered a bit," said Reynolds. "I've seen what these guys can do—they're barbarians, and Klurman doesn't give a shit about his own people or anyone else in his blast radius."

Payne clicked on the radio, only to have the side of the device crumble in his grip from him landing on it.

"Once they land that bird, they'll be coming after us," said Gus, brushing the grit from his face.

"They were on the ground a while ago and are probably already on their way," said Payne as everyone began studying the surrounding forest.

# CHAPTER 43

"How do you know?" asked Nolte, inspecting his rifle.

"Because there's no way Groh or anyone else made a single shot from a plane while doing a pass above us," said Payne. "Plus, there wasn't any engine noise during our conversation. They were dropped off, eliminated Gus' Cessna from the shoreline; then the pilot headed this way, awaiting orders from Klurman."

Reynolds sat up, rubbing his ankle. "Our only chance for getting help now is to get to the fire-watch tower to the northwest. It's probably three miles from here."

"Cross-country—that'll be more like five miles," said Micah.

Payne pulled out the topo map from his BDU pocket and unfolded it, tracing his finger along the probable route as the others huddled around. "We can follow this stream for the first mile, then veer west, skirting around this swamp until we hit higher ground."

"And that spot?" asked Nolte.

Payne tapped his finger on the black X he'd made earlier with charcoal in Burke's yurt. "The source of everyone's problems, it seems. Jenkins' old cabin site and his supposed pot of lost gold."

"Damn, so close and yet so far," said Micah with an obvious grin.

Nolte tugged on the girl's sleeve. "Before you get any ideas about lost treasure, our only goal is to get to that tower and radio for help."

"I know. I know," she said in a deflated voice.

Payne consulted Zandri's map one final time, tracing their route with a grimy finger, while the others gathered what supplies they could salvage from the devastated camp.

"One mile as the crow flies to Zandri's camp. We'll rest there, then plot the remainder of the route to the fire tower," Payne announced, folding the map carefully. "But we're not crows, and this country's going to make us earn every step. Plus, we'll have hunters on our trail."

Reynolds leaned heavily on a makeshift walking stick Nolte had fashioned from a dead branch. The weeks of captivity had left the geologist severely weakened, and the adrenaline from their escape was already wearing off. Gus fared little better, his arthritic knees protesting with every uneven step as they left the relative safety of the boulder field.

"How long before they catch up?" Micah asked, glancing nervously back toward the smoking ruins of the mining camp.

"Depends on how fast we move," Payne replied grimly. "Groh knows these woods better than most, but this terrain will slow him down, too."

The first obstacle appeared within a few hundred yards —a sprawling wetland that wasn't on the old map, which stretched across their intended path like a moat. The bog was too wide to circumvent without adding mileage to their journey, so Payne clung to the margins until he located semi-solid ground that wouldn't swallow a person to their waist.

He slung his rifle and tested each step with a dead poplar sapling before committing his full weight, constantly aware that every minute spent here was time gained by their pursuers. Behind him, the others followed in single file, using his footprints as a guide through the maze of hummocks and hidden sinkholes. Twice Reynolds stumbled, saved only by Nolte's quick reflexes. The trooper's uniform was soon caked with mud and decorated with cattail fluff, transforming him from a law enforcement officer to a bog creature.

"This is worse than basic training," Gus muttered.

"Basic training didn't have professional killers breathing down your neck," Nolte replied through gritted teeth.

"Since you mentioned the military—I've been wondering: did you learn to fly in the Air Force?" asked Micah, who was behind Gus.

The older man scowled, turning towards her. "Are you kidding me right now? Did Payne tell you to ask that?"

"No, I figured since you had your own plane and just said you were in boot camp, you musta been in the Air Force."

"Do you see any golf clubs in my pack or mints in my pocket?" snapped Gus.

"Here we go," said Payne with a grin. "You just lit another fuse, Micah. Take cover."

"Sorry. It was an honest question," whispered Micah.

"I think it's time for some operational silence, young lady," said Gus as he came out on the other side of the marsh and offered her a hand.

Payne gestured to the dense alder thickets ahead. "Get ready for round two."

The young trees grew so tightly together that passage required constant ducking and weaving. The flexible branches slapped at their faces, while hidden roots and fallen logs created an obstacle course that punished every misstep. Micah proved most adept at this terrain, her slight frame allowing her to slip through gaps that forced the larger men to push their way through by brute force. But even her wilderness skills couldn't mask the sound of breaking branches and rustling vegetation that would clearly mark their passage for anyone skilled enough to follow.

Twenty minutes later they emerged from the alders, their faces laced with sweat and mud.

"Another half mile," Payne replied, matching the undulating terrain with his mental recollection. "According to the map, the creek by Jenkins' place runs through that depression below."

The descent into the creek bottom proved the most challenging section yet, made worse by the knowledge that they were leaving another obvious trail in the muddy slope. The incline was steep and slick, forcing them to help Reynolds, while Gus picked his way down, relying on root handholds protruding from the bank. Each step sent loose stones clattering into the ravine below, creating noise that would carry far in the still air, and more than once Payne had to grab Micah's arm to keep her from sliding past him on the muddy surface.

"They'll hear us coming from a mile away," Micah whispered as another cascade of rocks announced their presence.

"Can't be helped," Payne replied. "Speed matters more than stealth right now."

But their persistence was finally rewarded. At the bottom of the ravine, a tea-colored stream bubbled over smooth stones. Nearby, Payne spotted the old fire-blackened stumps that marked the site of Jenkins' long-lost homestead. Scattered among the larger stumps were the unmistakable remains of a stone fireplace, the geometric arrangement a stark contrast to the organic chaos of the surrounding forest.

"This is it," Payne said, consulting the map one final time while constantly scanning the ridgelines above for signs of pursuit. "Clyde Jenkins' cabin stood right here, probably seventy years ago."

As they caught their breath, Reynolds suddenly raised his head. "There." He pushed through the undergrowth and pumped a fist up in triumph. Hidden beneath a tarp weighted down with stones was Zandri's cache of equipment: a folding shovel, metal detector, pick-ax, sample bags, and other excavation tools. Reynolds gazed skyward. "Damn shame, Ian. Sure wish life had turned out differently, old friend."

The pungent aroma in the air was overwhelming, and Micah pushed past Reynolds, zigzagging back and forth. "It smells just like the professor did that night at the campground. The gold jugs must be hidden in the ground around here."

The irony wasn't lost on Payne—after everything they'd endured to solve a seventy-year-old mystery that had claimed so many lives, the real treasure would have to be simply walking away alive before Groh could get them in his crosshairs.

# CHAPTER 44

Payne studied his GPS unit, then the topo map. He glanced back at Reynolds. "We've got two more miles, but it should be a little more flat than what we just did. You gonna be able to make it?"

The man held out his hand, asking for a lift up, and Payne hoisted the geologist to his feet. "Got any more Snickers bars?"

"Micah," said Payne.

She was on her knees, glancing through Zandri's tools. She paused and removed a half-eaten bar from her pocket and tossed it to Reynolds.

"We need to push on," said Nolte, kneeling beside Gus as they both scanned the trees to the east.

Payne pulled out his 1911 pistol and handed it to Reynolds. "It's cocked and locked, and I'm hoping you're no stranger to firearms."

"Got one just like it, but it's a twelve-hundred-dollar Kimber that I wouldn't dare bring out here."

Payne chuckled. "A safe queen—sounds like a Kimber." He moved past the geologist and tugged on Micah's jacket.

"If the treasure is out here, it'll still be there after this ordeal is all over, but that's only going to happen if we get to that tower."

She frowned, setting down the folding shovel. "This is tormenting."

"So is trying to pry a bullet out of your leg or gut."

"Yeah, no thanks."

———

PAYNE DIRECTED the group to their new route and led the way. Twenty minutes of slogging through the brush and muddy ground had already exhausted Reynolds, and he simply plunked down on a stump and hung his head low. "Go on. I'll hang out here. You're almost to the tower."

"Not a chance. If Groh doesn't get you, then some bear probably will," said Gus, pointing to fresh ursid tracks in the mud.

"No one could ever accuse you of being unconvincing," said Reynolds with an anemic chuckle.

A few dozen chickadees alighted from the trees to the east, and Payne and Gus swung around, staring at the forested ridgeline. Payne silently cursed, realizing he and his group were situated in a bowl-shaped depression about two hundred yards across and thick with vegetation and fallen trees—the perfect shooting gallery, and his enemies had the high ground.

The first rifle shot cracked through the air like thunder, bark exploding from a pine tree inches from Gus' head. He dove behind a moss-covered boulder as the echo rolled over the forest.

"Contact left!" Nolte shouted, his voice carrying across the scattered team. The lieutenant had taken cover behind a fallen spruce thirty feet away, his AR-15 already tracking a figure in the tree line.

Payne pressed his back against a granite slab, while Micah and Reynolds took cover on the other side of a large fallen tree.

Payne glimpsed movement—a figure in woodland camo sliding between the massive trunks like a ghost—the same figure he'd seen in Micah's video. Andre Groh moved with the fluid precision of someone who'd spent a lifetime hunting both animals and men.

"I count at least four shooters," Gus called out from his position near Reynolds and Micah, who had all taken cover behind the remnants of a large fallen log. The girl clutched her bear spray like a talisman; Gus flipped off the safety on his Winchester M70 hunting rifle while perpetually scanning the forest; Reynolds gripped the 1911, his hands trembling.

Another shot punched through the air, this one from a different angle. The bullet whined off the rocks near the geologist, sending stone chips flying. Klurman's team was spreading out, trying to establish a crossfire that would pin them down.

"They're trying to box us in," Payne muttered, studying the tactical situation. The killers held the high ground on three sides.

Payne spotted a muzzle flash from the ridge to his right. He adjusted his aim, leading the target slightly, and squeezed the trigger. The heavy rifle bucked against his shoulder, the .375 round designed for stopping charging grizzlies.

A scream echoed from the woods, followed by crashing vegetation as someone fell.

"One down," he called to Nolte.

A second later, another shot thundered out, and Payne heard someone shriek in the brush to his right.

"He's hit—someone help—TJ's hit in the neck," shouted Micah.

There was no way Payne could close the short distance without being exposed. "You remember your wilderness first-responder training you mentioned—apply pressure to the wound."

"Okay, okay," she said.

Payne was about to offer further advice when he caught a sliver of movement in the trees thirty yards behind Micah's position. He steadied his Ruger and waited. A flicker of leaves followed by a brief shadow. Payne fired.

A short guy in a green boonie hat collapsed to his knees and fell on his side, the hole in his abdomen leaking onto the ferns.

Nolte had worked his way to a better position, using the thick undergrowth for concealment. The trooper's tactical experience showed as he moved in short bounds, never exposing himself for more than a few seconds. Eventually, he hunkered down near Gus, both men scrunched near a cluster of car-sized boulders with their rifles fixed on the ridgeline.

A second later, the forest erupted in gunfire. Muzzle flashes strobed between the trees as Klurman's remaining men opened up with automatic weapons, the distinctive chatter of an AK-47 mixing with the deeper boom of hunting rifles. Bullets shredded bark and sent pinecones raining down like hail.

Payne crawled to his right, using a depression in the ground for cover. His knees scraped against granite and pine needles as he worked toward a flanking position. The familiar weight of the rifle in his hands brought back muscle memory from a dozen firefights in places whose names never made the evening news.

From his new position, he could see a guy with a prom-inent neck scar who'd just crouched behind a wind-felled tree forty feet away. The younger man sprayed rounds wildly, more concerned with volume of fire than accuracy.

Once he heard the man's weapon run dry, Payne leaned out, centering the crosshairs on the guy's center mass, and fired. The bullet struck just below the sternum, the impact spinning the shooter around before he crumpled behind the fallen tree.

"That's three," Gus called out, his voice carrying a note of grim satisfaction.

But the celebration was premature. Payne heard the unpleasant sound of a muffled thump from the ridge overlooking their position and could tell it was a suppressed weapon not an AK.

Either Groh or Klurman was closing in.

———

Sean Klurman had claimed the high ground, his German-made hunting rifle tracking their defensive line. The Blaser R8 Ultimate X rifle with integrated suppressor was his preferred tool for dispatching wildlife and, along with the Swarovski scope, had cost more than his employees earned in three months. The mining executive moved with the confidence of a man who'd stalked dangerous game on five continents, the custom weapon an extension of his predatory will.

He scanned the woods below for signs of the girl and Payne. He would end them both slowly with strafing shots to their extremities until they were in so much agony they begged for him to finish the job.

Klurman heard groaning forty yards ahead and figured it was Reynolds. He took a snaky route through the undergrowth, crouching and scanning until he finally saw the geologist—and the teenage girl beside him.

He squatted next to a charred stump, settling his sights on

the girl's right knee. But before he could shoot, he scanned the forest one more time for other threats, knowing his location was about to be revealed once he delivered the crippling shot.

———

GUS ABANDONED his position to help Micah with the geologist. TJ was conscious but bleeding heavily, his left arm hanging useless at his side. The bullet had shattered the clavicle and torn through the trapezius.

"Just a graze," TJ sputtered through gritted teeth, but his face was pale from shock and blood loss.

"Sure—sure it is," Micah said, pressing her jacket against the wound.

Twenty yards away, Nolte whistled in Payne's direction, then pointed to the northeast.

Payne scanned the terrain, finally picking out the lone gunman positioning himself for a shot.

*Klurman!*

Once the mining executive shifted position, Payne lost his opportunity. Using hand signals, he motioned to Nolte to take the shot while he flushed the man out. The trooper got into a crossed-ankle sitting position and rested the AR's barrel on his crooked left arm, which was supported on his upright knee.

The fact that Nolte easily slid into such an advanced shooting position confirmed what Payne had hoped about the man's rifle abilities. At least he hoped the trooper was as skilled as he seemed.

Once Nolte was ready, Payne leaned out and sent a round into Klurman's last known location. The bark shattered, causing Klurman to scurry to the left.

Payne heard Nolte's rifle bark out two rounds. Klurman

staggered to his feet, clutching his throat as crimson streaked onto his hands. Nolte sent another shot into the man's head, dropping him.

———

FROM FORTY YARDS AWAY, hidden behind a massive cedar, Groh could see the cluster of targets near a large fallen log. The girl and Gus Freed were completely focused on the wounded man. It would be like shooting fish in a barrel. Now he just had to steel his nerves after seeing Klurman's bullet-riddled body go down.

He realized the operation was over. Klurman was gone and his plans laid to waste. For a moment, Groh debated leaving altogether, but not before spilling the blood of Freed and Payne.

He brought his Weatherby rifle to his shoulder, the crosshairs settling on Gus' back. His finger found the trigger, taking up the slack with professional precision.

———

THE SHOT THAT SAVED GUS' life came from Payne's rifle, the bullet missing Groh's head by less than an inch. Bark exploded from the cedar as the poacher threw himself sideways, his own shot going wild into the canopy above.

"Groh's flanking!" Payne called out, already working the bolt of his rifle. "Forty yards, behind the big cedar."

"Klurman's down," Nolte shouted, intending to demoralize any remaining thugs.

The sudden silence that followed was deafening. No more bullets whined through the air. Even the forest seemed to hold its breath, waiting to see what would happen next.

But Andre Groh was still out there. The master poacher

had lost his patron and most of his team, but he remained the most dangerous predator in these woods.

# CHAPTER 45

Payne kept his rifle trained on the tree line where Groh had vanished, every sense straining for signs of the poacher's return. The forest had gone silent except for Reynolds' labored breathing and the distant sound of ravens cawing in the direction the poacher had run.

"How bad is it?" Payne called to Gus, not taking his eyes off the woods.

"Bullet went clean through," he replied. "Mangled the clavicle and maybe even the scapula on the way out."

Micah had removed the med kit from her pack and was applying a thick gauze compress to his wounds.

Nolte worked his way back from Klurman's location, returning with the man's pricey rifle and a big-bore revolver in a hip holster. "Now what?" he asked, looking at Payne. "If we head to that fire tower, Groh's just going to drop us one at a time."

"We can't stay here either for the same reason. He's repositioning himself and maybe waiting for reinforcements. We need to draw him out."

———

From Groh's perspective, hidden behind a wall of interlocking spruce branches, the tactical situation had become desperate but not hopeless. Klurman was dead, his remaining men were scattered or eliminated, and his main exfil route was cut off. He was sure Klurman's pilot had heard the ruckus on the comms and taken off. But Andre Groh had survived worse odds during his years as a fugitive and could live out here indefinitely if necessary.

The wounded geologist represented both an opportunity and a problem. Groh's enemies were pinned down by their need to care for him, but they were also more alert and defensive than before, and in a dense depression that would make target selection a challenge. Groh would have to wait for the right moment to strike.

Through a gap in the vegetation, he caught sight of Payne for a brief second but couldn't set up for a shot. *I'm going to take the top of your head clean off, you piece of shit.*

Groh shifted position, crouch-walking towards the cusp of a grassy field that stretched between two clusters of spruce forest. It was only a thirty-yard expanse, but it would be risky to cross. Once on the other side, he'd have a better sight line of the group, and then all it would take was patience to drop them, one by one.

———

Payne had positioned himself where he could cover multiple angles, and constantly shifted between the jutting rocks.

"TJ, stay with me. Focus on your little boy," Micah whispered, her compassionate voice carrying across the clearing.

The geologist's face was growing paler by the minute, his breathing shallow and rapid.

Nolte was behind the boulders again, his rifle covering the approaches from the north and east. He removed the two-way radio he'd retrieved off Klurman and handed it to Gus. "Play with the frequencies and see if you can pick up a signal from that fire tower. We need to call for a medevac."

The former conservation officer ducked lower beneath the rocks and got busy.

———

GROH WORKED his way along the open meadow, matching his movements to the wind to make it look like the grassy tops were being blown around. If he was spotted now, it was all over. Payne or Nolte would end him with one clean shot. He felt the familiar rush of adrenaline coursing through his veins. This was what he'd been born for—the hunt, the kill, the survival of the fittest played out in nature's most unforgiving arena.

He kept low and belly-crawled through the tall grass until he reached the forest on the other side. He crouched beside a stump and positioned his Weatherby's scope on the area he'd last seen Freed.

The master poacher had anticipated the move, figuring someone would go for the radios on the dead men, and he'd just caught a glimpse of the trooper handing Freed a radio.

Groh shifted position again, working his way to an angle where he could better intercept Freed before the man could call for reinforcements.

Now, he just had to wait for the old-timer to get sloppy. Then he saw Nolte's elbow stick out briefly from the rocks a few feet over from Gus, giving Groh another idea.

———

PAYNE CAUGHT the movement in his peripheral vision—a shadow that seemed slightly out of place among the natural patterns of the forest. His rifle swung toward the disturbance, crosshairs seeking the elusive target, but he heard a shot ring out from an unexpected direction, sending a ricochet off the boulders near Nolte.

"Contact rear," Payne shouted, spinning to engage the new threat.

*Shit, Groh somehow managed to crawl over a clearing to the left.* Payne had underestimated the man, figuring he'd never take such a risk along exposed ground, but now the poacher had a better shooting lane. His second bullet struck the ground near Nolte's boots, kicking up dirt and pine needles in a shower of debris.

But Groh was already moving, using the massive trees for cover as he repositioned for another shot. The poacher's rifle cracked again, this time targeting Gus' position. The bullet struck the boulders with enough force to send splinters flying, forcing the old man to scrunch back further.

Payne had pegged Groh's general location along a thirty-foot length of forest up top, but he couldn't get a fix on the hunter. *That's why he didn't attack us at Jenkins' old cabin—he wanted us in this kill box. Hell, even without his buddies, he'll win this little war of attrition.*

Payne found himself fighting a two-front battle, trying to protect the others while engaging an enemy who seemed to materialize and vanish like smoke. Every time he thought he had Groh pinned down, the poacher would appear from a completely different angle. Payne had only witnessed this type of guerrilla-warfare skill in seasoned fighters in Afghanistan who knew their region intimately from a lifetime of combat.

"He's using our own cover against us," Nolte called out

between shots; his face was now peppered with tiny lacerations from the rock shards.

The lieutenant was right. Groh was moving through the forest with ease and would just keep sniping and relocating until they were picked apart, he managed a deadly ricochet, or he ran out of ammo. And Payne figured the poacher was experienced enough to avoid the latter.

Gus finally tuned the radio, making contact with a voice from the outside world, but Payne wondered how much time they had left.

*I need to take the fight to Groh before it's too late.*

———

GROH WAS DOWN to his last twelve rounds and couldn't risk expending all his ammo hoping to get a glancing shot off the rocks by Freed and Nolte. But he still had one more card to play. He leaned back, removing a flash-bang he'd brought from Klurman's arsenal. The device would cloak his approach and give him the opening he needed for the killing shots.

He crouch-walked through the brush until he was close enough, then pulled the pin and counted off the seconds, his internal clock marking the fuse's burn. He lobbed the projectile toward the cluster of defenders, the metal sphere arcing through the air and clanking on the rocks by Payne's location.

———

"GRENADE—TAKE COVER," Payne shouted, scrunching into a ball next to the boulders.

The explosion shattered the forest silence. The concussive wave rolled across the clearing, stunning everyone within its radius.

Payne knew the poacher would be storming them and having his pick of stunned targets on the ground. The boulders had absorbed much of the force, but his ears were still ringing, and his vision was slightly blurry.

He peered out from the side, keeping his head in the ferns. With the smoke clearing, he saw Groh striding down the slope with his rifle fixed on Gus' position.

Even dazed, Payne pushed himself to his feet with his rifle leveled ahead as he blinked hard. His iron sights found Groh's center mass just as the poacher pivoted towards Payne, lining up his own shot. For a moment their eyes met across the battlefield, predator recognizing predator.

Both rifles fired, but Payne's shot was a microsecond ahead, catching the poacher in the shoulder and spinning him around. Groh's bullet missed by inches, chipping bark from the tree behind Payne's head.

Blood blossomed across Groh's camouflage jacket as he stumbled backward, his rifle falling into one hand.

Andre Groh shrieked and darted behind a large tree, melting back into the forest.

Payne staggered forward, his head still aching from the flash bang. He saw Groh darting between the shadows in the direction of the ridge.

"You hit?" asked Gus.

"No, just have scrambled brains," Payne said, dropping back to a crouch behind the rocks.

"You and me both," said Nolte.

"Did you get Groh?" asked Micah.

"No, but his arm sprang a leak, and he won't get far."

"We need to go after him and finish the damn job," said Gus, struggling to stand as his knees wobbled.

"Not we—you and Nolte need to get to that lookout tower. I'll take care of Groh."

"I already got through on the radio. The dispatcher said a helo can be here in an hour," said Gus.

"We'll need to move to a clearing—no way a bird can get down here," said Nolte.

"We can head to that large meadow back by the alder thickets," said Micah.

Payne grabbed Klurman's scoped rifle off the ground and handed Nolte the Ruger. "I'll see you all back at the lakeshore, hopefully by nightfall."

The trooper stood. "That's not smart, Payne. Wounded animals are dangerous as hell, and Groh knows these forests."

Payne studied the tree line where the poacher had vanished. "He's hurt and alone. This might be our only chance to end this. If he gets away, then all of us will be looking over our shoulders for years to come, and that's no way to live, trust me."

Micah finished lashing a makeshift sling around Reynolds' arm and glanced up at Payne. "Be careful."

Payne nodded, understanding the stakes. He dropped out the magazine on Klurman's rifle and noted seven .308 rounds, then reinserted it. Payne knew the German-made weapon was a lower caliber than the Ruger, but he needed something with optics so he could drop Groh at long range rather than risk another bad-breath encounter that had almost cost him dearly.

He did a partial chamber check on the weapon, seeing the .308 brass, and then headed towards the trail of blood waiting for him.

# CHAPTER 46

Payne knelt beside the large spruce, studying the crimson droplets scattered across the ferns like rubies against green felt. The pattern told a story—Groh was moving fast, favoring his left side where the bullet had torn through muscle and sinew.

*He's operating on adrenaline and sheer willpower to fight through that kind of pain. But how long will it last?*

The blood trail led northwest, farther from Pickerel Lake and the fire tower. Payne followed at a measured pace, reading the sign written in mud and broken vegetation. Groh was heading for higher ground, probably seeking a defensive position where he could use his knowledge of the terrain to maximum advantage so he could tend to his wound.

After two hundred yards, the blood drops became less frequent. Groh was either binding his arm, or the bleeding was slowing naturally. Either way, it meant the poacher would be harder to track.

The forest here was old growth, massive spruces and firs reaching toward a canopy so thick it blocked most of the sky. Undergrowth was sparse but treacherous—fallen logs created natural obstacles while hidden roots waited to trip the unwary. Payne had to remind himself that this was Groh's element—the wilderness that had sheltered him for fifteen years.

Payne moved with the patient precision of someone who'd learned tracking in places where mistakes meant death. Every footprint, every disturbed leaf, every broken twig told part of the story or shortened your own, if you were clumsy. The poacher was moving with purpose, not random flight. He had a destination in mind.

A mile in, the blood trail disappeared entirely. Groh had found time to properly dress his wound, or had reached terrain where tracking became exponentially more difficult.

Payne paused beside a massive cedar, studying the ground for any sign of his quarry. The forest was silent except for the whisper of wind through branches high overhead. The fact that no birds or squirrels were chattering was another indication that someone or something had just passed this way. In this unnatural quiet, every sound would carry, making stealth both more important and more difficult.

Payne closed his eyes, listening to the woods with senses honed by years of hunting human predators in the mountains of Afghanistan and the deserts of Africa.

Somewhere ahead, Andre Groh was doing the same thing —listening, waiting, and planning his next move.

———

FROM HIS POSITION among the fallen logs, Groh pressed his back against the rough bark and tried to ignore the fire spreading through his shoulder. The bullet had torn through the middle deltoid and scraped bone, leaving his left arm nearly useless and his rifle grip unsteady. Each heartbeat sent fresh waves of agony radiating throughout his body, but he'd learned to compartmentalize pain during his years in the wilderness.

Blood had soaked through his makeshift bandage, and he could feel his strength ebbing with each passing minute. He reached into one of the many internal pockets of his jacket and removed a small med kit. He tore it open with his teeth, then pulled out the QuikClot package and applied the combat gauze, which immediately helped stem the bleeding. Groh wrapped an oversized bandanna around his shoulder, wincing with each pass as it pressed against the clotting gauze. When he was done, he popped two Vicodin along with two caffeine pills. It took a few minutes to slide his shirt and jacket back on; then he rested his head back against the tree and tried to slow his breathing.

Through the maze of deadfall, he strained every sense for signs of Payne's approach. He knew the man was out there somewhere, moving through the forest with the patient precision of a professional killer. Groh had faced game wardens, rival poachers, and desperate men protecting their territory, but this was different. Payne hunted with the cold efficiency of someone who'd learned to kill others without flinching.

Groh thought about his next move. Hours ago, he'd never figured he'd need an evasion plan. And now there was no wealthy benefactor who'd cover for him or get him out of the country.

*Though I have enough dirt on the governor that he wouldn't turn a blind eye.*

He sighed, remembering Cartwright's recording, which was probably in Nolte's inbox by now.

*Fuck!*

He ran through the mental map in his head, knowing there was the small town of Skwentna to the south—if the census-designated place of sixty-two people could be called a town. It was twenty-five miles or so, but it was mainly forest and lakes in that direction, so he wouldn't have countless swamps to traverse. And there was an abandoned logging village at the halfway point that he could hole up in for a while.

*I could take a few weeks to get there. By then the search parties would have died down.*

He felt the Vicodin kicking in and knew he'd have to make wound-care management his top priority if he was to avoid infection, being in the bush for so long.

The terrible irony wasn't lost on him—these woods that had sheltered him for years during his youth now felt like a prison. Every tree seemed to lean inward, every shadow harbored potential threats, and every sound might herald Payne's arrival.

He made the decision to push south towards Skwentna. But first he had to survive the next few hours and take out the predator he was sure was on his trail.

———

PAYNE PAUSED at the edge of the forest, glancing across the small meadow that sloped up to a tangle of old-growth trees where he figured Groh was holed up. It was a dense island of spruce trees covering around thirty acres of land and was in line with the poacher's previous direction of travel. It was also the best cover out here for miles, so he figured the man was there managing his wound and figuring out his next move.

*But what's his plan? If he heads west, he'll be trekking into millions of acres of wilderness…which he could certainly handle long term, but he would be the subject of a massive manhunt and now, compared with fifteen years ago, there are drones, thermals, and satellite. Plus, he's not going to want to return to being a hermit again. He must have an exit plan out of this state and country.*

Payne glanced at the snowcapped peak to the north. *If he pushes that way, he'll run into higher elevation around Denali.*

He examined the topography to the left, where there were flat meadows interspersed with dense patches of birch and alder and the occasional pond. The route to the south would be the most calorie-efficient and quickest path to take, and eventually he'd end up hitting a logging road.

Payne scrutinized the patches of birch trees to the south, picking out a liver-shaped section about thirty acres in size peppered with young birch trees that would provide an ideal spot for setting up his own sniper hide. He reckoned it was a half mile away from the spruce forest where he figured Groh was hiding.

Payne had the tactical advantage of having an unbroken line of woods to his immediate left that he could skirt along for much of the way. He'd have to be trotting to get ahead of Groh. Then he'd have to sprint a few hundred yards across an open field to get to the birch stand, at which time he'd be totally exposed.

*But there's no alternative. If I keep pursuing him directly, he'll set up a shooting lane in a chokepoint and snipe my ass.*

Payne reached down, grabbing some mud and applying streaks across his face and neck. Then he returned to scanning the perimeter of the forest ahead one more time with his rifle scope. Once he was satisfied Groh wasn't backtracking, he moved up and began his slow crouch-run through the woods, pausing every few minutes to gaze at his surroundings.

He forced himself to maintain a medium pace to avoid stepping on a branch or busting an ankle in a marmot hole. Fifteen minutes of slow movement and he paused, kneeling beside a large stump coated with moss.

He got his first confirmation that his theory on Groh's

direction of travel was accurate a second later when he saw a lone coyote working the tree line near the island of spruce. The animal was nearly a quarter mile away and hugging the forest.

Through his rifle scope on the Blaser rifle, he watched the canid loping along, intermittently pausing to investigate a clump of shrubs or a hole in the ground. A minute later, it froze, staring directly into the forest. Then it frantically smelled the air while bobbing its head for a few seconds. Suddenly, it backed up and bounded back the way it had come.

*There's either a bear, some wolves, or a two-legged predator in those woods.* He ruled out a bear since he'd heard those leviathans crunching through the forest before, and this creature didn't have the telltale signs.

*And if it were wolves, they would probably have gone after that coyote already.*

Payne resumed moving forward, descending a slight drop in terrain and arriving at the crossing point to the patch of birch trees directly across the grassy slope.

Again, he glassed the route he figured Groh would be heading. Payne knew he'd only have a slight lead over the poacher and had to move fast to get into an ambush position. He sprinted across the grassy expanse, his legs and lungs burning as he raced to close the distance. Arriving at the edge of the birch forest, he slid to a halt before a tangle of raspberry briars, then crept low around the other side, coming to rest beside a car-sized rock.

Somewhere in the distance, a branch snapped, so faint it might have been his imagination. Payne's eyes fixed on the area ahead, the rifle coming up as he scanned the shadows between the trees. Nothing moved, but the sound had come from the northeast, maybe three hundred yards away.

He listened and watched. The sun hung low in the sky,

and there were only a few hours of daylight left. Thunder rumbled overhead, and the first fat raindrops began pattering through the canopy. Within minutes, what had been a light sprinkle became a steady drizzle, then a downpour that turned the forest floor into a maze of puddles and streams.

The rain was both a blessing and a curse. It would mask sound, allowing him to move faster, but it would do the same for Groh. Worse, it would wash away any remaining traces of the poacher's passage.

He pulled his jacket hood up, immediately regretting the decision as raindrops drummed against the nylon fabric. The sound was now advertising his position. He quickly tore it off and turned the jacket inside out, letting the fleece lining absorb the water silently. It was a small thing, but in a game where details meant the difference between life and death, every advantage mattered.

The rain intensified, turning the forest into a gray-green maze where visibility dropped to mere yards. Payne moved through this aquatic twilight, every sense straining for signs of his quarry. Water dripped from birch leaves with the steady rhythm of a metronome, masking smaller sounds.

Through the curtain of rain, he caught a glimpse of movement—or thought he did. A shadow that seemed slightly out of place among the natural patterns of the spruce forest ahead. Payne froze, studying the area through his rifle scope, but saw only trees and falling water.

He pressed on, the hours stretching like days, and each movement an eternity of careful stalking and constant vigilance. His legs ached from constant tension, and his shoulders burned from keeping the rifle at a ready position.

It was early evening when he stopped to rest and reapply some mud streaks to his face. That was when he heard a crow cawing somewhere ahead, the harsh sound cutting through the steady patter of rain. It was a scolding cry, and one he recognized from his youth hunting deer when the black birds objected to his presence.

Payne moved toward the sound, using a formerly dry wash that was now a small streambed. The bottom provided stable footing while the banks offered concealment.

The streambed curved left, then right, winding through the forest like a natural highway. Payne followed its course for several hundred yards before the corvid alarm call grew loud enough to pinpoint the source. Whatever had upset the black bird was just ahead, beyond a bend in the waterway.

He left the streambed and worked his way up the bank, using a fallen log for cover as he studied the terrain ahead. Through the rain, he could make out a small clearing where lightning or disease had felled several ancient trees. The crow perched in the surrounding canopy, its black eyes fixed on something at ground level.

Movement. A flash of blood-soaked fabric barely visible through the maze of fallen timber. Groh had holed up in the deadfall, using the tangled logs for both cover and conceal-ment. It was a perfect sniper's nest, with clear fields of fire in multiple directions.

Payne studied the position through his scope, looking for weak points in the poacher's defensive setup. Groh had chosen well—the fallen trees created a natural fortress with numerous escape routes. But they also limited his mobility, and the position had one fatal flaw.

The poacher was so focused on the approaches from the south and east that he'd left his western flank partially exposed. It wasn't much—maybe a foot-wide gap between two logs—but it was enough for a skilled marksman at the right angle.

Payne began his approach, moving through the alders and birch. Every step was executed with infinite care, his boots finding solid ground while avoiding the debris that might betray his presence.

The gap between hunter and prey closed agonizingly slowly as the sun hung low in the west. A quarter mile eventually shrank to the length of a football field. Then a hundred yards became eighty, then fifty. Payne could see Groh's position clearly now, the poacher's rifle trained on the eastern approach route.

Forty yards. Close enough to see the breeze flapping Groh's sleeve. The poacher shifted slightly, and Payne glimpsed his bearded profile through the scope. The crosshairs settled on center mass, but something made Payne hesitate.

For the first time in years, he wondered if execution was the only outcome. He wasn't on an assignment overseas for the agency. Was shooting Groh truly the best way to serve all the victims and their families? What if he returned to the shores of Pickerel Lake with Groh's wrists bound and turned him over to Nolte? Groh would have to answer for his crimes. Maybe a bullet was the easy way out for the killer.

But an image crystallized in Payne's mind with unwelcome clarity: within hours, the media and podcasters would transform Groh from a dangerous poacher into a backcountry rebel whose youth had been spent being persecuted and later becoming a victim of Klurman's manipulation and corporate greed. Social media would explode with #JusticeForGroh hashtags while Gus, Nolte, and Micah had their faces painted over the internet for years to come. And during his twenty-five-to-life sentence, Groh would be interviewed by countless reporters and biographers wanting to know more about the skilled woodsman who had bucked the system for so long, while becoming a folk hero to poachers and anti-environmentalists.

Payne centered the crosshairs and squeezed the trigger.

# CHAPTER 47

The morning sun cast long shadows across Pickerel Lake as Micah sat on a driftwood log, watching the controlled chaos of the incident command post taking shape along the shoreline. Alaska State Troopers from outlying posts down the peninsula had been arriving at the landing zone, where helicopters had been shuttling personnel and equipment since dawn.

The quiet wilderness that had witnessed so much violence over the past twenty-four hours now buzzed with the efficient activity of law enforcement processing what Lieutenant Nolte kept calling "one of the largest crime scenes in Alaska state history."

Micah pulled her borrowed jacket tighter against the morning chill, her eyes constantly drifting in the direction where Payne had disappeared into the forest, pursuing Andre Groh. Every minute that ticked by made his survival seem less likely. She'd barely slept, startling awake every time the wind shifted or a branch creaked, hoping to hear his voice calling from the woods.

"Coffee?" Gus offered, extending a steaming cup he'd

obtained from the mobile command unit they'd airlifted in at first light.

"Thanks." Micah accepted the cup gratefully, wrapping her fingers around the warm ceramic. The coffee was bitter and strong, but it helped chase away some of the coldness that had settled in her hands.

Lieutenant Nolte approached from the communications trailer, his face grim despite the tactical victory they'd achieved. Three separate forensics teams were working the decimated mining site where Reynolds had been held captive, documenting evidence that would ensure convictions for anyone connected to Klurman's operation who might still be alive. The mining executive's body had been recovered along with those of his hired killers, and Reynolds had been flown to the Anchorage hospital the previous evening, where he was reunited with his family.

"Any word from the docs about TJ?" Micah asked, though she could read the concern in Nolte's expression.

"He's stable. The bullet missed the major arteries. Poor bastard's been through hell, but he'll live to testify against anyone else connected to this operation." Nolte patted the iPhone in his vest. "Which it sounds like involves Governor Slattery, who, along with Klurman, was behind Detective Cartwright's death."

"Sorry to hear that," said Micah. "I didn't really like her, but she deserved better."

Gus patted her on the shoulder. "On the bright side, Reynolds is alive because of you. If you hadn't been able to take care of him while the rest of us were busy with those shooters, he never would have made it. You're a hero."

Micah lowered her eyes. "Thanks, but not so sure about that."

"Take the compliment, kid," said Nolte. "Especially since it's true. You did great."

She held her head up and smiled, unused to standing in the spotlight of approval but surprised by how much she didn't want it to end.

Gus sat on a folding chair, rubbing his left knee. The old conservation officer had refused medical evacuation, insisting his injuries predated recent events and that he needed to see this investigation through to the end.

"What about Jimmy Dean?" Micah asked. "When will he be released?"

"Process is already started. With Klurman dead and the real killers identified, the charges against him will be dropped within forty-eight hours."

The activity around the command post continued as the morning progressed. Crime scene photographers documented every angle of the mining site while another team took pictures where the firefight had taken place south of the fire tower. The sound of generators hummed along the shoreline, powering the equipment needed to process such a complex scene.

Near the forest's edge, coroners were preparing the bodies of Klurman's men for transport. As they loaded one of the corpses onto a gurney, the dead man's arm fell out, revealing his wrist. Micah's attention was caught by something dark against the pale skin.

"Wait," she called out, approaching the gurney. "Can I see his right arm?"

The coroner looked at Nolte, who nodded. The man pulled back the sleeve fully, revealing a small tattoo—a crucifix with its side arms angled downward instead of horizontal.

"I've seen this before," Micah said, her voice growing excited. "When I visited Jimmy Dean in the hospital, he told me about the woman who drugged him at the bar. He said she had a tiny tattoo just like this."

Gus had moved closer, studying the unusual crucifix with a frown. His weathered face suddenly went pale. "Son of a bitch," he muttered. "That's a Russian Orthodox cross. Old style, from the communities that came over in the early 1900s. Yancey Groh had one."

"What of it?" Nolte asked, moving to examine the other bodies.

The older man's eyes lowered. "Jasmine has one, too. Said she got it when she was growing up in the Russian Orthodox community near Razdolna, east of Homer. Always said it reminded her of her grandmother."

Micah felt her stomach drop as the pieces fell into place. "She knew I was at Payne's cabin that first night."

Gus glanced at them. "And she also knew I was flying you and Payne out to look for your missing phone with the video footage."

Nolte's face hardened. "Her part-time cleaning business. She mentioned once that she handled houses all over the area, including some of the old-timers who lived off the grid, and even serviced my post. She probably bugged the place and put the tracker on Payne's vehicle that he told me about."

"Stanley Hirovicz," Gus said grimly. "She's been cleaning his place for years. The old man trusted her completely. She probably overheard everything about the gold legend and Zandri's research." His hand clenched into a fist. "She was in the perfect position to feed intel to Klurman about everyone involved."

"That's how they knew about Zandri's trips to Pickerel Lake, about Reynolds being hired by the Jenkins family, about everything," Micah said, anger building in her chest. The woman had seemed so harmless and concerned about her welfare. But she'd been playing them all along, providing information to the people who butchered her friends.

Nolte was already moving toward the communications

trailer, keying his radio. "Dispatch, I need some troopers sent to Wolf Lake Lodge immediately to arrest Jasmine Cook on charges of conspiracy to commit murder and accessory to kidnapping. Consider her armed and dangerous." He set down his radio, glancing back at Gus with a sympathetic look on his face.

––––––

As THE HOURS passed without any sign of Payne, the mood grew increasingly somber. Radio checks every thirty minutes had yielded nothing but the usual check-ins, and ground search teams were beginning to return to the incident command post.

Nolte walked up beside Micah again as noon approached. "We need to talk about the possibility that Payne might not be coming back."

She had been dreading this conversation. "He's alive. I know he is."

"Andre Groh survived in these woods for years. He knows every tree, every hiding spot, every advantage the terrain can provide. Even wounded, he's incredibly dangerous."

"So is Payne." But even as she said it, Micah felt doubt creeping in. Groh was fighting on his home turf, and life had taught her long ago that it was far from fair. Sometimes evil prevailed.

"How long do we wait?" she asked.

"Until dark. Then I'll have to pull back the remaining search teams until sunrise."

Micah stared at the tree line, willing Payne to emerge from the shadows. He'd saved her life multiple times, protected her when she had nowhere else to turn, believed in her when everyone else saw only a troublesome runaway. The idea that he might be lying dead somewhere in those woods, another victim of the violence that had consumed so many innocent people, made her chest tighten with an emotion she couldn't contain.

"There," Gus called from the steps of the communications trailer, pointing toward the northern edge of the clearing. "Movement in the trees."

Every head turned toward the forest. For a moment, Micah saw nothing but swaying branches. Then a figure emerged from the undergrowth, moving with the tired gait of someone who'd traveled far.

Payne.

His face was streaked with mud and dried blood, his clothes torn from pushing through dense underbrush. Dark circles under his eyes spoke of a sleepless night in the wilderness, but he was alive. More importantly, he carried his rifle in a relaxed position rather than at the ready.

Micah was moving before she realized it, her legs carrying her across the uneven ground toward the man who'd become the closest thing to family she'd ever known besides April. When she reached Payne, she threw her arms around him in a fierce hug.

"Easy, kid," Payne said softly, his voice hoarse with exhaustion. "I'm sore as hell in places I didn't even know I could be sore."

"I thought—" She pulled back to look at his face, reassuring herself that he was real. "I thought that bastard might have gotten you."

"It was close," Payne admitted, his eyes finding Nolte, who was approaching with several other troopers. "But it's over. Groh's dead."

Nolte extended his hand, and Payne shook it firmly. "Where's the body?"

Payne pulled a GPS unit from his jacket pocket, reading

off coordinates, which the other troopers began plotting on their own devices. "About five miles northeast of here. He made his last stand in a deadfall clearing near Raven Creek."

As the activity around them resumed with renewed purpose, Micah found herself staying close to Payne's side. The nightmare that had begun at Birch Lake was finally over.

But more than that, she'd learned something about herself during these harrowing days. She was capable of surviving anything life threw at her.

The sun was hanging over Pickerel Lake, turning the surface into a mirror of glacial blue, and Micah Brezny was aware of something she hadn't sensed in years.

She felt like she could breathe again and finally stop running.

# CHAPTER 48
## TWENTY-FOUR HOURS LATER

The late afternoon sun filtered through the towering spruces surrounding Wolf Lake Lodge, casting dappled shadows across the upstairs porch, where Payne found Gus sitting on a wooden recliner.

"Hell of a thing," Gus said as Payne passed through the open door, gesturing toward the empty administrative office down the hallway, where Jasmine's desk sat cleared of personal belongings. "Hired her after my wife passed, trusted her with everything. State troopers found her trying to board a flight to Seattle when they arrested her yesterday. Had a suitcase full of cash and a fake ID—cash from my account and then some. Even had a red wig in her luggage, which Nolte figured was the same one she wore in the bar that night she slipped something into Jimmy Dean's drink." Gus shook his head, his voice heavy with betrayal. "Guess Klurman paid her well."

Payne settled into the chair beside him, both men staring out at the pristine lake, which had somehow remained untouched by the violence that had consumed the surrounding wilderness. "We're all walking contradictions, capable of both kindness and cruelty. The trick is figuring out which side someone will choose when it matters."

Gus waved a hand out to the lake. "As if I didn't have enough problems keeping this business afloat, now I gotta figure out how she handled the books and all the marketing stuff."

Payne chuckled. "I'm sure you'll figure it out. You've been adapting to changes in these woods for decades. One computer system shouldn't be too much of a challenge for someone who used to track poachers through terrain that would kill most people."

"Difference is, poachers don't come with instruction manuals."

"No, but they're usually more straightforward about wanting to kill you."

Both men laughed, the sound carrying across the porch. It felt good to find humor again after the darkness of the past week.

"You know," Gus said, studying Payne's face, "I never did thank you properly for everything you did. Hiring you was supposed to be a simple work-trade arrangement, and instead you ended up saving all our hides."

"I should be thanking you. This place gave me exactly what I needed when I needed it most." Payne gazed at a flock of geese overhead, remembering his first morning here when the biggest concern had been splitting firewood and maintaining trails. "Though I'm sorry I brought so much trouble to your doorstep."

"Trouble was already here, we just didn't know it yet. At least now it's finished, and that girl can get on with her life without looking over her shoulder."

Payne reached into his jacket and withdrew a leather pouch, its weight substantial in his palm. The bag was stained with mud, but the contents had remained secure during his journey back from Pickerel Lake. "Speaking of getting on with life, I brought you something."

Gus raised an eyebrow as Payne set the pouch on the small table between their chairs. "What's this?"

"A little something from Jenkins' spring that I retrieved on my return trip after eliminating Groh. Call it a parting gift." Payne loosened the drawstring and let a few gold nuggets spill onto the wooden surface.

Gus' mouth hung open as he picked up one of the larger pieces, turning it over in his weathered palm. "Jesus, Kyle. How much is in here?"

"Enough to keep this place running for a long time, and I left you another pouch down on your desk. Maybe you can use it to upgrade some of those cabins, fix that dock that's been listing to starboard, and hire proper help instead of relying on drifters like me."

"I can't accept this. This belongs to the Jenkins family or the state or somebody with a legal claim."

Payne shook his head. "Jenkins has been dead for seventy years, and his only surviving relative is gone, too. This is probably going to end up in state or federal coffers. Besides, after what Klurman put everyone through, I'd say you've earned a finder's fee."

He paused, turning to face Gus. "There are two favors I'd like to ask in return, though."

"Name 'em."

# CHAPTER 49

The Indian motorcycle purred beneath them as Payne navigated the winding coastal road toward Homer, Micah's arms wrapped securely around his waist. The Kenai Peninsula stretched out before them in all its rugged glory—snowcapped mountains rising from dense forests and the vast expanse of Cook Inlet shimmering to the west.

After two hours of riding, they crested the last hill, and Homer spread out below them like a postcard image. The famous Spit extended into Kachemak Bay like a narrow finger, its length dotted with charter boats, restaurants, and tourist shops.

Payne parked the bike near the end of the Spit, close enough to the water that they could hear waves lapping against the wooden pilings. The evening air carried the salt tang of the ocean and the distant aroma of grilled salmon from the nearby restaurants.

"April always said this was the most beautiful place in Alaska," Micah said softly, pulling off Payne's helmet and shaking out her blonde hair. "She wanted to bring me here for my birthday to watch the sunset."

"She had good taste," Payne replied, studying the girl's face. The hard edges that had defined her features when they first met had softened. "Come on, let's walk out to the end."

They strolled along the wooden boardwalk, passing fishing boats heavy with the day's catch and visitors snapping photos of the dramatic backdrop.

Micah paused at the railing, staring out across the bay toward the Kenai Mountains. "I keep thinking she should be here," she said quietly. "April, I mean. We made so many plans for this trip and talked about all the things we were going to do after graduation. Seems wrong to be here without her."

"I think she'd want you to see this and to remember your good times together."

They found a bench near the end of the Spit, away from the crowds of tourists and fishermen. The sun painted the sky in shades of orange and pink, reflecting off the calm waters of the bay. In the distance, a pod of beluga whales surfaced and dove, their white backs gleaming in the golden light.

Payne reached into his jacket and withdrew a small bakery box he'd purchased during their brief stop in town. Inside was a chocolate cupcake. "Happy birthday, Micah. I know it's a few days late."

Her eyes widened with surprise and something that might have been tears. "You remembered."

"Hard to forget someone's eighteenth birthday, especially when they spent half the week reminding everyone about it." He produced a candle and lighter from his other pocket and carefully lit it, shielding the flame from the ocean breeze. "Make a wish."

Micah stared at the flickering flame for a long moment, her face serious with concentration. Then she leaned forward and blew it out with a decisive breath.

"What'd you wish for?" Payne asked, pulling the candle from the frosting.

"Can't tell you, or it won't come true. That's the rule, right?"

"That's what they say." He handed her the cupcake and watched as she took a bite, chocolate frosting smearing across her lips. "You know, turning eighteen is supposed to be a big deal. A fresh start—a chance to decide who you want to become."

"Feels more like an ending than a beginning," she said, though her tone lacked the cynicism it once carried. "Everything I thought I knew about my life turned out to be wrong. Foster family who didn't give a damn, friends who are gone, plans that'll never happen."

"The hardest thing I learned after my friend's death last summer was that goodbye doesn't mean gone. April's stories and laughter and friendship will always be with you. *She* will always be with you." He turned towards her. "You survived something that would have destroyed most people. That kind of strength doesn't just disappear when the crisis is over—it becomes part of who you are."

"So, what am I supposed to do with it?"

"Whatever you want. That's the beauty of being eighteen and having your whole life ahead of you. Remember what you told me about Costa Rica? The monkey sanctuary, the treehouse, all those dreams you had?"

"That was just fantasy. I don't have the money or education for something like that."

He grinned. "Gus is going to have some resources available very soon, and he's specifically setting aside money to help you get to wherever you want to go, along with providing you with my old cabin in the meantime."

Payne pulled a folded piece of paper from his wallet. "This is the name and email of a friend of mine who runs that jungle training school in Belize. He knows everyone down there in the conservation field and will connect you with the right people."

Micah took the card with trembling fingers, studying the words. "You're serious? This is real?"

He nodded, an easy smile emerging.

"But I don't know anything about biology or research methods or—"

"You know how to survive in the wilderness, how to work hard for what you want, how to adapt when everything goes wrong. That's worth more than any degree when you're living in the jungle, studying primates."

The sun had nearly touched the horizon now, turning the entire bay into a mirror of molten gold. Seabirds wheeled overhead, their cries mixing with the distant sound of boat engines.

Micah was quiet for a long time, alternating between staring at the piece of paper and watching the whales in the distance. She leaned against his arm. "Where will you be after this?"

"Out on the road for a while until I get the urge to settle some place for a bit," he said, gesturing toward the vast expanse of ocean and mountains. "Following my own second chance, I suppose."

"Any of that involve getting in some halibut fishing before you go? Gus told me that's been at the top of your list here since you arrived."

He held a hand over his stomach. "Think I'll just settle for having some grilled halibut in one of the towns up the road tonight."

"Sorry you didn't get to do that. I feel bad."

He nudged her with his elbow. "Don't. Life reeled in a friend for me instead."

She brushed the hair from her cheek and smiled.

They sat together in comfortable silence until the sun finally disappeared behind the mountains. The first stars were beginning to appear overhead, and the lights of the fishing boats created their own constellation on the dark water.

"I should get going," Payne said finally, standing and stretching. "I gotta drive to my motel and repack a few things before I leave on the ferry at sunrise, and you've got April's family to meet tomorrow."

Micah nodded, tucking the paper carefully into her jacket like a talisman. "Thank you, Kyle. For everything. I know I was a pain in the ass most of the time."

"Try all of the time." He grinned.

They walked back toward the motorcycle, the boardwalk now lit by strings of lights that swayed gently in the ocean breeze.

"You sure you'll be okay getting to the hotel?" he asked.

"It's three blocks, old man. I think I can manage." She threw her arms around him, and he pulled her in for a bear hug. Finally, Micah stepped back, her hands shoved deep in her pockets. "Hey, Payne?"

"Yeah?"

"When I'm down in Belize studying monkeys, I'm going to name one of them after you. Probably the grumpiest, most stubborn one I can find."

"I'd be honored," he said, laughing. "Just make sure it's one that howls the loudest."

"Deal."

Payne put on his helmet and swung his leg over the seat, kicking the engine to life and pulling away from the curb. In his mirror, he watched Micah grow smaller as he rode back toward the main road, her slight figure silhouetted against the harbor. Coming to a halt at the first stop sign, he pressed his right arm against his jacket pocket, assuring himself that the handful of gold nuggets was secure.

The Indian ate up the miles as he headed toward the ferry terminal in Seward, the headlight cutting through the gathering darkness. The salty air whipped past his helmet, carrying the promise of a fresh start in the lower forty-eight.

For the first time in months, the road ahead felt like a beginning rather than an escape to the next town. The engine roared beneath him as he accelerated, chasing whatever lay beyond the horizon.

# ABOUT THE AUTHOR

Did you enjoy *Savage Game*? Please consider leaving a review on Amazon to help other readers discover the book.

———

JT Sawyer is the pen name for author Tony Nester who writes survival and vigilante-justice thrillers. Before becoming a full-time writer, JT spent 30 years teaching survival courses in the American Southwest for the military special operations community, at the university level, and for a variety of federal agencies. He also served as a consultant for the film industry and provided training in mantracking and fieldcraft for actors Josh Brolin and Emile Hirsch. Nowadays, JT prefers having a roof over his head and placing his fictional characters in dire straits. He lives with his family and several rescue dogs in Colorado.

———

Want to connect with JT? Visit him at his website:

www.jtsawyer.com

## ALSO BY JT SAWYER

Printed in Dunstable, United Kingdom

72796005R00181